CONTACTS

Mark Watson is the acclaimed author of eight novels, which have been published in twelve languages. He is also a stand-up comedian and has won numerous awards in Britain and Australia. He regularly appears on TV, has had several Radio 4 series and been named the Edinburgh Festival's highest achiever of the decade by *The Times*. He lives in North London.

Also by Mark Watson

A Light-Hearted Look at Murder
Bullet Points
Eleven
The Knot
Hotel Alpha
Dan and Sam: A Graphic Novel
The Place that Didn't Exist

MARK WATSON

CONTACTS

HarperCollins*Publishers*

HarperCollins*Publishers* Ltd
1 London Bridge Street,
London SE1 9GF

www.harpercollins.co.uk

First published by HarperCollins*Publishers* 2020
1

A catalogue record for this book
is available from the British Library

ISBN HB: 978-0-00-834696-6
ISBN TPB: 978-0-00-834697-3

This novel is entirely a work of fiction.
The names, characters and incidents portrayed in it are
the work of the author's imagination. Any resemblance to
actual persons, living or dead, events or localities is
entirely coincidental.

Typeset in Dante MT Std by
Palimpsest Book Production Ltd, Falkirk, Stirlingshire

Printed and bound in the UK by CPI Group (UK) Ltd, Croydon CR0 4YY

MIX
Paper from
responsible sources
FSC
www.fsc.org **FSC** C007454

For Coop,
who changed my story for good.

PART ONE

THE TEXT

1

8 MARCH 2019

23:55

I've decided to end my life. I know this will come as a shock to some of you and I'm sorry if it upsets anyone. Sorry, also, if a text message is a strange way to find out. I am not sending this for you to try to change my mind; I know what I'm doing, and I'm fine. I just wanted the chance to say goodbye and to thank you for the things we have shared. James x

2

9 MARCH 2019

LONDON–EDINBURGH TRAIN, 00:02

Texting 158 people at once was a strange feeling – stranger than James had expected. The task of drafting the message hadn't been difficult at all. In fact, it had been cathartic to write it. It was as if he didn't fully believe he was capable of taking this dramatic action until he'd committed it to the screen. It was the difference between making a mental vow and saying it out loud. And now, telling every single one of his contacts: that was the final step. You didn't tell 158 people you were doing something and then duck out of it. This was sealing the deal.

Most people would probably have a more tech-efficient way of spreading the news. WhatsApp, perhaps.

Even as recently as five years ago, well after he'd left the tech world, James would still have found it difficult to imagine not having a Facebook account. But then, he would also have found it difficult to imagine not having a girlfriend, or best mate, a healthy relationship with his sister, a purpose. He'd come off Facebook, and everything else like that, as soon as Michaela left.

This was his final act of sharing, you could say. It was a bit of a clumsy way to do it, he reflected, reading the message which was about to be dispatched to his entire phone book one more time. The 'James x' looked ridiculous to James's own eyes. He never normally signed off with an 'x'. He'd been left behind by the age of over-familiarity between virtual strangers. Only recently, before he got sacked, a passenger he was picking up – a total stranger – had sent him a GIF of a goat eating a chocolate bar whole, with the caption 'SWEEEEET!' Again, at one time James would have found that funny, responded with something similar. But when you were lonely, fake displays of friendship made things feel lonelier still. And fake was all he had, now. A brief smile exchanged at the table with his flatmate, a friendly nod on the way into work. They weren't enough. You couldn't be almost forty and be living off these crumbs of affection. And now he wasn't going to, any more.

They can have the 'x', he muttered to himself, with a private little smile. He felt the lightest he'd been for a long time: light both in the head and in this flabby body he'd come to despise. Neither brain nor body mattered so much, now that he was almost done with them. *They can have the 'x' just this once.*

He could feel his heart skip against his ribs as his finger slid onto the screen. This was it. There was no recalling this message; it would be out there immediately. Everyone knew how unforgiving it was, the instant-contact world they all lived in. Michaela had once written the sentence 'my tits feel like they've been through a mangle' and sent it by mistake to a colleague. He could remember how she described the realization, the dizzying rush of stomach into mouth. James almost smiled again at the memory of his ex, but this time the smile died, and he took a deep breath and pressed send.

The moment itself was curiously undramatic. It wasn't even one single 'moment', as James had imagined it when he'd looked ahead to this night – which he had naturally done a lot. Some of the numbers in the phone book were out of date, some phones were switched off this late; exclamation marks immediately started appearing on the screen. It was not immediately obvious who had got the message and who would remain ignorant of his plan until he was already gone. But he wasn't about to find out. The phone was going onto flight mode and would stay that way.

Of course, nobody could find him here – he had planned it well. Nobody could physically stop him; that had been a given as soon as they pulled out of the station. All the same, he didn't want to be bothered, over the next few hours, by people's responses. This wasn't a proposal: it was a done deal. Flight mode was a good compromise. He didn't want it off altogether, because the phone was his only timepiece, for a start. It would be reassuring to keep an eye on the time. To know how close he was to half past seven in the morning, when it was going to happen. The phone would be by his side, but surrounded by a force-field. Nobody could touch him, now.

A little aeroplane icon popped up at the top of the screen to confirm that it was no longer possible for any of James's contacts to speak to him. This time, the moment *was* as rewarding as it should be, *did* feel as significant as it should. Admittedly, it wasn't quite the end of his interaction with the rest of humanity. It was possible he'd have to speak a few words here and there before 7.30 a.m. But no real conversations. Those were done with. No more opportunities to mess up, to disappoint others, or himself. It was done.

James rummaged in his plastic bag, bringing it up onto the narrow bed with him. For his final meal on this mobile Death Row he had brought two pork pies, a six-pack of beers and a packet of plain chocolate digestives. *What a spread*, he could hear his sister Sally saying, in the mock *Famous Five* voices they used to adopt in their early twenties: the youthful person's mockery of the only-just-past. He removed the biscuits from the bag. Tearing off the yellow strip to open the packet, stuffing the first biscuit into his mouth, provoked the usual rush of guilt and shame. It was a conscious effort to remind himself that those feelings were obsolete now, that he was free, he could eat whatever he wanted. Do whatever he wanted, for the whole of this ghostly night that was left to him.

It had surprised him a little, how slow the adjustment was. The way that, even though he had made his decision weeks ago, the body and mind kept on with their business. That was what life was like, he supposed. An amazing amount of it was lived almost automatically, and could be for many years, unless one found the courage to change it – or do what he was doing now, escape it.

James's actions this afternoon wouldn't have looked to an outsider like those of a man about to kill himself. He'd approached it like any other day off work. He'd cleared up the crumbs of cheese left from his mid-afternoon snack, polished the kitchen surfaces, hoovered, straightened the jumble of shoes by the front door and hung up his flatmate's jacket, which was lying in the hall. Before leaving the flat for the last time, he had gone into the bathroom and made sure the shower dial was turned tight to the top, because the shower had a habit of spewing water out of its pipes at unpredictable times – noisily and sometimes for several minutes, as if it had an invisible user standing under it. Admittedly, these actions hadn't been for James's own benefit – it made no sense to talk about 'benefit' when he wasn't going to be alive this time tomorrow. But there was his flatmate, Steffi, to consider.

'Flatmate' was a generous way of describing their relationship, as was the case with all the people who had moved in and out in the three years since Michaela left. The two of them weren't close; they'd barely had a detailed exchange until that recent night, still mortifying to think about, when she'd seen him crying. James generally came home from work at the station at around seven, and usually Steffi was already out, waiting tables, by then. Their main transactions revolved around the Amazon packages which Steffi was always receiving early in the morning, and which James collected for her because he knew she would still be asleep.

Sometimes he thought he had more conversations with the delivery man – who always said the same thing, 'just a signature here please, chief' – than with Steffi herself. But he certainly didn't want her to think badly of him now he was gone. That was why, as well as making sure the flat was nice, he had left her an email with detailed instructions: how to contact Michaela, who was still the landlady, and what to say to anyone who got in touch.

Steffi (there was no denying it) would be inconvenienced a little by what he was about to do. It was bad news logistically if the other person in your flat killed himself. But she was a capable, practical woman – he knew that much about her. She'd be fine.

Everybody would be fine. In a few cases their lives would be better, in fact, as a result of this. If James hadn't believed that, he would not have made this decision. He helped himself to a second biscuit, turning it upside down as usual to enjoy the hit of the chocolate coating a couple of seconds more quickly.

'God, that's nice,' he found himself muttering, and grinned at the oddness of the situation. It was so freeing to have made this decision. *I feel alive*, he thought, *somewhat ironically.*

A third biscuit. Eighty-six more illegal calories. He could still remember the figure from the weight-loss app that used to patrol his and Michaela's diets like a prison guard. Eighty-six calories, astoundingly, in a single biscuit. But it wasn't illegal any more. There could be eight million calories in a biscuit, he thought, and it wouldn't matter. Nothing was a problem any more. He visualized for a second an insanely large biscuit, himself eating his way through it, and almost smiled again as he realized where the thought came from: Sally had once helped him get off to sleep with a made-up story in which he was trapped inside a giant peach, like his Roald Dahl namesake. But the thought of her gave him a pang of sorrow – they would never be young and full of in-jokes and cynicism again, never be brother and sister again – and he forced it away. There was no room for that stuff now.

He yanked a cord to pull the blind, revealing a grubby little square of window. It was midnight: indistinct shapes went by in the darkness. James thought about all the texts, the messages-in-bottles, shuttling invisibly through the night sky. Some of the recipients would be asleep by now, wouldn't see the news for hours yet, perhaps not until he'd done it. Others would half-read the message through sleep, or glance at it but fail to absorb it.

But a few people would already have read it, and some perhaps were trying to contact him right now, hammering in vain on the screen-door he had pulled shut across his phone. James wasn't so detached from his life that he couldn't see that. If Michaela and Karl saw the message, they would certainly try to get in touch. Their brains would shine a beam on everything good about James, everything (as his message said) they had shared. The mad escapades of years gone by, like the time they raced around all the Monopoly squares in London; or that night they spent grovelling around on hands and knees to capture a frog that had found its way into the flat during a storm. Michaela would remember how he always brought her a morning coffee although – in his own words – he felt like an absolute dingbat trying to say 'matcha latte' to the youthful, band-T-shirt-wearing baristas who probably discussed him after he'd gone. Karl would remember watching middle-of-the-night foreign films after a shift, joining the action an hour late, debating who the killer might be only to discover at the end that it hadn't been a murder mystery in the first place. Both of them would remember the fun things, the filtered memories, and the hysteria of the moment would make them forget that they were the ones who'd helped to cast him into this grim place.

Even people with less invested in James, which was almost everyone else amongst his contacts, would be concerned. Humans were naturally programmed to think that way, for their own protection. They'd say that he 'wasn't in his right mind', that he was a 'danger to himself'. They would convince themselves that this was a tragedy which needed averting, from which they could emerge as a hero. They would be reacting, in other words, not to James's actual situation, but to the drama. So their reactions would be fished out of the first-aid kit everyone had for dramas. And they would be wrong. It was a long time since he'd felt so decidedly in his right mind: so calm and in control. As for being a danger to himself – no, it was the opposite. He'd been a danger to himself when he was alive, when he was still trying to make out that he could cope with what that required. He was safe now.

He put the phone down on the sad little ledge that passed for a bedside table here. It was odd how small the phone looked, all of a sudden – a trick of the mind, perhaps, now that it had been stripped of its powers. It was an object again, inert like a brick, rather than an ever-watchful second brain. It might as well be a toy.

3

9 MARCH 2019

LONDON–EDINBURGH TRAIN, 00:06

James had a momentary flashback to his first encounter with an iPhone. It was 2007 and he'd just moved in with Karl and two other coders. Karl had brought the phone home from an Apple event which they'd all been invited to because, at that time, their start-up had been regarded as a pacesetter.

'Look at it, man,' Karl had said, holding it out like a bar of gold on the kitchen table. 'You just touch the screen, like this. *Not* you.' He playfully swatted James's hand away. 'Compulsory hand-wash before you even go near it, fam. This thing cost an arm and a leg. Look at it. You flick through – beautiful, isn't it. Your conversations, it shows you like this. You've got all your apps, you've got all your music on it, like an iPod. It's like a computer but the size of a phone. These things are the future, man, for sure. Ten years' time, they'll own *us*.'

'How did you . . .' James almost stepped back from the

question, feeling it was the sort of thing his mother would ask – much too square for conversation with Karl. Karl wasn't much like the programmers James had met while getting his degree, or in the past couple of years touring as a freelancer around the IT departments of companies which had only just upgraded their equipment from abacuses. Karl had pecs like Argos catalogues, his black skin was covered in tattoos of objects that James thought you could probably do violence with, he was keen on romantic adventures which always backfired. On their first week in the flat together, a woman had turned up in their kitchen shouting that Karl would be 'judged by history', and yet half an hour later they'd been having sex so loudly that James had to try to drown it out with a documentary about someone he didn't recognize touring India's railways. Yes, Karl was a lot cooler than James. Still, sometimes the cool found it useful to have the less cool around. James considered himself difficult to beat when it came to knowing the rules of board games and how long to put things in a microwave for.

'How did I afford it?' Karl raised his eyebrows. 'Is that what you were going to ask?'

'Sorry if it's a rude question.'

'It's a fair question, fam. Because it actually brings us on to something I wanted to ask you about. This is a bit difficult. I got the phone by making use of my credit card, right. But that does bring me close to the credit limit, which I didn't realize, so I'm going to have to ask you a favour.'

James smiled. It was promising, having this man who hardly knew him, ask a favour. James felt he was at his best when helping out, being a *steady pair of hands*, as his school report described him – something which Sally criticized as faint praise ('you're better than that') but which James himself was pleased with. 'How close to the credit limit, and is the favour helping you with the rent this month?'

'Close to the point of being, arguably, over it,' said Karl, 'and yes, although I feel like a dick, I'm going to have to ask you if you could pay a bit of it on my behalf.'

'How big a bit?'

'A very big bit,' Karl conceded, 'by which I mean, all of it.' James laughed out loud, and Karl brandished the phone by way of explanation. 'Again, yes, I probably shouldn't have bought it, but: look at this, right. This app is a fishpond and you can *send fish to people* who have the same phone. We need to copy this idea. This is what everyone is going to want.'

'Imaginary fish?'

'Connection. Networks. The world is one massive team, fam. We don't know the half of it yet.'

The James of then nodded, agreeing as he always did, thinking sheepishly that although this was almost certainly true, he himself didn't need much of a network beyond what he already had: his family, a couple of friends, and now Karl himself. The James of now, ten years on, winced at the crack of the ring-pull, which sounded rather dramatic in this enclosed space: as if he was trying to make some sort of point by opening the can. When in actual fact he wasn't trying to express anything at all. He, 'James', was nothing any more – that was the idea. He was passive here, with the creaking and moaning of the train's body around him. Everything could just carry on without him. This wasn't an act of aggression, just withdrawal.

He swigged from the can, feeling the metallic taste crawl across the back of his tongue. The moment of sensory engagement brought James back into being himself, and he looked at the gagged phone and thought how strange it was that you could go, so quickly, from that to this. From being protected, feeling that you had a place in the world, to this: sitting on a sleeper train, with a bag of beers, knowing you were going to commit suicide shortly after the sun came up.

'Suicide'. He wrinkled his nose. It was a very attention-seeking word. And notion. James remembered the way he'd once had to stop the car because the radio reported that a friend of James's celebrity passenger, Hamish, had 'taken his own life' in Los Angeles. Hamish had sat, thumping the window over and over again, while James reached back and offered him a hand, an intimacy he would never normally risk with a customer. 'Suicide' was for people like that: depressed millionaires, or rock stars. It wasn't for people like James, people who went to work every day, feeling progressively more invisible, feeling fat and hot and useless. Nobody was going to sob in the back seat when they heard about James. No, 'suicide' was an overblown word for what this was. 'Taking his own life', likewise. Taking it from whom? You couldn't steal from your own bank account, could you?

It was more like resigning, as you would from any job which you had proved unequal to. *I resign from life*, muttered

James to himself, with a half-smile. It was almost fun, this. The sensation of a load released. And it didn't really matter, in the end, what name you gave to what he was about to do. After it, there would just be a full stop, and relief.

4

MELBOURNE, 11:25

SALLY CHILTERN

Twenty minutes until the interview, Sally's ever-eager phone reminded her. Twenty minutes till the *Age* journalist showed up. That was fine. She'd be at the office in ten. After that, the phone could say what the hell it liked, because it wouldn't be with Sal any more. She would have given it to her personal assistant, Meghan, who would deal with anything that came up – any calls, emails – while Sal was busy. As usual, Sal's husband Dec had all her appointments in his diary, and he knew not to send dirty messages outside what they called the Filth Windows, or FWs. He was much more into rude texting than Sal was, but she did miss it a little bit when the phone wasn't with her. In all other ways, though, not having it for a couple of hours was a blessing. It was great having Meghan to shear through the weeds that grew ceaselessly in her inbox. Invitations to speak *unpaid*, for Christ's sake, like she was still 21. 'There's no budget, but the girls would be so thrilled to have you and we'll feed you well!' Emails from struggling restaurants, her name dumped in the subject line in a hollow attempt at chumminess. 'Sal, we haven't seen you in a while!' You had to turn down the background buzz, sometimes. *Background buzz. I like that. I could use that in something.*

It was definitely a thing you heard more and more about, the effect carrying a phone everywhere had upon humans. She'd heard on a podcast that scientists were already recording a change, for the worse, in global sleep patterns – even among people who switched their phones off for the night. Just the presence of the devices created a sort of subconscious twitchiness, an unease. It was a product of the slavishness which the world had wandered into; of the mental pattern established by checking a single device hundreds of times in a day. Asleep or awake, the brain reached insatiably for the phone.

Still, it was amazing what they could do, you had to admit it. Right now, Sal could see from the screen that it was twenty-five degrees – beautiful early autumn weather, although she had never got used to thinking of the seasons the wrong way around. She could see, if she opened the relevant apps, the stock markets, a range of sports scores. Neither finance nor sport was a big interest of hers, but she found it useful to have a bluffer's knowledge of both, as she did with a huge range of subjects. If she flipped on to WhatsApp she could follow the excited chatter of three of her mates who were organizing a trip down to Lorne for Easter. The chief organizer was unemployed, so the build-up to this three-day holiday had become her major undertaking in life: she'd set up the chat group as early as Christmas and it had now produced more than a thousand messages in total. Sal rolled her eyes indulgently at the latest dispatch. *Still so pumped for April, girls!* What was Bridget going to do when it was all over? She'd jump in the river.

You didn't need a phone, of course, to see that it was a glorious day. The sky, over the dashing art-deco façades of Bourke and Collins streets, was a confident blue, Australian blue. Weekend shoppers were out; in rooftop bars, weekend drinking had begun already. Some people would find it weird going into the office, doing promo, building up to a big speech, on a Saturday. Melbourne, even more than other cities, reminded you at every turn it was *fun time*: crowds flocking to the stadium, rowing boats slicing their way upriver. But Sal didn't mind it at all.

She'd always liked the feeling, in fact, of working when others weren't. As a high-flying teenager she used to help James off to sleep by making up an adventure – do you fight the monster or hide, the same as his computer games but without the computer – and then, when he was snoring, return to her desk, her midnight essay. Being active while others slept: it had felt like a superpower of some kind. Even now, she hadn't entirely lost the buzz that came from being many hours ahead of Britain, something she was able to discuss on a weekly basis because Mum never seemed to tire of it. *Now, what time is it there? Breakfast? Goodness!*

Near the top of Bourke, Sal paused, as she occasionally

did, to enjoy the sight of all the bustle. Melbourne often reminded her of those Richard Scarry books they'd had as kids. Of course, it wasn't always that smooth. On almost this exact spot just before Christmas, a tram driver had had a bust-up with his wife, let his mind wander, hit someone who was checking the cricket score on her phone. She survived, but the streets around Sal's workplace briefly went crazy. Police tape everywhere, one of the city's central arteries clogged up, two hundred people made late for work or doctor's appointments or dates. In one of her columns, Sally had used it as a salutary example. There was nothing an individual could do about the potential for mayhem that existed when humans tried to carry out their plans at the same time as one another. So you had to outsmart it, leave more time, plan well. Expect things to go wrong.

It was lucky she'd survived, or Sal would probably have felt bad using her as an anecdote.

Already in her mind's eye, Sal could see the peninsula which she and Dec were driving down to next weekend. A spa, a wine tasting. Dec would undoubtedly overdo it at the winery and be all over her before they even got back to the room, which had a hot tub and a 'romantic terrace'. He was a bit route-one sometimes, Dec, but at least he still fancied her, which was more than was true of some people's husbands. One of the girls in the WhatsApp group was the only person in Australia not to know that her man was gay and regularly getting spanked by a sommelier. Sal was planning an intervention next week. Everyone agreed she was the one to do it. The trouble with being a business expert was that people seemed to think you could sort out pretty much any other type of business, too. Just like the way that, because she'd written a bestseller on time management, people thought it was hilarious if she was ten seconds late anywhere.

'See the footy last night?' asked Arnie, the concierge, rising very slowly to usher her to the lift. Although Sal had been working in this building for three years, a recent security overhaul meant that you now had to be bleeped into the lifts with an ID card which he alone, in the building and perhaps the universe, possessed. She had a suspicion that the 'overhaul' had been effected purely to give Arnie some duties to carry out, but if so, he hadn't exactly risen to them. As always, he shuffled across the hall as if it didn't really matter whether Sal got upstairs today or tomorrow.

'Bombers were a shambles,' said Sal, glancing at the phone. Two minutes. Perfect. 'Thought they were meant to be good this year.'

'Believe it when I see it,' said Arnie, with a low laugh, raising the magic card to the sensor.

Meghan was already at work, looking – as usual – like she'd slept in the office overnight. Hair unwashed and hanging listlessly at her shoulders; owlish, unflattering glasses. Meghan was one of these girls who could probably look great with even twenty minutes' effort: she had great boobs, her skin had that smooth uncomplicated quality of someone who hadn't been kicked too hard by life yet – but she would never go to that effort. And Sal was aware of the irony of thinking these thoughts, when half her life was spent steering people away from objectification, so she naturally never said a thing about it.

'So just to flag up, you've got the ABC interview after lunch, and then a car is coming to pick you up for the rehearsal, and there's that other interview, which is a phoner, which is about women heroes in the workplace?'

As usual, Meghan laid no particular stress on the final five words, exciting as they might have sounded to an outsider: Sally often thought that she could have the phrase 'rescue drowning man' in the diary and Meghan wouldn't read them with any emotion. Tonally, the only thing that differentiated her from a robot assistant, like Alexa, was the modern tendency to slope upwards at the end of sentences, as if everything was a question.

'OK,' said Sal, 'and then we head for the dinner at . . .'

'At six-thirty, they want you there seven for the drinks reception, your actual speech is nine?' said Meghan, not even glancing down at these details on the screen in front of her. 'I'll be with you obviously, but the cars are all booked. And Andrew, the guy you're speaking to now? Just a heads-up that he's arrived?'

'Send him up.' Sal slid the phone across the desk. She didn't expect to see it again for a couple of hours, but then, very little of the day from now on would go as she had imagined.

*

'. . . and why do you think we *do* obsess over running late? Shouldn't we all be more chill about it? Do you worry people read your book and get judgey?'

Sure enough, straight for the cliché questions. It wasn't

a surprise; as soon as they shook hands, he'd made a quip about how he'd been scared to get coffee on the way here, in case he was late. Also: 'chill'. 'Chill', as an adjective. The guy was in his forties, like her.

'Well, it isn't about "obsessing". Time management is just one of the ways I try to help people focus on what's most important. If you learn to prioritize, divide your priorities into simple lists of five, it's—'

'So this speech tonight, will you be nervous? Do you get stage fright?'

I mean for the love of God, thought Sal. It was one of her favourite inner cries.

'Well, I've been giving speeches for quite a few years. Obviously, it does have its challenges, and part of what I try to do in my work is coach people who aren't – sorry – who aren't experienced in it.'

The hesitation had been provoked by the appearance of Meghan in the doorway, for the second time. With a slight angling of her head, Sal sent her away, as she had done ten minutes ago. Whatever it was, Meghan was experienced enough to sort it out, and Sal didn't want to be in this room a minute longer than she needed to be. If she knocked the interview on the head by one, they'd have proper time for lunch, and she could go out and look at her speech notes and maybe even nip into Myer for foundation. Meghan's eyes flickered behind the big round lenses, but she shut the door, noiselessly.

'Tell me about Mind the Gap,' said the journalist, at last, and Sal went gratefully into her bullet points. Women were still paid fourteen per cent less than men across Australia.

So the point of this campaign . . . The journalist was nodding, making the occasional note, but it didn't seem like much was going in. He was very likely wondering why he'd been nailed to do this on a Saturday lunchtime when he could be in a beer garden. Sal could see a doodle of a shark in the corner of the page. This was going to be one of those pieces that were super-light on content, heavy on what-I-did-with-my-weekend narrative. *'Chiltern, unsurprisingly, calls me into the office at eleven-thirty on the dot.'* *'Chiltern sips her green tea as she tells me that addressing an audience can sometimes be challenging.'*

'And that's why – even though I do know it's not the sexiest subject – I feel like for anyone with a woman in their life they care about, which is hopefully everyone . . . can I help you with something, Meghan?'

It was a jarring sentence to say out loud, an inversion of their natural relationship. Meghan wasn't there so that Sal could help *her* with stuff. Sal wasn't going to start being PA to her own PA. And yet here she was, in the doorway for the third time now, the hat-trick as Dec would say, glancing between the floor and Sal's phone in her left hand. The overall effect of all this pantomime discretion far more distracting than if she'd just bloody come out and said whatever it was when she first walked in.

'So, there's a message you – I think you'd want to deal with it?' said Meghan.

'To do with what?' It came out brusquer than Sal intended. But this wasn't good. The journo was doodling, again, and Sal knew he was enjoying this, the human angle, the comic relief. He'd end up putting this in his piece, the prick. *'Chiltern – famed for being in charge of her time – is visibly rattled when her assistant . . .'*

Meghan hesitated.

'Give me a clue at least, darl,' said Sal, working hard to keep her tone humorous.

'Your brother's about to kill himself?' said Meghan.

5

BERLIN, 01:27

MICHAELA ADLER

Michaela Adler's phone was in her handbag. The incoming text lit the whole interior of the bag for a second, like a torch in a tent, but she didn't read it straight away. *I need to turn off some of my notifications*, she told herself, once again. All her chat threads, Facebook, the pushy running app which still piped up every couple of days – 'let's go run! The best time is right now!' Phillip didn't like it when she was glancing at it all the time. Even though it was very often gallery business. And even though, as she liked to point out, 'People do tend to do things by text sometimes, because it's not 1995.'

Phillip was only four years older than her, just like James had been, but he enjoyed his caricature as a grumpy old man; played up to it with a certain glee. He feigned ignorance of Justin Bieber's life and work, however many times

31

the name came up; he went to the local government office to register to vote, even though you could do it in five minutes on the internet. He visited Facebook no more than once a week, which in this day and age meant you might as well be living on a desert island.

In this place, they probably *were* the oldest people. Phillip with his thick-rimmed Tom Ford specs slightly misted over in the warmth of the club. Michaela in a dress she would describe as pretty revealing, but which by the standards of the 18-year-olds here might as well be a spacesuit.

The place had been a power plant before the Wall came down. The mezzanine was lit by bare bulbs that poked out on wires between the exposed girders of the ceiling. Michaela and Phillip often came here for late drinks. The throb of music from the floor below always made them grateful they didn't have to dance, didn't have to 'go out', try to meet someone. When they finally did go home they would joke about how they'd outlasted all the teenagers, who came out full of talk but by one in the morning were slumped in alleys outside, texting, sobbing, vomiting.

Maybe this would have to stop if Michaela got pregnant. When she got pregnant. But this was a good consolation prize for now. There was time. Occasionally she did get scared that there wasn't as *much* time as there should be. People on the internet told horror stories about what happened if you left it past 35. If you had to have treatments. But, as Phillip said, 'Everything is horror stories on the internet. Remember when you googled the pain in your side, it looked for half an hour like cancer, but it turns out you just had a pain in your side.'

She'd never met anyone whose opinion she deferred to so automatically, *wanted* to defer to. When they came out of a film she waited to hear what he thought, and tinkered with her own review automatically. If there was a weird noise in the night, she would nudge him awake just so he could say it was nothing, it was just the building. None of this was very feminist, probably, but in all her previous relationships – including with James – she'd always been the one to take the lead. It was tiring, being that person. It had been a fun couple of years on the other side of it. Couple of years and counting.

Of course, she hadn't been able to articulate all this to James when she left him for Phillip. The conversation, the horrible bombshell dropped over a dinner: it had all been a mess. Her explanation had been a mess – *it's not that he's better than you, I just need to see what's out there, I can't live not knowing.* Her face had been a mess, too – mascara all over it like a kid's crayon strokes. He hadn't known how to react because she hardly knew what she was saying. Her reasons for running away to Phillip had only become clear months after the event. In fact, they were still becoming clear now. But if she had to describe what she loved about him in one sentence, it would be something to do with this – with the way they never ran out of stuff to talk about; they just saw five new conversational doors with every one they walked through. It was like a feast where, the more you ate, the more dishes reappeared. Mum used to tell her a Dominican folk tale which went something like that, though she couldn't remember the moral.

Tonight, they had been talking about a friend with an

online gambling problem so bad that there was talk of a plan to confront him for his own good. He'd just lost €2,000 in five seconds by betting online on a netball match which he wasn't even watching. They'd also touched briefly on the Brexit debacle. Whether it would ever be sorted out or, as Phillip put it in his wiry voice, 'the same people will be arguing the shit out of it until we all die from the temperature anyway'. In the last few minutes they'd been discussing a new exhibition at the gallery called 'Denim World', which featured nothing but a hundred pairs of jeans, worn by people in a hundred different countries. As with most work of this kind, Michaela wasn't really sure whether it was interesting, or absolute horseshit, but as usual she'd written a press release which went big on the former.

It was twenty minutes after James sent the text that his former girlfriend glanced down to see the phone light up again in the bag, as it kept doing at intervals if you ignored a text – as if to say *excuse me, I thought we were a team*. She pulled the phone out, still only half-curious.

The sight of James's number was a real surprise. Any interactions between them these days – minor queries about the upkeep of the flat – were conducted by email, and with no discussion of anything other than the matter in hand. She'd even officially deleted his number, because of a commitment to Phillip that this would be a fresh start for both of them. All the same, she naturally recognized those last three digits: 997. There was the satisfaction of having been thought of, and a little intrigue. Then she read the words and went cold.

'I'll just, I need to . . .' she said, rising a little too quickly. Phillip nodded, taking a final contented sip of his beer. As she headed down the spiral staircase, he was inspecting the brickwork, etched here and there with the names of old lovers.

The toilet stalls were all taken and there was a queue, and a soundscape familiar to Michaela even though it wasn't her language: high, urgent chatter, amped-up Friday-night emotion, over the shadow of the music from outside. She propped herself against a sink and read the message again.

I've decided to end my life. I'm fine. The understatement of it was so like him, in a way. But the actual sentiments couldn't be right, couldn't be real. He couldn't have written this – she checked – almost half an hour ago, almost half a fucking hour. She pictured his round, earnest face, the curly fringe he was always toying with, to no real effect. She jabbed at the green icon to call his number.

The person she had called was not available. What did that mean? Where *was* 'the person', she asked herself, adrenalin hammering its way down her neural pathways. Was the phone at the bottom of a ravine with him? Was it wedged in his pocket in some hotel room as he hung from. . .?

No, this was stupid. Michaela was good in these situations; at least she thought she was. She might not be well organized, she might once have called the police to break her into her house when the keys were in her bra all along, but she believed in herself when real crises arrived. She was a go-to for panicky friends; she could do CPR and sometimes fantasized about becoming a hero by carrying it out, normally on the film star Tom Hanks. She'd even put 'crisis management' as a skill on her job application to the gallery. During the interview it had, sure enough, come up. They asked her what she'd do if fire damaged an exhibit the night before opening. 'It's a stupid question,' Phillip had scoffed, 'how often do they think that comes up? Why not ask what happens if a dinosaur gets in?'

Anyway, this was likely not a real crisis. He didn't mean it. It was some sort of a stunt, or a drunken gesture.

Michaela's stomach told her she didn't believe herself. James never really got drunk, and it was hard to think of someone less likely to attempt a 'stunt'. James was not a stuntman; he was a ponderer. He'd once caused a Monopoly game to be abandoned by deliberating so long over a hotel purchase that their guests went home.

'Do you think we ruined Kath's night?' Michaela had asked as they washed up together afterwards.

'She ruined her own night,' said James, as they fought a tug-of-war over the tea towel. 'How can she be married to someone who puts houses down without any sort of strategy?'

And two years later, when she marvelled over his shoulder at a spreadsheet showing that their new company had made a monthly profit for the first time, despite all her night terrors, he turned and grinned. 'See? There's no better way of choosing a partner than Monopoly skill. Never mind looks or being slim, or. You know. Having good one-liners at a party. No: Monopoly, clean driving licence. It's all you need.'

It didn't seem possible that the same person who'd spoken

those words was the person making dire threats by text, threats to *himself*. She pressed green to call again. The recorded message repeated itself. She brought the phone down hard on the dirty-white edge of the sink. The petulance of it surprised her. It crossed Michaela's mind that she was more pissed than she'd thought. She eyed herself uneasily in the mirror and moved aside to let a Goth girl wash her hands.

There was no point in panicking, she told herself again. Her legs felt leaden, as if the staircase was ten times as long as it had been on the way down. The reason it went to voicemail was that someone else was already talking him down. Yes. That was it; that made sense. Karl would be on it. Or Sally. Michaela gritted her teeth at the memory of the sister. Well. Someone. Someone would be dealing with this.

Phillip had ordered more beers and was already well into his. James would never have done that. He would have ordered the drinks, yes, but he would never start without someone else. He could be at a banquet in the last days of the Roman Empire and he still wouldn't have touched so much as a dormouse until everyone was served. It was something she liked about him, one of the things she noticed first. *An old-fashioned gentleman,* her mum had said.

'What's up?' asked Phillip.

'Nothing.'

'Clearly it's not nothing.'

She hated it almost as much as she liked it, the ease with which Phillip could read her.

'I just had . . . I had a weird message. From . . . James.'

Phillip raised his thick eyebrows. There was no reproach in the look – more a sort of quizzical amusement – and you would have to know Phillip as well as she did to realize that he was slightly hurt.

'I thought that you didn't . . .'

'I *don't* have his number. Any more. I can't stop him having mine, can I? It wasn't even to *me*. It was to . . . well, it looks like everyone.'

Her boyfriend's eyes went rapidly over the text. It was easy to forget that English wasn't his first language. She'd worked hard even to get to her passable level of German, and almost everyone at the gallery spoke English with a proficiency which made that effort seem pointless. They sprinkled English phrases into their conversation: *online*. *Hanging out*. Sometimes when Michaela was around, they spoke in English to each other, as if it was such a minor adjustment it wasn't even worth mentioning. Last week her boss Anneka had used the English phrase *cognitive dissonance* in a meeting, and nobody flinched; Michaela had had to google it in the toilet later.

Phillip looked up from the phone with an expression whose rancour was a nasty surprise to her. It was such a handsome face, though, that even scowling suited him. He looked like a king disappointed with his dinner.

'That is absolutely a dick thing to do,' said Phillip. 'That's not fine.'

'I know, but . . .'

'He needs to grow up instead of sending something like this for attention.'

'But I'm . . . that's why I'm worried. I don't think that's

the sort of thing he'd do, at all. I'm worried he might mean it.'

'He doesn't mean it,' said Phillip, handing back the phone.

'He might mean it. He isn't the type to . . . he's not melodramatic at all.'

Phillip blinked. Again, he didn't have to say anything. *Why are you defending your ex?* his face asked. Most people in his position would ask the same, she supposed. Michaela was even wondering it herself, and perhaps that was what James would want. So maybe it was true; maybe it was manipulative of him to be doing this. She wondered fleetingly what James looked like these days; whether he had put all the weight back on by now.

'Well, do you want to call him?' asked Phillip.

Michaela moistened her lips with her tongue. Her throat felt dry. Below, there was a gap in the music; then a thudding beat came in, louder than anything before, and there were faint whoops from the dance floor. She could see James in the doorway for a second, as she had left him in the doorway of the old flat, shoulders drooping, and head held between his big hands. Her feeling of guilt and relief as she walked away.

'It's fine,' she said. 'He'll be fine, I'm sure.'

6

STEFFI BERMAN

Now that the underground was running through the night at weekends, Steffi's commute home from the restaurant was easy. Tonight had been a raucous one, a party of twenty businessmen loudly and repeatedly toasting someone who seemingly went by the nickname Billy Bollocks. One of the diners had called her 'darling' too many times, and for a moment Steffi had entertained a bizarre fantasy: of taking the red mullet off his plate, the whole fish, lifting it from its bed of rice, and putting it down the back of his neck. The mental image was so strong that Steffi laughed out loud, as if she'd seen it in a film rather than dreaming it up. The would-be fish victim had taken this for some sort of flirtation, as men of this kind often did when she laughed, smiled, or looked at them. But they had tipped quite heavily, drunkenly – at La Chimère they let you keep

41

individual tips – so she was in good spirits as she walked to the tube.

If anything, in fact, the journey home almost wasn't going to be long enough, given the entertainment Steffi had lined up. For the past couple of months her spare minutes had been mopped up ruthlessly by a phone app called 'Sheep Wars' – created by one of James's successors in the game-tech business, though she had no idea her flatmate had ever worked in that field. Sheep Wars was so addictive that it was difficult to remember a time when she hadn't played it at every opportunity. You were a wolf and your mission was to eat as many sheep as you could; if you caught enough of them, you went on to the next level. In the early rounds the game was boringly easy; the sheep were so slow and stupid that a 4-year-old could capture them. Steffi had been annoyed with Emil, the colleague who'd recommended it to her: did he think girls couldn't play games? Or that she specifically was useless, just because of that one time she slipped on a bit of pulped avocado and smashed all the glasses?

But as the stages of the game went by, your prospective prey became faster, and more cunning. They armed them-selves with weapons; they built fortresses. Last night she'd played it until 3 a.m., as usual, and to her amazement the sheep, who normally just shuffled around like real sheep, had escaped from her by jumping into a sports car and driving off laughing. This was level seventy-four and she hadn't yet worked out how to respond to the sheep's new cunning. Nobody online seemed to know how many levels there were; you couldn't find anyone who claimed to have finished it. There was a theory, in fact, that the invisible creator was perpetually adding to the game; was a mad genius who had them all indefinitely enslaved.

Sometimes, on the tube, she glanced across at other passengers hunched over their own phones, and wondered if they were on Sheep Wars, too – unwittingly part of a community, even as they all played the game alone. People always looked so serious, but you never knew what was in someone's head. Steffi remembered once sitting next to a man who was studying his screen with one of the most intense expressions of concentration she'd ever seen. When she sneaked a look over his shoulder, it turned out he was watching a GIF in which someone had made Beyoncé appear to turn into a pizza. Watching the five-second film over and over and over again, like someone newly arrived on the planet, grasping fruitlessly for context. Quite often she thought that everyone except herself was insane. The thought was half-ironic – but only half.

On the escalator up to the street, Steffi's gaze was still fixed on the little sheep as they danced around, taunting her. She knew that before too long she would work out how to ambush the car and finish this level. And then two contradictory things would happen. She would feel a little swell of satisfaction, followed almost immediately by disappointment that this was not a real-world achievement, something that anyone else alive would care about. Steffi was not a zombie gamer, an addict, in the truest sense. She was aware that there should be more substance to life than working as a waitress in a restaurant whose online reviews were struggling to match up to its pretensions, and then spending every other moment engaged in the hunting of imaginary animals. It just wasn't clear how to get out of this loop.

As she came out onto Pentonville Road Steffi glanced at her phone. Slightly surprisingly at this time of night, there were two new notifications. One was from Emil, the line chef, asking the staff's WhatsApp group if anyone wanted to 'get a drink somewhere Euston or whervr'. The proposal was backed up by emojis depicting glasses of wine, beer and champagne, as well as a dolphin; Emil was a profligate emoji user and rarely stayed on-topic. The other message was a text, from her flatmate and landlord James. In the instant before she read it, she registered that it was unusually long; she couldn't remember him ever writing more than a few words before. Even after the bad night, the crying night, he had only messaged to say, 'I am very sorry about all that'. She hadn't even replied; too awkward to know how.

She read the text, read twice through the words 'end my life'. She stopped dead outside a kebab shop, where a huge skewer of meat was rotating in the window and a couple of customers waited at the counter.

'What the fuck,' said Steffi out loud, to the nearly empty street, 'what the actual fuck.'

She touched the screen to call James. It was hard even to remember the last time she'd called someone, actually called them on the phone like in the Seventies or something. With Mum it was always Skype on a Sunday. She was in constant contact with friends, but it was all instant messaging. Even with her best three or four buddies back in Holland, one of them actually phoning would mean something seismic was happening.

But now something was, or at least could be. There was a brief pause as the call tried to connect, and then the same recorded message that Michaela had heard minutes earlier. There was no option to leave a voice message and Steffi experienced a guilty twinge of relief that she wouldn't have to.

What now, though?

Where are you? she wrote. Unlike Emil, she preferred – even in her second language – to text in proper words and sentences. Your screen looked ugly otherwise.

She stood looking at the screen in case the messaging dots popped up, in case there was an immediate reply. Within thirty seconds she knew in her heart that there wouldn't be one. Well, she hardly even knew James, really, did she. Other people must know him. Someone else would know what to do.

But no one else was heading home *to* James. There was no escaping that. If he had done something to himself in the flat, Steffi was going to be the one to find him. The knowledge flipped her guts. Although she was only seven minutes away from the flat, it seemed impossible all of a sudden to imagine going in there, finding . . .

That wasn't a thing that just happened, though, she told herself. Your flatmate did not spring something like that on you. Even if you kept to your own space like the two of them did, you couldn't be living with a person and not know that they were on the verge of something so drastic, surely. Steffi thought about the suicides she'd

45

seen in crime dramas, which she often bulk-watched when the insomnia was getting her down and her eyes wouldn't focus on the sheep any more. Gun in the mouth, rope hanging from a beam. A politician blackmailed, a lover rejected. These characters had suffered some disaster, they'd lost their minds; there was nowhere else to go. That wasn't James. Yes, he'd perhaps been down recently, but he was hardly a guy to ram a gun in his mouth. She'd seen him decide against going to the cinema because the weather app said there was a 60 per cent chance of rain.

A little rain was falling now, too; a drop landed squarely on the screen, distorting the green and grey boxes of text. She shivered. It wasn't winter any more, but March in London didn't exactly seem to be spring, either. Steffi swallowed hard a couple of times. *I could do with a drink*, she thought. *A drink would be nice.*

As she rounded the corner onto their street, the noise of the main road fell away as quickly as ever, and so did the big-city feeling. It would have been hard to guess now that it was a Friday night, or that they were so near a major transport hub. Some windows offered glimpses of warmth: a dinner party that had extended its run past midnight, a couple in front of a late movie. Steffi told herself that if James *had* done anything, there would be some activity, some visual sign of it. Police would already be here. Concerned neighbours would be hammering on the door, like they did on Netflix. But no, not necessarily. He'd sent the text under an hour ago. She could easily be the first actual witness.

She wet her lips with her tongue, went down the four stone steps, took a breath and put the key in the lock.

The place was as neat as ever, James's hat and coat hanging where they always were, next to the denim jacket that she'd decided was too much like old-school Madonna, and which she hadn't bothered to pick up from the floor because she was worried about being late for work. That was a good sign; it must be. You didn't worry about tidying the hall the same day you went and did yourself in. But the odd calm of his message came into her head again. *I know what I'm doing.*

'James?' she called. 'James? Hello?'

She was almost sure from the dead way her words landed that nobody was here. It didn't diminish her sense, though, that she was in a TV show, one where a minor-key soundtrack was building subtly under her footsteps. She never liked coming back alone, really, not since the burglary at her old place in Clapham. One of the girls at La Chimère had been assaulted on her own doorstep the other week, violent crime was up in London; although not normally a jumpy person, Steffi had bought a 'panic alarm' and a small knife online in the past month. Knowing that James was almost always in – that he was almost certain to be in his room when she got back from work – had always been a little bonus about living here, although this was the first time she'd ever consciously had that thought.

His bedroom door was wide open, giving an unaccustomed glimpse of the bare floor, a neat little pile of books; so was the bathroom door. All clear in the kitchen. Steffi approached her own room with a trepidation she had never felt before. Christ, imagine if he'd done something in *there*. That really would be fucked-up. She'd have to move, again.

A lean on the handle, and the door was open a crack; she pushed it a little more, then all the way. Everything was where she'd left it. The clothes scattered across the floor like wreckage from an accident, the dormant laptop at the end of the bed. Wherever James was, he was not here.

On the kitchen table was a note.

Hi Steffi. Really sorry for any fuss. I've scheduled an email which you'll get in the morning, re. the flat. You can stay, of course! It shouldn't be too complicated. Good luck. James.

The fridge was still full of his stuff: the blocky cheeses he seemed to like; the full-cream milk she couldn't stomach. A big green box of eggs. Again, it didn't make sense. You didn't buy eggs and then two days later overdose or something. 'It shouldn't be too complicated.' Was he taking the piss? What was this?

She sloshed some gin into a wine glass, topped it up with partly flat tonic water. The phone lit up with a message and she jumped. No. It was just Emil again. He'd been drinking on his own since he sent the last one, he said, with six crying-face emojis, three winking ones, and a watermelon. He couldn't believe nobody else was out, he added.

In a series of purposeful swigs, Steffi saw off the drink. She always drank quickly, not out of greed, she thought, but because her brain tended to see it – like everything – as a task she had to complete. She pushed the glass aside and messaged Emil.

You want to do something with me?

She saw him begin typing at once. She and Emil didn't know each other especially well. His English was poor, nowhere near her level. He was small, with dark eyes and a fluent, almost mesmerizing kitchen technique. Sometimes as she came in with orders, she would watch him for a second, drizzling rings of pesto like green blood onto the ice-white plate, turning a mountain of herbs to confetti in seconds. It was very attractive watching someone do something with such ease. If you didn't look at his face too hard. Anyway, it was only ever a moment; that was all you got, in the kitchen, before someone screamed at you.

Do what? Emil replied. He followed up with a fusillade of emojis which included a face deep in thought, a couple of drinks, a detective with a magnifying glass, a dancer, a guitar and the flag of Iceland.

Can you meet me Kings X station? Got some shit going on.

Emil accepted the cryptic invite with a line of girls in tutus. Steffi went to the bathroom and looked in the mirror. Her pupils were dilated; a bit of colour had risen in her normally pale face. She blinked and rubbed her eyes. She was surprised to have invited Emil into this; she was surprised to find herself in any sort of drama. But here it was, and she could hardly just pretend it wasn't happening – that she hadn't read the message. She'd get those jeans off the floor, go back out. And see where this took her.

She was worried for James, however passive their relationship. The guy couldn't be well. He needed help. She was worried for herself, too, because never mind what he said: if he *did* turn out to be dead, her life was surely going to get all kinds of complicated. She felt the prickly edge of guilt that he had cried in front of her not long ago, and she had taken it as a mere bad night rather than a sign of something more significant.

But there was something else, as she looked in the mirror, some other emotion stirred up by the bizarre turn this night had taken in the past half-hour. Here, at last, was something that was not a game. Steffi felt bad admitting it to herself, but the feeling was a little like excitement.

7

LONDON–EDINBURGH TRAIN, 00:49

Branches, like gnarled old trolls' nails, scratched at the train on its way past; small handfuls of rain were thrown at the windows. The train didn't sound like it was enjoying it. It was surprising, James thought, how noisy sleeper trains were, given that you were meant to sleep on them.

He'd always loved buses, planes, trains. A train barrelling past, a plane swooping as close as a bird as he negotiated the M25 interchange with some important client: getting right over their heads, so they could see the underside of the fuselage, the little marks in the metal. As children, James and Sally had a whole series of books in which animals bustled around a town, putting out fires or teaching kindergarten classes of smaller animals. The junior-level computer games he wrote as a nerdy child were always about things like being an air-traffic controller ('press A to reroute the flight; B to never compromise with terrorists'). Even when he first met Karl, he was working in idle moments on a game called 'National Rail', where you had to get around the country as fast as possible using real train routes – something Karl had found hilarious. 'You're making a game about something that isn't even fun in real life? What's next, Jamie, a game about getting your central heating fixed?'

Sure enough, it had never seen the light of day, just like James's similar pet project 'Bus Magnate'. But he never lost enthusiasm for the sight of a train zipping past, a plane soaring at its almost impossible angle into the sky. These sights meant people had places to go, places that might be better than here. Transport in action still gave him something of the warmth of those old Richard Scarry books, of their agreeable sense that there was *a plan*. Or had, at least, until recently. Until the sacking. Until he began to lose faith in the idea of plans altogether.

And yet he had been on a sleeper train only once before: with Karl and Michaela, on a trans-European holiday jaunt which was only a bit more than five years ago but might as well be fifty years, as the memory, along with all his others, receded into the darkness down the track. Even though James and his dad had gone to Edinburgh every year by tradition – right up until Mr Chiltern's death – they'd never done an overnighter. Largely this was because of an intuition on James's part that sleeper trains were something of a thin man's game. That had been backed up by his experience tonight so far. The bed he was lying on was barely wide enough for a healthy-sized child. The word 'cabin' on the website had possessed a certain grandeur, evoking the *QE2*, that sort of thing; the reality was a room which, to a man of James's dimensions, felt a little like a cell. His plan had been to put away two or three beers quickly and then fall asleep until the moment came, but it was already clear that might be more difficult than he'd imagined.

Still, the beer was helping; as the first can signed off, he could already feel its contents nudging the dimmer switch of his mood. It was quite a while since he'd really enjoyed a drink. When they got on the train at Euston – each passenger checked in by a vigorous, curly-haired Welsh woman who said things like, 'We'll be in at seven, but you can occupy until seven thirty', there had been a large number of benign beer drinkers, in red scarves and rosettes, on the way to some sporting event that James wouldn't know about at the best of times, and would certainly now miss as he would be dead. He'd eyed them for a second, listened to their oiled, jolly bantering, with what was almost regret. Might things have been different if he'd been more of a drinker – if he was a bit better at *relaxing*? For some people happiness, or at least a sort of hazy, zoned-out contentment, seemed that easy.

But, as he reminded himself now, he had been that person once. He'd had a gang, even if it was a smallish one, and largely drawn from friends Karl introduced him to. In his years working for the tech start-up, they used to go to the pub almost every night. Karl – because he was working on a web encyclopaedia, as part of the project – would entertain the group with his knowledge of various historical figures' lives, and James – because he paid more attention to detail – would quietly correct that knowledge.

'This woman, can't remember the name; they reckon *she*

was the one who came up with DNA, but being a bird, they took the Nobel Prize off her . . .'

'Rosalind Franklin. Actually, she never got the prize.'

'What's his name, Neil Armstrong, the geezer that walked on the moon: do you know, he said the "one small step for man" bit slightly wrong; he messed it up because he'd got the yips being up there – fair play, really – and also did you know he once punched a bloke who claimed that they never went to the moon at all?'

'That last bit was Buzz Aldrin, I think.'

The start-up, where Karl and James worked in their mid-twenties, had been creating a platform called OnLife: a portmanteau of 'online' and 'life', which Karl feared was a 'dogshit name for something that's supposed to be cool'. Karl had tried to point this out once to Jacob, the handsome dimpled blond whose company it was – but unfortunately, he had used exactly those words, and had been drunk, and Jacob was from some nebulous but severe American background which meant he disliked both swearing and drinking. Even if the name was always a bit tin-eared, though, the actual project had at one time seemed very exciting. It was based on the notion that the internet's best things would not remain free for ever. Email couldn't always be free; nor could massive resources like Wikipedia, nor connection tools like Facebook. One day, in Jacob's view, there would be a single hybrid of all these entities – a single place you went to do, as he put it, 'everything you want to do with a computer, and some stuff you don't even know you want'. When this megalith came along, people would subscribe to it in their masses.

So James and Karl's job had been to write code for a sort of web encyclopaedia which could also use algorithms to predict the sort of facts you probably wanted to search for. Other people in their office and flat-share were responsible for building other parts of this internet planet. A Taiwanese man called Yan – who never spoke a word of English to them – was creating a messaging service. Katarina, the only woman in the set-up, was coding a personal organizer which would allow your computer's diary to sync with your mobile. There were twelve people employed by the company, and all of them were working on good ideas, ideas that would become very popular. But the overall conceit – that people would one day pay for what was currently free – proved a disastrous one. The consumer testing went badly. And even as Facebook's share value was darting upwards like a spider climbing a wall, Jacob's funders, whichever rich Californians were bankrolling his experiment, pulled out overnight. James was grumbling to himself over a line of code, something he'd wrestled with for three hours already, when Karl shuffled into the office, late as usual. He began a good-natured reproach – Karl averaged around half as much time actually working as James did – but Karl cut him off with an unusual edge to the humour in his tone.

'I wouldn't be sweating over that too much, Jamie, my man. I don't think Jacob's going to show up for the meeting.'

'And what makes you say that?'

'It's a hunch,' said Karl, 'based on a couple of clues in the voicemail he's just left me, which said he was about to get on a plane, our company didn't exist any more as of this morning, he'd already got a job lined up for the Federal Reserve back home, and he was sorry but he didn't think we'd ever meet again.'

All but James and Karl moved out of the flat after that, and by now James's core friendship group was scattering too, on the various winds that always blew groups apart in their late twenties: marriages and children, New Zealand holidays that became permanent stays, nervous breakdowns triggering dramatic career changes, and so on. But even well into his thirties, now driving cars for a private hire firm and helping people fix their computers on the side, James would have said he was broadly happy, most of the time. There were still the nights out with Karl, when Karl came back from whatever monstrous job he was currently trying out. There were the Edinburgh trips; there were dates and little tentative romances. By now there were certain mental ulcers, too, rubbing away at him, flaring up. He was aware that he was a little heavier than he'd like, that a decade and a half of sitting down had left its mark on his body; he worried that it was getting late to meet the right person, that it was never going to happen simply by having pleasant chats with people in the back of his car. Once Michaela had entered his life, these problems, along with all other remaining ones, disappeared. But in time Michaela herself had then disappeared.

Despite being dumped by her, and thrown aside by Karl, James had never imagined himself as a person for whom unhappiness could be this thick and choking; a person who would go home at night and simply not know what to do with himself. He understood there would be crises, even in an unremarkable life, but it turned out there was something worse than the adrenalin of a crisis: the endless flat grey afternoon of depression. The terrible night he had cried in front of Steffi, three months ago, had been the first time he'd really understood how hollow he felt, and had been feeling, and would keep feeling. Even after googling 'depression' – an act which released a flood tide of pop-ups that said things like, *It's OK not to be OK* and *Take a mate for a pint*, he would have thought it impossible that he would ever be desperate enough to call the Samaritans. Until the morning, midway through January, when he'd gone ahead and done it.

He'd woken at eleven on a Saturday, having slept badly, and the emptiness of the day ahead descended on him as if the plasterwork had come crashing down from the ceiling. He had no plans; nobody would want to see him. Everyone had kids, or they were in couples having brunch, or they were just mysteriously away as people so often seemed to be when you were yearning for them. His last online date had ended in a humiliation so complete that he couldn't imagine opening the app again; it felt as if everyone else there could see him, pitied him. Thoughts like that were irrational; they were not the sort of thoughts James was used to having – not until he lost the job, if it was possible to identify a turning point. Since then, they'd been more and more common, and it was exhausting to carry them around.

He went into the hall, made sure Steffi was out. His body felt heavy, his legs reluctant to carry him even this couple of dozen steps. Her bedroom door was open – chaos inside, as usual, as if she'd had a fight with herself in there. In the bathroom, the shower was dripping. James went to turn it off, returned to his room, picked up his phone and typed the strange word into Google. S-a-m. The algorithm finished it off for him. The future Karl had once predicted was here, now; maybe the phone knew you were miserable just from the way you sat on the edge of the bed with it.

His fingers went over the numbers on the screen. 116 123. It felt too short for a phone number. Even as the dial tone sounded in his ears, James doubted that he was going to go through with this. He wasn't even certain he expected it to be answered. Calling the Samaritans felt like something you did at midnight, not before lunchtime. But it *was* answered, almost straight away, and it was too late to go back. It was a woman's voice. She asked what he wanted to talk about. James swallowed and clawed at his scalp and managed to say that he was very lonely, and that he'd been thinking about . . . not being here any more.

The Samaritan did a good job of sounding surprised and concerned, even though this must be how many of her calls began. In her kind, Home Counties voice – a voice he could imagine speaking authoritatively on Jane Austen, or the need for better cycle lanes – she gently steered him towards more concrete discussion. James found he was, if not enjoying it, at least pleased to be able to answer the questions. He'd once remarked to Michaela, during the cult for Scandinavian murder shows, that he quite liked the idea of being a witness. Being quizzed by the police, 'helping their investigations'. She'd laughed. 'How are you going to infiltrate a criminal gang?' she asked. 'You literally phoned the Revenue this morning to tell them you owed them more tax.'

'When were you last in a relationship?' asked the Samaritan.

'About two and a half hours ago. I mean, *years* ago.' He was annoyed with himself for the slip of the tongue. 'Two and a half years ago. And that relationship was four years long. It was the only proper one I've had. If you see what I mean.'

'With a woman?'

'Yes.'

'Can you say a bit about her?'

'Her name was Michaela.' Straight away he thought he should have kept her anonymous. 'We met doing a weight-loss course. We were both, er . . . Overweight. And then we set up our own health-and-fitness business, which was successful. But she left unexpectedly.' Unexpectedly, he thought, even to Michaela. It was the way Michaela always did do things. He'd believed her when she said that she never planned it this way, she never meant to hurt him so badly.

'She's in Berlin now. With someone else.'

'That must be difficult,' said the Samaritan.

'It is.'

A silence seemed about to fall, but the woman caught the conversation expertly and tossed it back into the air. 'And do you have a support network?'

'A . . . ?'

'People you can talk to, people you trust.'

'It's difficult.' James scratched his scalp, fingered one of the untidy curls. He was more than due a haircut, he was starting to look like someone you'd move away from at a bus stop. But even this had been beyond him, the past couple of weeks. He remembered last time at the barber's. The awful creak of the chair as he settled into it; the way he caught, in the mirror, the stylist eyeing his body in a way he was used to people eyeing it. Like a house that needed some work. He'd have to go to a different place next time. All this took time and mental energy. 'My – er – main friend. Well, he became my boss. And recently sacked me. So we haven't been – we haven't spoken much since then.'

'And close friends, family?' asked the woman.

The word made James think immediately of being young. 'Family', like 'Christmas', was an idea that belonged to his past, not his current situation.

'I was very close to my dad. My father. But he's dead – he died.' *He's dead* had never stopped sounding brutal, winding him, in the saying or the hearing of it. 'My sister and I, actually, were close too, but we had a disagreement.' James felt that he wasn't holding up his end of the conversation very well, even though that was a strange thing to think about a Samaritans call. His list of setbacks didn't seem substantial enough to justify having called; having confessed to being in despair. He searched for a way of explaining why the thing he was trying to tunnel through felt thicker than the sum of these parts.

'You know – Tony Hancock, when he . . . well, when he died,' said James. 'He just said *too many things seemed to go wrong*. Something like that.'

'I'm afraid I don't know who that is,' said his younger listener, 'but I do understand the feeling, of course. And it can seem like that for a long time – but also, life can change very quickly for the better.'

The slight easing that James felt, after the chat, lasted about a week – maybe more. But it wore off like aspirin, a little at a time, and he didn't feel he could call up again. They must have more urgent cases to deal with, and he didn't want to become a *regular*; he wasn't a hypochondriac bothering a GP. What he needed was someone to sit and talk to. What he needed was to have friends again. And that urge had led to his 'opening up' to Steffi, someone who wasn't really a friend, and that had been a terrible misjudgement which embarrassed both of them.

Well. It was gone, now. James listened to the footsteps padding up and down in the corridor; the lilt of the Welsh woman's peppy voice as she chatted to the sports fans. 'Yes, be a good game, I should think! You should get some sleep though, mind!' People he didn't know; people who couldn't affect him. Nothing could really affect him any more. It had been as easy as the single touch which slid flight mode into action.

Departing from his own life, he could look back on it like one of Karl's pub biographies. *This fella, can't remember his name. Girlfriend leaves him for a geezer in Germany. Best mate gives him the sack. He gets the hump, jumps off a bridge.* It was a comforting thought, James reflected, allowing himself to open the second beer. That everyone ended up being a minor curiosity, given time; all lives ended up as footnotes, often full of factual errors. He needn't have seen himself all this time as a major character, every decision triggering grave consequences. Everything he'd done wrong would pack down into an anecdote for future Karls. Something to pass time between rounds at the bar; something very quickly forgotten.

8

JEAN CHILTERN (MUM)

It had to be Sally calling. At this time of night. It had to be one of the children, Sally or James. Or at least, more worryingly, it had to be *about* one of the children. But James would be fast asleep. No, it would be Sally in Australia, and that must mean something major was happening. All this went through Jean's head in the ten seconds after she was woken by the phone. The thoughts didn't arrange themselves one at a time; they coalesced into a pang of disquiet, something Jean felt before she was even really thinking. It had been years since the children were actually children, but the feeling was cold-stored in her core and could kick in again in a matter of seconds.

'Wassit?' muttered Lee.

'Shush,' she said, 'it's nothing, go back to sleep.'

Lee turned the other way and half-folded the pillow over

his head. Jean felt for the light switch in the hall, found the banister with her left hand. These instincts, once more, were more or less automatic, hard-wired by years of maternal nightshifts. Sally with her nightmares about being buried alive; James, fretting over not being able to sleep. What a fine state of affairs, as they used to say, when Alan was still . . . With her free hand she picked up the trailing edge of her nightie, a recent purchase. Jean had picked it because, although practical, it would also be reasonably stylish if worn in front of strangers in an emergency, like a fire alarm at a hotel. This had happened years ago to Jean on a weekend break in Glasgow, and it continued to affect her nightwear choices.

The phone was on its table by the front door, in almost exactly the same spot Jean's parents had had the phone in their own house. In the final few seconds before she reached the bottom stair, Jean had a momentary flashback to her father bemoaning its installation. *What's it going to be next? A brass band in the front room?* He'd refused ever to use it; if the house was burning down, Jean's mum used to joke, he'd probably write the fire brigade a letter. Imagine if he'd lived to see this world, where everyone carried a phone in their pocket, or bag. Well. Almost everyone. Not Jean. She was her father's daughter, still.

'Hello?'

'Mum? I'm sorry to wake you up.'

So it was Sally. It wasn't a policeman or someone from a hospital, as it had been on the awful night when Jean's sister, Pam, had died – suddenly, incomprehensibly, even though she was still describing her leukaemia as a 'nuisance' and had bought them concert tickets for the next week. It was Sally, in Melbourne. And so perhaps after all this was going to be *good* news. Perhaps . . . Jean had almost stopped hoping for it. But women did wait a lot longer these days, didn't they: they had careers first. Which Jean had mixed feelings about, but, well, the world changed, didn't it?

'There's a situation with James,' Sally was saying, and Jean's daydream evaporated.

'What do you mean, a "situation"?' Sally talked so much like a businesswoman, these days. *Was* a businesswoman, of course. You just never got used to it, with your own kids: having them speak to you like bank managers discussing your overdraft. Not that Jean had ever been near going into her overdraft.

'I've had a message from James.'

'What sort of a message?'

'A text, Mum.' Sal's voice crackled with impatience and Jean had the feeling, more and more familiar these days, that *she* was the junior one. 'He's made a threat – and it could be some sort of joke, or . . . but he's talking about . . .'

Even when Sally had explained it, Jean couldn't understand it, not really. Even when Sally had hung up, promising that she'd find a way to get hold of James, telling her things were going to be all right and that she'd call back as soon as it was sorted.

Jean stared numbly at the phone numbers of her children, the strange long numbers they had these days – especially Sally's, with the international code, the foreign-looking

'0061' at the start. They were written in biro on a strip of paper which never left the phone table, was held down with a kangaroo paperweight Sally had bought her. There was no point in trying James if Sally was doing it. Jean didn't want to tie up the line, or whatever the phrase was. She would only get in the way. And yet, *not* to call him. Her son. James. Not to call him, if he was in danger.

She had sat down on the stairs while Sally was talking, but now she stood up again, and her fingers went shakily over the buttons. Nine-nine-seven. Her fingers left a clammy film across the handset and she looked at the phone cord quivering gently as she extended the receiver. No dial tone. 'The person you are trying to call is not available.'

Jean put the receiver back into its cradle and took a deep, uneven breath. All right. She was going to get dressed. She would get dressed and put the kettle on. There was no point in trying to address this, this baffling emergency, without at least making things as normal as they could be. She would get dressed without waking Lee – not that he wouldn't be sympathetic, but she needed to wrap her head around this alone. And by the time she had done all this, Sally would surely be on the line again, to say it was all fixed.

But it didn't feel as if she could go back upstairs, somehow – not straight away. Jean's heart was beating at a speed which she couldn't remember it reaching for many years. These had been fairly quiet years, after all. An even keel. Some fresh air would be good, she thought, and went to the front door. The lock, the bolt, all the things you continued to do every night in case of some intruder, some wolf at the door. And yet now the wolf was here, had come in down the telephone line.

She peered across at the Bradshaws' nice new drive. The silver cars all slumbering as you looked down the hill, ahead of the supermarket trips or drives to country pubs which would make up their Saturday duties. The neat shuttered houses, green and brown bins outside; the absolute normality of it all. No reason, when she and Lee had gone to bed last night, to imagine anything outside that normality could jump on her like this. Of course not. Lee had watched a documentary about Pink Floyd, whose songs went on a bit, if you asked her, but he was happy. Jean had read a bit of her novel, which – like almost all the books chosen by her book group – was about a missing child. WHAT WOULD *YOU* DO? the blurb had asked, and Jean had thought how distant, how far from one's real experience, the question seemed. How far-fetched these books always seemed.

And now this.

But the danger here was not of a kind that you could call someone to come and stamp out; it wasn't in a shape which she could hold in her hands. Jean felt the swirling of her stomach again. Talking about *ending his life*. Why? He must be depressed, Sally had said. Or in 'some sort of trouble'. And Jean had felt it like a slap, heard an accusation. She was always there for James to talk to. But how long, in fact, had it been? He wasn't chatty on the phone. He wasn't someone you could call for a weekly bulletin in the way she did with Sally.

Depressed about what? In what sort of 'trouble'? It was

appalling that she didn't know, couldn't even guess. Well. She could *guess*. Perhaps he still wasn't over the mixed-race girl, if you were still allowed to say that; lots of things you weren't allowed to say, nowadays, according to the younger members of the book group. Perhaps it was the job, money. She gathered that he wasn't working for the taxi company any more, and even *that* job had been a bit of a comedown because the business went wrong, or he fell out with Michaela, or whatever exactly had happened there. But she could have given him money. She could have come up with job ideas for him, he could move back to Bristol, there were people hiring at the gym where Jean did Pilates, and at Boots, and that was just off the top of her head. Or perhaps it was his weight that was getting him down – but if that was the problem, there were so many diet plans.

It hadn't been easy to tell, at Christmas, what sort of shape James was in. To her concerned eye he had looked a little overweight and dishevelled, and he'd been evasive when she'd asked about his love life (while trying to avoid that phrase) and what avenues he might explore work-wise (while feeling she was twenty years too old for that phrase). Evasive, but not unhelpful. He'd got involved basting the turkey, chopping vegetables with so much force you'd think, as Lee said, that they'd done something terrible to him. When the Bradshaws had come round on Boxing Day with, as always, a new-smelling and complicated general knowl-edge board game, James had done his usual trick of getting the first five questions right and then deliberately playing less well when Mr Bradshaw began to get grumpy and swig the port like regular wine. She had glanced across, proud, wondering wherever he got all these facts from. But prouder still that he knew when *not* to use them. When James had left for London on the 29th, she'd taken both his hands in hers, her boy, and said, as always: look after yourself.

How empty that sounded in her head, now. And how negligent it felt, that she hadn't seen James since Christmas. Nine weeks, ten? They went by so quickly. But of course she wouldn't have let nine weeks go by if she had thought he needed something. Whatever was wrong, she could help him; that was the point. It was her job to help him. Yet she had somehow neglected that job. And now – without what felt like fair warning, without anything except this dizzying distress call in the middle of the night – now, things were on this knife-edge, and she felt sick.

She went back into the house. The cool past-midnight air had made her shivery, if anything. She went to fill the kettle. The kitchen felt smaller than it usually did. Jean took a deep breath, opened the dishwasher and began to make little piles of plates and bowls on the worktop, to be transferred into the cupboards. Just something to do that was normal. A neutral taste to offset the acid of this, of the thing there was no possible way of digesting. *James has sent people a message that he might do something terrible. James has been talking about – something happening.* She couldn't even quite frame it as a phrase in her head.

If only she had a mobile phone, she would at least have seen the message with her own eyes. It might make no practical difference, but she wouldn't have this terrible sense of having been wrong-footed. Of being so negligent that dozens of people – by the sound of it – were aware of her own son's despair before she knew the first thing about it. She'd just never got used to them. She was the wrong generation. Lee had a mobile, and the few times she'd tried to type out a message on it, it had taken so long that she might as well – like her father – be popping a letter in the post. It was the same with all of it. Her Facebook page, set up by James, had gone unmonitored for months; it was too much, the way it kept telling you about new features, and she hadn't really recovered from the laughter of her children when she asked how to 'befriend' people on the site. Emails, Jean tried her best with, but she'd always found typing laborious: her fingers just wouldn't fall into the right patterns, it was like trying to play the piano. Talking was so much easier. People just didn't seem to be so keen on that, these days.

The kettle had boiled, and Jean looked blankly at it. It was one of these new ones with a transparent body, so you could watch the water – under a blue light – frothing and bubbling right up to the second it clicked. It was no better at the actual job than the shrieking kettle she'd had for years, before Alan died. But Sal had said that was 'on its last legs' and that this one had the best reviews.

Jean flipped the top of the Kilner jar, got a teabag out, tossed it into the mug. Milk came last, no matter what anyone said. She rubbed her eyes. She didn't even want the tea, not really. Of course not.

She saw James as he had been at twelve, a chubby, polite boy in a smart grey jumper, off to Edinburgh with his father. With Alan, her soulmate. She experienced a quick and lacerating sense of loss for those days, of the time when they were a family. It wasn't fair to Lee to think like that. It didn't do any good, either. But this again was not really thinking, it was just feeling; it came from lower than the brain, from somewhere not so easily located. And the loss became a longing, to know where James was, to know what to do to help him.

It was absurd to think it, but without a mobile phone it felt as if she was further away from him than she should be. The decision not to own one of these devices – which she'd never had the slightest desire for – all of a sudden seemed careless to the point of selfishness. And the darkness outside, in the garden barely lit by the fingernail of moon, felt like a big solid wall between Jean and her son.

9

M1 NEAR LUTON, 01:23

KARL DEAN

At about the time James stabbed the screen to dispatch his news, Karl had been waiting to pick up an important passenger from the SSE Arena, formerly Wembley Arena, and take him all the way to Newcastle. This should be just short of a five-hour drive at this time of night, if he kept to the speed limit, which of course he wouldn't. Newcastle was a fair old schlep, as Karl was fond of saying – but he was happy doing it himself. There weren't many drivers he'd trust with a VIP job. There were even fewer these days, without James. And besides, there weren't many drivers who he'd be happy to see earning the money, when he could earn it himself. Yes, Karl was the boss now, so every journey was arguably earning him money. But when he was at the wheel, he was essentially making money for his own business *and then paying himself pocket money from that business.* It was like being, as he'd recently said at a party, both the ringmaster and the elephant. It didn't really make sense because elephants in a circus didn't get paid, and in fact circuses weren't allowed to have them any more, but it had gone down well with the table, and the reception sometimes meant more than the truth.

Anyway, you didn't know how long it was going to last, this job, any job, not even when you were in charge. Not in – as radio hosts were always saying – 'the current climate'. There were plenty of younger drivers who would have taken this in a heartbeat. Karl had been at the bottom of the ladder long enough. He knew that hunger.

There was lots of it about. That hunger. Some of the young ones would keep going till they fell asleep at the wheel, if he let them. Everyone needed the wedge. The fella who'd replaced James had recently done an eighteen-hour stint, which wasn't technically illegal, but also wasn't technically a good idea at all. By the end of the shift, his texts had read as if a dog was walking across the screen. Yes, there were a dozen of them who'd do the big schleps. It was where the proper money was. And some of these gold card clients, like the DJ geezer who was currently in the back of Karl's car, were also capable of coming out with fairy-tale tips. A footballer had once given Karl a pair of trainers, brand new, and – as it turned out – worth £400. Just handed them over at the drop-off. 'Do you want these, pal?' Karl had put them on eBay, and someone had paid the reserve price before he got home.

A story had done the rounds about a female driver – little bit of a rarity, in this industry – who'd got a pop star to

Gatwick against a very tight deadline and, the next morning, found ten grand in her account. No reference. No sender name. Just a set of life-changing digits. And she'd gone well over the limit, by all accounts. She could have lost her licence, game over. Or, of course, lost more than that. Someone pulls out at a corner, she goes into the back of them, lights out. But the point was, none of these things did happen. She won the gamble and she won the ten thousand big ones. And that was what you were in this job for.

How many other jobs could you watch money coming in every time you got a text, any time the phone hummed in its little perch on the dashboard? And how many people like Karl, whose dad used to wallop him, who dropped out of school at 16, could have built an app like that? Or rather a whole empire, powered by an app?

Yes, life was sweeter than he'd ever thought it could be. But tonight – tonight, as he and James used to say, had not been the dream.

First: the customer, the DJ, had an attitude on him. He wanted to sleep, in fact he *had to* sleep, that was his thing. As soon as he got in the back. 'I have to sleep, mate. All the way, yeah? Wake me up at the hotel, I don't want to wake up at all till then. At *all*. Yeah?' Fair enough, it was late: though from what Karl could make out, the geezer had only been on stage for an hour. You'd think he'd been doing mountain rescue the way he talked, you'd think he'd been doing mountain rescue and working a pizza oven at the same time. Still. Fine. Customer always right. But Karl didn't have the power to guarantee that the guy could 'just sleep' all the way. This wasn't a magic carpet service. This was two hundred and eighty-two miles of bloody tarmac.

And tonight, crossing even a tiny area of that tarmac had been the ball-ache to end all ball-aches. More than half an hour to get away from the Wembley area. The stadium, the arena, all of it, absolute murder to get away from. If Karl had three wishes, he'd use one of them to set the whole place on fire. Not with people in it; he wasn't a psychopath. And anyway, the genies couldn't kill people, could they – at least not in *Aladdin*. That was one of the terms and conditions. Yeah, wish one would be to tear down this whole area. Wish two, that he'd never given James the job of driving Hamish Elton, so he'd never have had to sack him. Wish three, thought Karl, glancing in the rear-view mirror to make sure the guy was asleep, would be the old 'infinite wishes' trick, but they probably had a procedure for that, so that people couldn't take the piss. Well. Karl wasn't going to wait around for genies. He was used to working his own miracles. He wasn't going to fuck about rubbing a lamp when his phone contained the riches it did.

A slalom of temporary traffic lights, hi-vis jackets carving up the roads. Like most drivers in a big city, Karl had long stopped associating workmen with any sort of improvement or even change. He barely saw them as people. He just saw a sort of cartoon figure, a helium balloon with a grinning face on it, who'd come out with a spade just for the fun of it, to make a great big hole where Karl wanted his car to go.

The satnav was already showing forty minutes later than its original estimate. Karl always felt like he was losing a game when that happened; he loved steaming into town ahead of the original time. No, they weren't looking at being in Newcastle till the thick end of 5 a.m. at this rate. Bit of McDonald's or something, another Red Bull, turn around, back to London for mid-morning. And that was if it went well. It would be Saturday morning coming back, normally not too bad, but you never knew. If he got caught up on the M1 coming back into London, if there was an accident or something, he might as well stop off and buy a Santa hat for nine months' time because that was roughly when he'd be back at his gaff.

He sighed as the fake traffic lights stopped him once more and swigged from the can in the drinks' holder. Karl was proud of himself for giving up coffee, which made you too jittery, but if he was honest he was now equally addicted to energy drinks, which also made you jittery and cost four times as much. Also, he'd overdone it: he would need to piss like a donkey well before Newcastle, at this rate. But never mind. The DJ fella was worth it. The money, transferred by his management, was already in the company's account. Karl didn't know much about the man: he hadn't signed up for the app, as some passengers did, unwittingly granting Karl access to a huge amount of their personal information. But he was obviously a big deal and his management company was worth about ten of these jobs a year. Yep, this geezer – whoever he was – was getting to Newcastle asleep if Karl had to chloroform him and charter a private jet.

When he was driving, the business essentially ran itself. The app, its central nervous system, paired passengers and drivers instantly. Drivers knew to contact passengers directly if there was a problem. In an emergency they could go to Karl's assistant, Hugo, who was always awake when Karl was asleep or at work. Hugo had psoriasis and it came on like buggery at night, which was a shocker for him but made him perfect for these shifts. In short, it would take what Karl had once termed a 'double emergency' before he had anything to worry about at the wheel. Like the one he'd had to sacrifice James for.

So when James's suicide text slid onto the screen, it was displaced within sixty seconds by four notifications, and disappeared. A year ago, this would not have happened, even with all the noise on Karl's phone, because anyone on Karl's 'favourite contacts' list was fast-tracked by another app; their messages would stick at the top of his inbox. This allowed him to make sure that his mum, for example, could always reach him when he was out and about. But Karl had had to remove James from the favourites list when he removed him from the job, because James's pleading texts had made him feel bad. Karl wasn't in the business of feeling bad; he'd felt awful quite enough when he was growing up – when he lay awake sobbing at night, when he came back with his school report shaking in case it wasn't good enough.

That was the past. The present was about good vibes. The vibes from James, since he had to leave the company, were not surprisingly less than good. And so the two of them hadn't been in touch for a few months now, and that record continued as Karl continued towards Newcastle, and James's train – for the time being, on a similar route – proceeded towards what would be his last ever appointment.

10

EVERYWHERE, 01:45

It was a strange time of night to send a text to one hundred and fifty people, and it was – as James had acknowledged himself – a bit of a strange thing to do full stop. One consequence was that a peculiarly mixed cross-section of his contacts became the first to learn of his suicidal intentions. While someone as pivotal to James's recent life as Karl remained ignorant of the message, it reached a number of people who had no idea what to do with the information.

The message was read, for example, by a former passenger of James's, who owed him £50 she would never pay back. She was in a hospital in Birmingham, stuck in the frustrating stage of labour before anything really happened except widely spaced spurts of discomfort. It was read by Michaela's former accountant, who gave it little thought because she was about to make love to an artisan ketchup and mustard entrepreneur. It was seen by one of James's former colleagues at the start-up, known at the time as Exploits because of his CV of drunken disgrace, which included throwing a curry off a bridge into traffic and making a near-successful attempt to kidnap rocker Jon Bon Jovi. Heavy drinking had served Exploits very much less well in his thirties than twenties. He now slept on a friend's sofa in Cumbria, was unemployed, and had gone back to being called Ricky. He glanced for a second at the message, took in none of it, and dropped the phone back over the side of the sofa, where it had been before it disturbed him.

Between this bracket of contacts and those (like Steffi and Michaela) most affected, there was a bank of people who found themselves worried to think of someone like James being so stricken, but worried in a manner too passive to interrupt their plans – which mostly involved drifting into sleep. Almost all of them had a memory of something generous James had done, since he'd accrued a reasonable résumé of small kind acts simply by living forty years as that sort of person. They remembered him giving them a lift because he was the only one not drinking that night; or even coming to pick them up in his private hire car, and not charging them. They recalled taking credit for a pub quiz answer James had come up with, or owing him a drink because he'd gone for a round without even being asked. He had made a kind comment about someone's haircut – although fearing it was a gauche thing to say in the flesh, he'd done it by text, and so long after their meeting that they had already booked their next haircut. He became friends with older people whose computers he'd fixed; helped them to write emails to family members; went out shopping for them, took them to hospital. A solid guy, you might say. Enough so that it was a shock to learn he was thinking of doing something so rash, or talking about it for effect, or whatever he was up to.

Some of them did attempt replies, in tones of wary but genuine concern. *Hope you're OK. Call someone. Things aren't as bad as you think. Please speak to someone for help if you're serious.* A couple of them even tried impulsively to ring James, but were not surprised when the call went straight to the 'not available' brush-off. They consoled themselves with the knowledge that someone higher up James's chain of acquaintance must, surely, be sorting this out. Most of the recipients, as they finally went off to sleep, had either got the weird little incident out of their minds altogether; or convinced themselves that whatever was going on, it would probably be fine when they woke up.

There was another category of people, of course: those who did not receive the message, were not on James's phone, but would find that their lives were affected by James's even in the time he had left. These people could be anywhere, because of the paths technology had built, because nobody was very far from anybody any more. Indeed, one of them was on his train.

PART TWO

THE CONTACTS

11

LONDON–EDINBURGH TRAIN, 02:05

The train groaned again as it carried James and his unknown companions through an empty station. Although sleepers didn't take on passengers, they did seem to stop for frequent short rests, as if worn out by galloping up the country. Like Dad carrying the kids on his shoulders, across the Downs, grumbling cheerfully. 'Oh, mind your back, Alan!' Mum fretting, to no avail. 'Honestly, watch your father's back!' 'I *am* watching it,' said James, 'I'm right on top of it!' Sally screamed with laughter. It was her favourite thing her little brother had ever said. All of them had laughed for ages, in fact – even Mum, who often didn't come out on those excursions because, as Dad explained, she got very tired doing things around the house and sometimes needed a bit of time to herself.

James took a slug of the second beer and wiped his mouth with the back of his hand. He tried to delete the memory like a file on a computer desktop, drag it over to the bin. It wasn't his intention to spend the whole of these last few hours wallowing in *This Is Your Life* mode. If his life were worth sentimentalizing like that, he wouldn't be finishing it this way. But it was hard not to think of them at all, of course it was. Especially Dad; this trip was the one they'd always done together.

The tradition had begun as early as schooldays. James's dad was a meteorologist. That was the word James and Sally both learned when they were very young – because if they said 'weatherman', their classmates thought he must be on TV. Alan Chiltern was not on TV but, as their mother often liked to remind them, he was more important than those people; he was the one who looked at the satellite pictures and actually worked out what was going to happen in the skies. One evening during the Easter holidays, Dad had announced that he was off to Edinburgh the following week; there was a retirement dinner for one of his old colleagues.

'Can I come?' asked Sally. It took James's breath away, the boldness of it. Sally was fourteen by now; she wore lipstick, her bedroom boasted its own TV and its walls had disappeared behind posters. She talked extensively about a band called New Kids on the Block – often implying, although James didn't really understand how this could be the case, that she was on close personal terms with them.

Mr Chiltern raised his eyebrows. 'I don't honestly see why not!' he said.

James took a deep breath. The kettle screamed in the kitchen; Mum was making gravy. He was almost too nervous to get the words out; he prepared himself, even as he voiced his wish, for disappointment. To be told he was too young.

'And could . . . I mean – what about me?' he asked.

'Well,' said Dad, 'I don't . . .' James's heart was on a seesaw, about to be launched towards the sky or the ground. 'I don't, to be absolutely honest, to be *completely serious with you*, James . . .' It was almost too much for the boy to bear, and then the punch line. 'I don't really see why not, either!'

James's heart soared. He could still remember the excitement when Dad brought the little green tickets home from the station. He could remember telling everyone he met that he was going to Scotland on a train and would have to stay in a hotel because it was so far away.

It was remarkable to him that so many other people were travelling by train, and that they were acting as if it was completely normal, even when the whistle blew to send them off and a fanciful list of stations was read out. Wakefield Westgate. Chesterfield. Durham. These places, for all James knew of the country, might as well be on Jupiter. Sally was wearing a New Kids T-shirt and pale, ripped jeans. James watched the countryside speed by out of the window, feeling the world getting bigger every minute. Sally listened to her Walkman. Dad, reading, clapped very softly a couple of times. This was a habit he had, though normally he knew better than to do it in public – had been told off before. At home it was different. Once a joke in a P. G. Wodehouse novel had caused him to applaud so sharply that James spilled his hot chocolate on the rug, and Jean lamented, 'White was a mistake, I told you, Alan; white is always a mistake.'

But today they weren't at home, and more unusual things kept reminding James of that fact. Mum had made sandwiches, as always – Philadelphia and ham – but to James's surprise Dad instead bought them all much bigger ones from the buffet car, having been unable once more to see why not. He had a can of beer, even though it was only lunchtime, winking to them as he fizzed it open; James had had the idea it was illegal to drink before night-time, because pubs always seemed to be shut until then. 'This is the life!' Dad said, and Sally immediately agreed – 'Yes, this is the life all right' – and so James adopted the phrase, making sure to say it as often as he possibly could in the weeks that followed.

Even when the train slowed and stopped altogether for a little while, and there were announcements about the delay, Mr Chiltern was unconcerned. 'This is a fine state of affairs!' he said, earning an irascible look from the man across the aisle.

'What if something's wrong?' asked Sal.

'You can't stop a train,' Dad remarked, with a relish in the words, as if letting them in on something not many people knew. 'You can hold it up, you can get in the way if you're daft enough, but it will always get where it's going.' And even as the sentence finished, the train had jolted forward, settling almost immediately back into its thoroughbred trot, and James had rested his face against the window and felt the miles thumping by.

At the dinner itself, James wore the stiff white shirt Mum had sent him with, but Sally didn't tease him because she herself was in a velour dress which she claimed several times was velvet. He could no longer remember what they ate, though he did recall Sally's being offered a glass of red wine, which she drank with a display of insouciance but with shining eyes.

The main memory James came away with, and which he still held even now, was of how everyone seemed to love Dad. Red-faced, hearty men ruffled his thick black hair, calling him by a nickname – Sergeant – for reasons James couldn't guess at. They asked James what he wanted to do for a job, and he said he wanted to make computer games, and they all said no no, you want to be in weather, pal, and young James laughed so eagerly at everything that his face started to get sore.

In the hotel room, which they returned to at an intoxicatingly late hour, Dad slept on the floor on an arrangement of sofa cushions, giving his children the bed. They lay side by side, wakeful, aware it was a little odder now to be sharing a bed than when they were really young. Although it had been a very long day, its events had elevated James to a high from which sleep was a distant prospect. He lay on his back, shuffling about, occasionally hearing Sally grumble and tut. He was almost certain that she was asleep, though, and that he was alone to face the unthinkable hours of the morning, when she rolled onto her side and took from the bedside cabinet the notepad and ballpoint pen. He saw her back arch as she began to scribble on the pad, and in the half-dark squinted to see what she had been working on. It was an analogue version of the games he liked to make.

You are in a spaceship bound for the Moon on a mission to

collect rocks. Out of one window you suddenly see something
strange. It looks like a planet that's never been discovered before.

Write 'A' to carry on to the Moon as per your orders
Or
'B' to change course to check out this new place.
Please write your answer below to continue the game.

Long after Sally was too old to improvise role-play games
to help him sleep, James was still making the Edinburgh
trips with his father – once a year, either in summer or at
Christmas. By booking in advance, James always secured
first class – something Dad commented on every time, since
he'd gone the first sixty years of his life without ever getting
into what he called 'the Rolls-Royce area'. The two of them
would sit at their table with books; in the quiet space that
this created, they conducted some of their most successful
conversations. Many of the key changes in James's life were
revealed to Mr Chiltern on those five-hour journeys.

'So, yes, I've started work as a . . . a driver.'

'A cabbie?' Dad's eyes were still on his annual Bill Bryson,
but his eyebrows – thick and black, like his hair – twitched
in interest.

'Not a cabbie exactly; private hire. You have to book us
in advance.' James said this proudly. Sometimes on Saturday
nights, when people flung themselves at the locked doors,
he took a certain satisfaction in pointing to the driver's side
window, below which it said PRIVATE HIRE ONLY. It
wasn't a foolproof way of communicating with people who
had had fifteen Sambucas, but he liked the passenger to
feel safe.

'That sounds fun,' said Mr Chiltern, the same thing he

said about almost any new proposition that wasn't signing up for a war. 'And how did you get into that?' James replied by talking about how he'd helped someone get to hospital in an emergency recently and realized that driving could be a good way of meeting people and making himself useful. He spared his father the details, the drama. Mr Chiltern, glancing up from the Bill Bryson, nodded approvingly and said that perhaps James could drive them up to Scotland one of these years. Both of them knew they didn't really want that; the train was part of the ritual.

A couple of years later, Dad became the first of the family to hear about Michaela. 'I think I'm . . . well. In love with her,' said James, aware that he would never be able to come out with this sentence if the cover of Bryson's Australian travelogue hadn't put up a little wall between them. Dad clapped his hands together softly, almost unnoticeably. 'Excellent,' he said. 'Your mother has high hopes for this Michaela. I mean, both of us do,' he added after a few moments, rubbing his hair. 'But she's the one who tends to have the stronger opinions, as we know.'

'What – what does she think of Sally . . . Sal marrying Declan?' James found he was able to ask.

Dad nodded at the page as if the verdict on his daughter's fiancé was to be found there. 'Solid chap, very sporty. Seems to care for her. But Australia is an awfully long way away. That's one of Mr Bryson's insights.'

After the diagnosis, James wasn't sure how to ask whether the Edinburgh trip was still on, but Mum insisted. 'He doesn't want anything to be different.' And so up they went, towards the end of August 2014. The train was full of festival performers, cello cases and accordions clogging the luggage racks; pale, earnest young men with hoodies advertising their shows. 'I wouldn't have minded being a performer, an actor, you know,' said Dad, although this had never come up before. Bryson had apparently decided even Australia wasn't enough for him: this year's book offered the entire history of the earth.

'An actor?'

'Used to do a bit at university,' said Dad, 'messing around, revue, that sort of thing. Would have liked to be on the weather-report side of things, on the telly. I did try out for it once.' James looked across the table at his father. His hair had been thinned out alarmingly by the treatment, and gone grey, bone-white in places. There were liver spots on his hands that hadn't been there before. He didn't like the tone of reminiscence; didn't like the past tense that Dad was starting to apply to himself.

'Did an all-right job of it, too,' said Mr Chiltern, sipping his tea. 'But the chap making the decision was a – what's the word. Stupid bastard.' James had never heard his father speak like that before; he snorted some of his own cup of tea and took a moment to recover as Dad went on. 'Good luck to this lot, going up there and performing. That's my point. Takes some nerve.'

'How have you – how are you feeling?' James managed to ask, after several minutes' inner consideration.

'Oh, not bad, not bad at all most of the time,' said Dad, and James slipped thankfully back into the mental space he'd occupied for the past few months, in which his father's illness was a regrettable but unchanging state, a problem which could be deferred for ever. A heavily tanned man in a flat cap went down the aisle with a folded-up unicycle over his shoulder. James stood up to help him jam it into the overhead locker, and the conversation spotted its chance and moved on, Dad giving a nearly silent clap to some witticism about cosmic destiny as the train flew up the spine of the country.

During the trip, they saw the man again, this time on his unicycle, with two flaming torches in his hands and one sticking from his mouth like a fish from a seal's. It was near the top of the Royal Mile. The street performer – now dressed in a striped shirt, like an American sports referee's – spotted them before they even had time to react. 'My friends from the train!' he shouted, in front of the large crowd, tourists with their wriggling children, the rubber-neckers that always built around a dangerous-looking stunt. 'Come here and hold the ladder for me, sir!'

'It's you!' said Dad in undisguised delight. 'What are you waiting for, a barn dance to start? He means you!'

James found himself, in front of all the pairs of eyes, clutching the stepladder as the performer mounted it, torches in his hands and mouth, one of them brushing close enough to James that he could feel the heat on his arms. 'Let's hear it for my volunteer!' yelled the performer, and, taking James's name, hectored the crowd into chanting it. *James! James! James! James!* chorused the strangers and, in the middle of it all, he saw his father clapping his hands together vigorously, a huge smile on his face. And he simul-taneously saw that Dad was forming a memory he would treasure, and also understood there would not be many more like it, and James had to look down at the cobbled street beneath his feet and think about something else.

That evening as they stood in their favourite spot, near the end of North Bridge, Dad referred for the first time to what was coming.

'I'd like it if you would scatter me off here, James, old man,' he said, resting one hand on the low wall and gesturing into the sky with the other.

'What do you mean?' asked James, feeling an internal tightening, as if he were small again, and something bad had come into the room at night.

'Not immediately.' Alan Chiltern smile-frowned. 'Not right this minute, I think there'd be a scene if you chucked me off now. But my ashes. You know.'

'Your . . .?'

'After they cremate me. After the funeral.'

James felt his fists ball up tightly. He looked out at the sky. It was like a cocktail poorly mixed, with three distinct layers. Thin, almost translucent blue at the top. Then a bolder, deeper blue, broken up with narrow ribbons of cloud. Then, low down, over the castle and the Tattoo floodlights, was a stripe of butterscotch. The sunlight was off-yellow: it turned the solemn buildings of the Old Town a variety of golden-brown shades. Because it was impossible to reply, James made himself list the clouds. Wispy cirrus up high, taking on the brittle blue as if it were paint leaking onto them. Further down, layers of stratus like long bread-sticks. James wanted his dad to nod approvingly, he wanted him to say, 'Excellent work!', though of course he hadn't spoken the names out loud.

'Well,' James said, forcing brightness into his voice, 'I don't think we need to talk about it just yet!'

'I don't know how long it will be,' said Dad, 'but perhaps not *all* that long.' He coughed, and James had the sensation that he'd been preparing this speech, something so out of character that it only added to the head-swim of this moment. Dad's hand was on his shoulder. 'But what it would mean, you see, is you could pop here and see me, in a manner of speaking. Keep me abreast of things. The wedding. Whatever's happening in your job – and I know great things will happen for you.'

He raised his eyebrows: a human at the mercy of the march of events, a way James could not remember seeing him before. 'Not quite the same as being here in the flesh. But, all the same. We'd be sort of meeting, wouldn't we?'

James nodded, numb, and glanced to his left. The sunlight, fizzing like a firework before it died, beamed off the golden letters of the Scotsman building. It was at that instant James decided he would leave the flat he shared with Karl. Move in with Michaela. Focus less upon the driving, more upon helping with her new fitness business. Probably, with hindsight, it had not been a perfect time to make any sort of decision. But he'd had to do *something*. His brain had needed to put up some sort of shield against the way the moment was being crushed, as if in a big hand, between past and future. The past, so rich with small joys that weren't theirs any more; and the future which, in six months, would require James and Sally to watch as a green curtain – closing bit by bit, inching around the rail – took their father away from them for the rest of time.

Their grief, in a three-person huddle at the front, had been wildly and inevitably out of proportion with anyone else's: with the kind-faced celebrant who was on his third funeral of the day, with the family friends and conscripted half-relatives who, Sally had said bitterly, were all just relieved not to be in the casket themselves. *Yet*, she added. James had grimaced at that. 'I'm not sure we should use the day as – you know. As a recruitment drive for the next person to go.' Sal had grinned through her tears, briefly. She and James had been texting each other dozens of times a day in the run-up to this horrible event, and he felt as close to his sister as he had since they were children. He squeezed Sally's arm even harder and – because the curtain was closing, the final few seconds in Dad's company were upon them – said, under his breath: *I'll make you proud, Dad. I'll do something good.*

When he looked back on that later, James hadn't really known what he had meant by it. But, over the last year or so, he'd known with a deadening certainty that he was getting further and further from making it come true.

★

He could hear the conductor, if that was a phrase still in use, holding a conversation right outside his door. She'd been so full of energy when they boarded. 'You're in number four, and the toilets, if you need them, are. . .' 'You've got a first class there, which means you're going right here, and then sort of back on yourself. . .' He'd even wondered if she was always this chirpy; if, perhaps, working on a midnight train meant that the night became your morning. But the past couple of hours had seemingly taken a toll of some kind. Her voice was a stage whisper, hushed and intrusive at the same time. The voice of someone conscious of the need to be quiet – people were sleeping, after all – but constitutionally unsuited to the task. 'There's nothing I can do,' she said, several times. 'There is *nothing* I can do.' The confined nature of the space – James's head against the back wall, the Welsh woman just the other side of it – made it feel as if she were having the conversation in the same room as him, had wandered in for some reason.

He could only pick up fragments, something about being out of options, being 'backed into a corner'. *I mean, it doesn't really matter*, thought James, raiding his plastic bag again for the first of two Melton Mowbray pies. He bit into the claggy pastry. *It doesn't matter at all.* The whole point was that the time of things mattering was over. The misery of it, the physical ache in his muscles that had come from failing, over and over again – those were a few hours away from being over, for good. There had been a version of himself that tried to solve people's problems, that drove people where they needed to go, knocked on doors to ask if everything was all right. But that person had turned out not to be good enough – and had been spat out.

It doesn't matter any more, he told himself again, brushing pie crumbs into his cupped hand and depositing them in the tiny bin under the ledge. That much, he could do. Someone else would have to tidy this up, after all. It was still common courtesy not to make a stranger's life more difficult than it had to be. Beyond that small principle, though, James no longer had to care about other people. All that mattered was his own welfare. And with every clatter and lurch of the train, he was getting closer to the point where that welfare would be permanently taken care of.

12

MELBOURNE, 13:05

The first thing Sal had had to do after calling Mum was get rid of the interviewer, pretend that both she and he were not being shat on by the elephant that Meghan had introduced into the room. She'd seen the glimmer in his eyes; she knew he'd got ten times what he could have imagined from this appointment. *'While we're talking, Chiltern's assistant suddenly changes the game big-time ...'* He had at least had the grace to say that he wouldn't mention any of this, and maybe it was true. But that wasn't even the point. It was the fact that he'd laid hands on this personal information at the same time Sal had. It felt like someone going through her knicker drawer. And not even by snooping, but by Meghan flinging open the bedroom door and saying, over there, bottom left – or the dirty ones are in the wicker basket if you prefer.

Meghan was a great PA and she was learning, and Sal loved to promote women in the workplace and pass on some of what she'd learned, but also, Meghan was a fucking idiot. 'Your brother's about to kill himself.' Was that a way you began a conversation with someone listening? Was that a way to break the news? At least she'd seemed to sense she'd messed up. Sal had gone wordlessly past her, out into the laneway to call home, ignoring Meghan's half-question; Meghan had flinched as if someone had slapped her. Sal was angry enough that she *could* have slapped her.

The day was hot, the chrome and glass twinkling like the ocean in the sun. The city was exactly as it should be. The city that was her home now. Growing up, Sal had often read books where the heroine ran away to become queen of an animal kingdom, or was adopted by mermaids. In adult life she had found that alternative universe, here, the reverse side of the world. She'd refused to play the game her schoolfriends wandered into, the two kids and stolid relationships, the soft-play and date nights 'to keep the spark', a world that stretched no further in any direction than the week in Majorca every August. She had made up a different game and played it like a pro. Her teenage self would have rubbed her eyes in joy to see 2019 Sally. Right down to the way she'd chopped off those last two letters.

That was how she would have summarized her existence, in total, if asked to do a self-assessment even an hour ago. And yet now, standing in an alley under a blue-purple mural of Jimi Hendrix, surrounded by the high spirits and profitable activity of others, she was being asked to believe that James was threatening suicide, or conceivably had even done it already, and she could not even get him, her brother, on the phone.

No. He couldn't. He couldn't have done anything. This could still be fixed, and would be fixed, by Sal.

'The person was not available.' Christ. This was such an irresponsible thing to do. It wasn't like James, not the James she knew. Used to know. They used to text nearly every day, when she first started living in Australia. 'It doesn't have to be a big deal, the distance, not with a phone,' she'd said, when he almost – almost – made her cry by surprisingly showing up to see her off at Heathrow. (She held back and had a short sob hours later, when she was safely over Uzbekistan.) They'd met up any time she came back to the UK to see Mum or look for wedding venues.

But the thought of the wedding, and the way he and Michaela had missed it, stopped her mind in its tracks. Michaela had a lot to answer for, she really did. With her fucking pantsuits. Talking about how she'd 'discovered' quinoa as if she'd stumbled upon it on the banks of the Amazon or something, when in fact she hadn't even mastered pronouncing it. Calling herself a businesswoman, who'd invented the concept of 'plus-size running'. James had never been the same once he was with her. If they hadn't met, if she hadn't driven Sal and James apart, would they be in this situation right now?

All right. Anger was not the right response. Nor was sentimentality. The present was what counted. Sal was good at this stuff. Mentally, she sketched out a five-point plan.

1. Make this list. (This was a little joke of Sal's. She'd put it in all her time-management books. Sometimes, readers tweeted her pictures of lists

with this at the top. It wasn't just a gag; it was meant to relax you, release a bit of the tension that held you back from making good gut decisions.)

2. Go back to office, grab laptop, delegate anything high-priority to Meghan. (Not 'hi-pri'. She wished to God she could stop Meghan saying that. Australians loved to abbreviate, but this was a millennial buzzword too far.)

3. Get out of office. Breathing exercises.

4. Reach out to James's network, see who can help.

5. Go for a walk, assess it in an hour.

It was pretty simple. There was no wizardry to her lists, ever. The opposite. They were about simplifying. You could solve any problem in five steps.

All the same, as she headed back in towards the lifts – Arnie rising, with his infinite slowness, once more – Sal felt an unfamiliar doubt gnawing at her. Who *were* James's social circle? Once more it dug her in the heart, the fact was that since the wedding debacle, they'd barely communicated. Three years lost that way. She didn't know if James had a girlfriend these days. There was still Karl, the black guy who talked so much like a contract killer she was never sure if he was putting it on. But James didn't work for him any more, she'd gathered from Mum. Although the details escaped Sally now. It was hard to take much concrete information from the weekly phone calls, because of Mum's tendency to approach them as if Sal was a recently escaped hostage (*oh, you've missed so much, now, what did I have to tell you*) and to ricochet between unrelated topics, like a social media feed in a Laura Ashley cardigan.

'Going to work somewhere out of the office?' said Meghan, her tongue flicking out and playing around her lips, as it sometimes did when she was anxious.

'No, Meghan. I'm off to inspect a building site.'

'I don't have that in the schedule?'

I mean for the love of God, thought Sal.

'I was joking.'

'Aw. Right.'

Sal looked at Meghan, peering out through her glasses, spreadsheet of Sal's activities in front of her, and felt the usual admixture of fondness and frustration. Two-thirds frustration. Actually, four-fifths right now. Nine-tenths. Meghan was a nonsense figure, she really was. In Britain you'd never get a job in an office environment if your grasp of sarcasm was as bad as hers.

'I'll be back for the pick-up later.'

Meghan stared down at the desk, those big round lenses looking as if they could bore a hole in the workspace. Sal knew she wanted to ask if everything was all right with James, if she could do anything. When Meghan *almost* said things and bottled it, it was worse than when she did say them. One day Sal was going to take her out for margaritas, do some mentoring. Work on this side of Meghan's game. Communication. Empathy. But not right now. There was more than enough going on today, it turned out.

She went down Bourke a couple of blocks in the weekend sunshine, waited for the green man and the clock-clock-clock of the 'walk' signal, thinking as usual of that sloppy cow getting nailed by the tram. Just being out of the office was helping, already. There was no need to panic. She was exactly on schedule, still, because her schedule had built-in contingency time. She wouldn't be late for the pick-up or the interviews or anything. She looked at the wide Myer shopfront, one of the first things she'd seen when she came to Melbourne. *This is like your John Lewis*, Dec had said, *but just sort of less depressing*. Saturday shoppers with big white bags. A row of red flags announcing the arrival of *West Side Story*. A Japanese man was playing a sort of electronic harp, a little crowd of children watching him. The sky was still promo-photo blue, just a couple of high, skimpy clouds: cirrus. She thought of the word and thought of Dad who'd point up in the sky, on the Downs, and test them: 'What do we call this one? And what about that nasty grey blighter over there? Excellent work.'

The confident black letters – M Y E R – seemed to swirl in front of Sal for a second, and she felt the grip of something nameless and frightening, something strong enough to pull her right through the pavement, into nothingness. She put out a hand and grabbed a railing, earning a look from a skinny guy, absurdly sporting a bobble hat on this thirty-degree day, whose coffee she nearly knocked over.

'We're going to take a breath,' she muttered to herself. And again, the body obeyed; the shaky seconds passed, the floor was solid. She'd been very cynical about all this – breathing, meditation, mindfulness. But Dec had been right. It never lasted long, the . . . that feeling. Sal addressed herself, mentally now, as if she were talking to someone at one of her workshops.

OK. Look. There are only two scenarios. Either you can solve this problem, this insane James problem, or you can't. If you can't, there's no point spending another second thinking about it. But the likelihood is you can.

Sal got out her pocket-mirror, the one that used to belong to Jean. She would call Mum again and tell her everything was going to be fine. Then she'd work out how to make that into the truth.

13

Emil wasn't sure what he'd been expecting when Steffi's message had come through about 'shit going on', but it definitely hadn't been a missing-person search. If he was honest, he'd hoped for a small personal drama, maybe a dumping; something that could be ironed out reasonably easily over a few drinks. Back in San Sebastián he'd specialized in those. He had far more female friends than actual girlfriends. That was what happened if you were a good listener, but not very tall. He'd hoped, in London, where nobody knew him as a serial loser in love, that he could make a fresh start – as a man you could talk to, have a drink with, fool around with maybe. As a fun guy and a considerate, gentle lover, which he knew he was, if he could get anyone to sleep with him, which so far he couldn't, over here.

The London rebrand of Emil into sexy, man-about-town Emil hadn't really worked out so far. He struggled with the language; the restaurant's hours were unsociable; he often left work smelling of parmesan or fish – none of this helped. And maybe restaurant culture had just become blander. If you read books by the famous chefs, they were all perpetually off their tits and shagging like Vikings. They were jumping each other on the worktops, they were snorting double lines off the butcher's block; it was surprising they ever got any food onto the pass at all. After service here, people mostly seemed to go home and watch *Game of Thrones*. Emil wanted to be having sex; he didn't want to be watching other people having sex with elves, or whatever the fuck it was. He'd only seen the first episode, and there were so many characters he'd had to take a nap afterwards.

And now finally he got to hang out with a girl from work. But it hadn't turned out to be a small personal drama; it was weirder and more complicated. Her flatmate, or whoever he was, was threatening to do himself in, and Steffi was making Emil play real-life Cluedo at two in the morning.

As soon as they'd met, and with minimal explanation, she had dragged Emil into King's Cross, which was in its bleak closing stages. We have to start somewhere, she'd said, and this is where he works, so who knows? But at this time of night it wasn't really where *anyone* worked. The last trains had gone, the huge departure boards were all empty. The GNR bar had finished chucking out. A security man in a blue Puffa jacket was trying to wake a couple of people who'd gone to sleep not far from the ticket gates. One of them protested angrily. From what Emil could understand, she was catching an early train in the morning and had nowhere else to go. 'I'm not hurting anyone, am I?' she kept saying.

Emil had watched, curious and willing but mostly confused, as Steffi marched up to the security man and asked if he could help them. 'We are looking for someone whose life is in danger,' she said. Emil was impressed by the grandeur of it, and obscurely pleased to be caught up in something which sounded like a film. *A life in danger*. But it was cold, the miserable English cold-in-your-bones he hadn't been prepared for even though everyone talked about it. And the quest made no sense. There was no chance of finding him here, surely, if he'd sent the text so long ago. There was no chance of finding him anywhere, without further clues. And there weren't really any clues because Steffi hardly even seemed to know the guy they were searching for. He didn't understand why she was taking it quite so personally.

Steffi went through the identifiers. 'An overweight guy, sort of wavy dark hair, a bit . . . sometimes a bit – a bit sweaty,' she added, guiltily, knowing she had to say anything that might help. The security man nodded gamely but with a show of regret; his face suggested he was used to hearing people out and then disappointing them. 'I'm afraid I haven't seen anyone like that on the concourse tonight. And I do check all over the concourse. And that does include the toilets, I've had to knock on doors before now, I've had to wake people who've fallen asleep on the job, as it were, so it's not just the concourse I check.' Emil had never encountered the word 'concourse' before, but the station man seemed to be getting paid per use of it, and Steffi was becoming visibly impatient at the repetition. 'I think you should probably call the police,' he said.

Steffi had already done this, she said. She gave the man her number and asked him to call her if he happened to see anyone who could be James. She supplied her name.

'Like Steffi Graf! German?' said the security officer, and Steffi agreed, even though she was actually Dutch with German parents, and even though she only knew who Steffi Graf was because of the number of people who had said the same thing since she moved here.

*

'I've already called the police, obviously I have done that, I don't have shit in my brain.' Steffi's eyes were bright with annoyance; her cheeks were a little pink in the sickly street-light. 'But what can they do? Search the whole of London? We have to reach out to whoever knows him. Knows where he is.' Steffi glanced at her battery. It was down to 16 per cent, the red-bar zone, the road to Hell. Even looking at the screen seemed to cost another percentage point each time. The sheep game had drained the battery like a thief. 'His . . . friends or his ex, something.'

'Can we do it indoor, in a place?' asked Emil.

She looked guardedly at him. It *was* getting chilly, she had to admit that. There was still a stealth drizzle, only just visible as an orangey swirl in the lights, brushing like a fellow traveller against their skin. But she wasn't taking him back to hers, if that was what he meant. He hadn't been particularly good value so far; he wasn't shaping up as much of a Watson to her Holmes, unless in the original books Watson was always shivering and thinking about getting into Holmes's pants, which she doubted.

'You know anywhere?'

'Yeah, the Mixer. Open, like, nearly ever.' Emil had once hit the tequila here till 5 a.m., on one of his few successful nights out in London. They'd only left in the end because the barman – having put the lights on and killed the music in a vain attempt to encourage patrons to go home – had moved on to Plan C, which involved smashing his fist on the cash register and using phrases like 'I am at breaking point', which the friends did not need Duolingo to grasp the general sense of.

Steffi hesitated. 'I don't want to get stuck.'

'You can stay in mine.' Emil realized how eager this sounded; regretted that his English was such a blunt instrument. But if you didn't ask, you didn't get anywhere. 'I have, how to say it, a bed, it hangs.'

He mimed the hammock which hung as a sort of ersatz spare bed in his landlord's flat, because the landlord was a 23-year-old whose rich parents had bought him the place as a 'start in life', and he had spent a post-uni travel year filling it with international artefacts – rattan blankets, drums, weird-ass skulls – which Emil and four others lived around, like squatters in a museum, for £700 each a month. Like a reluctant charades partner, Steffi guessed the word but had to google it to make sure. Emil had googled it too, and for a strange moment the two of them stood, far from their birthplaces, in the small-hours grey, looking at pictures of hammocks on their mobiles.

'All right,' said Steffi at last. It was hard to see what other option she had. She couldn't go home, with the situation as it was, and she wasn't going to trail around the city on her own. 'I will get us an Uber to this bar. We will message people and do whatever and find him. Then I'll get an Uber home.'

Emil watched her fingers skip across the screen to summon a car and then share James's number with him, in case her battery went. The series of digits – under the name James Flat – went on their way up into space and back down onto his phone, less than a foot away. Her nails were painted different colours, pink, red, black, but most of them were chipped away. Working in a restaurant, even just as a waiter, killed your hands. Emil had heard on a podcast that head chefs never appointed a sous if their hands were too pretty; it showed that they were scared of proper work. The day after he read it, Emil deliberately plunged his hand into a hot pan. It had stung for a week, but he was proud of the scar. Maybe one day he'd get one on the other hand.

'What's even up with him? A girl, or no money, or . . .?' Emil tried to imagine what other problems you could have, but the effort of empathy was too great.

'Both of those, a little,' said Steffi, waving to get the attention of the driver. 'I'll explain when we get there.'

The car conveyed them through the nightscape dotted with other strangers: a drunk guy being helped along, a couple bickering next to an old stone church. They went past a place on the right whose name she recognized, some sort of club or rock venue she thought; she didn't go to music shows much because it was a lot of standing and also very loud music made her teeth hurt, which she had never told anyone. She had a lot of minor secrets; everyone did. She wondered exactly how much of James's despair she could 'explain'. What did she actually know about him? Well, more than most people would probably have picked up, thanks to the combination of detective instinct and insomnia. She knew that James was paranoid about personal hygiene, because she'd once caught him googling a product that kept you sweat-free. Not *caught* him, just glanced at the screen, walking into the kitchen, and he'd jumped as if she'd seen him logging on to a terrorist chatroom. That he wore dark shirts when he went out on dates; that he was on at least one dating app, hadn't had a serious girl-friend since he was dumped, or a serious job since his friend screwed him over: this much she knew just from the bad night, the night with the crying.

James had always been a pretty easy person to live with, if that was even the phrase for it. Their lives only intersected through an Amazon package handed over, a *how are things* in the kitchen. The reassuring crunch of his key in the door late at night. His behaviour recently had been a little erratic. He would get up in the early hours and do things that made no sense at 3 a.m., like heating up a lasagne or spraying himself with aftershave. He paced up and down, sometimes, between the kitchen and her bedroom. He couldn't have imagined she was awake to witness any of this, because he didn't know how little she normally slept.

The polite exchanges of their mornings and evenings; the strange, unacknowledged shadow-routine of the nights.

Several times recently Steffi had wondered about it. Whether he was all right, whether she should ask him somehow, in one of the tiny windows of conversation they had. But it didn't really feel like – as the English would say – any of her business. And that night when they did meet, the night with the crying, was embarrassing to recall, largely because she sensed *he* was so embarrassed by it. It was easier not to refer to it at all. It had been easiest of all to assume that whatever emotional strain he was under that night, it had passed by now. It was a pretty reasonable thing to assume. If he needed some sort of help, somebody else would be supplying it.

With that assumption in her head she had left the house in the early afternoon, saying no more than the briefest hi and bye to James, who was in the kitchen, preparing some sort of stodgy snack. She hadn't spent more than a few moments wondering why he wasn't going in to work today. She didn't really know his schedules; it was obviously a day off. There was nothing in what he said or did, in that brief period of their last interaction, to make a normal person worry about him.

Yet just a few hours after that, he'd left the same building with what sounded like the genuine intention of killing himself. Steffi, without ever having asked for a responsibility like this or feeling she deserved it, was perhaps the last person to have seen him, said hello, had the chance to change his path. It was mad, and awful, but still . . . not *exciting*, that wasn't it. But there was the chance to do something. To solve a puzzle that meant something real.

The barwoman had hair like Steffi wanted hers to be: spiky, a bit punk-looking. Bleached, and then dyed red at the tips. It was tiring even to think about how long it would take to do all that. She allowed Emil to order her a beer and sighed inwardly as he tried to get a fuller grip on the situation.

'He's fired because he's bad driver?'

'No, I don't think it was that.' James had said – in that terrible conversation – that he had always been an impeccable driver, and Steffi hadn't just been humouring him when she said she believed it. He wasn't the sort to build himself up unduly, and anyway, you only had to see how he got the hoover into corners. 'It was something more complicated. His boss, his boss was his mate, and they had, they fell out or something.'

'Fell . . .?'

Steffi sighed. Why would you be here a year, two years, and not make an effort to learn the language. It made her look bad by association; it gave fuel to all these people, more of them every week, who said things like 'Britain is full'. The people who had said to her Czech friend, the dishwasher, who'd been here nineteen years and had two kids with an English boyfriend: 'You must be going home soon.'

'The boss said James did something wrong. James said, no, I didn't. But the guy didn't believe him.'

'Well, why don't you call him,' said Emil, as the barwoman thumped down the beers in front of them. 'You know his name?'

She didn't, but there *was* something James used to say: what was it? When people called him directly for a ride. He used to say the name. 'Hello . . .' and then the name of the company. What was it?

'Anything else?' asked the barwoman.

Steffi refocused on the present. 'That's all, thanks. I like your hair.'

'It's for Keith Flint,' said the server, and Steffi remembered the dance music guy who'd died that week – it popped up several times on her Twitter feed – and then by some sideways mental skip she remembered the word James used to say. 'Cruiz!'

'Cruise?'

'With a z. I think that's the name. He used to say, "Hello, Cruiz".'

'You want to call them? You want my phone, battery more?'

They moved to let someone else get to the bar. There was the usual odd sensation attached to handling someone else's iPhone, a stranger's, knowing how much of their life was inside it. But then it was still weird to be holding a phone to her ear at all. To be *calling* someone. She might as well be in *Friends* here.

Emil watched her face: tense, focused. She reminded him a bit of an animal. Her features were a little like a . . . squirrel, maybe? Alert, intent. A smallish face. She looked like she could dart into the trees any time. He probably wouldn't use the squirrel comparison out loud.

'Hello, no, I don't have a destination,' said Steffi. He saw her jaw clench. 'No, I don't have a reference number. Listen to me.' She would be a bad person to annoy, Emil thought; she had steel. Although he never really *wanted* to annoy anyone, of course not. It just seemed to go that way a lot.

'I need to speak to whoever is in charge,' Steffi demanded. She made a gesture and Emil handed her the pint. She sipped it and shook her head.

'No. Listen. That's not it. I need to speak to the guy, whoever it is, who fired James Chiltern.' Her eyes changed; yes, it looked like the name had had an effect. When she spoke again it was in the tone of someone pressing home an advantage, someone on a TV quiz who knew they had the right answer.

'I need to get in touch with him, because James Chiltern is about to commit suicide.'

14

Michaela's contacts had always been a bit of a mess. Even though her family name was Adler and so her mum and brothers should be right at the top of the list, they were instead saved as (for example) Jerome Brother, or Mum Mum, and lived in different parts of the alphabetical list. The top name on the list – a name she saw, without processing it, every day of her life – was therefore someone she and James had once purchased a piece of equipment from, who was saved as Exercise Ball Adnan. She called this stranger accidentally from her pocket three or four times a year; once he'd been at the Rio Carnival, once in a hot-air balloon. It had always amused and incensed Michaela that she was in James's phone as 'Michaela Adler', rather than as just Michaela or Michaela Girlfriend or, as she had once suggested, Michaela, Queen of My Heart and of Universe. 'First name, surname is just how I have everyone,' James had said, laughing. 'But I'm not *everyone*, am I,' she'd protested, tweaking his nose, grabbing his lovely puppy-fat.

Karl was saved as Karl James Mate; Michaela had been drunk when she put the number in her phone. It was a number that, for a while, she had used multiple times every day. Around the time of that European train adventure, and in fact for a couple of years afterwards, she and Karl James Mate messaged each other more frequently than James and Karl themselves did. In-jokes, observations on James's latest anti-sweat tactic, on his mania for keeping his new phone out of the rain. They were his entourage, his left and right hands. Their opinions on James were the only ones which held any validity; everyone else was on the outside. They'd do it at 2 a.m., sometimes. Her in a cab home from a health and fitness event which free booze had turned into a health and fitness hazard; Karl out in the car. There'd been something so rare about it, about such a keenly felt friendship with a bloke which was nonetheless completely innocent, had no prospect of turning into anything else. James had never felt insecure, she knew that; he didn't flinch if her phone pinged at an odd time. He, after all, was what they really had in common.

Now, dwelling midway down the contact book among the Ms, Karl James Mate was a name she barely noticed from week to week any more. He was in the chapter of life she had closed by moving here. But that chapter wasn't quite closed after all, it turned out; it had opened again tonight, violently and without warning. And Michaela was sitting in her newly renovated kitchen, past the tail-end of a drunken evening, dialling and redialling the number from her supposed past, while the man at the middle of her present sat with a whisky and an expression she was starting to find intolerable.

*

When the phone lit up for the fourth time, Karl took a deep, peevish breath. This was just as they were finally getting up a bit of steam, clear of the drab post-London stretch with the hangar-like furniture warehouses, the stadiums, all the big yellow storage units which looked like you could hide a dead body in them. The M1 nice and clear, the rain drifting off. Less than three hours now if there were no more clowns sticking their spades in the road.

Four calls, though – not texts, calls? It was time to pay some sort of attention. He pulled over on the hard shoulder, removed the phone from its base, and opened the door with great caution. He glanced worriedly at his passenger. The cars thudded by, incredibly fast, as motorway cars always seemed when you weren't in them. But the guy appeared to be properly asleep, breathing through his mouth, his face serene.

Karl rustled his way over to where the undergrowth was thick and flopped his penis over his waistband. He wasn't going to mess about with the buttons. Whatever joker invented the button fly, Karl would see him in Hell. He heard his stream patter against the foliage. He unlocked his phone with one hand, brought up his missed calls.

What the fuck is this? he thought.

There was a call from Australia, for a start. There was another one from . . . Michaela, of all people. Michaela! And then two missed calls from Hugo. And finally, a recent text from Hugo, which said that he didn't want to alarm him, but he really did need to get in touch ASAP. With him, or with James Chiltern. James? Why were people on about James? What was the fucking beef here?

As he walked back to the car, finger working to unearth more and more of his inbox in long swipes, stealthy fear began to fill Karl. It was like turning on the news hours into their reportage of some tragedy, trying to piece together what was already known to many other people. He remembered the morning of the tube bombings in London, hungover and uncomprehending, people on the telly huddled outside stations, reporters saying things like 'difficult to guess exactly how many casualties'. Wondering if it was one of his mum's days to get the tube to work. It was a cold, churning feeling, then and now. He slid into the driver's seat, his bowels suddenly heavy, and found at last the message from James himself.

I've decided to end my life.

'No, no,' said Karl, softly. 'Oh, no, no.'

He pressed the screen to call James, but with no expectation of hearing anything other than what he did: the same recorded message that had fended everyone else off. 'The person you are calling . . .' Before it had even finished, he pressed the red button. He sat nauseous in the leather seat, the driver door still slightly open, listening in a daze to the cars whizzing past.

A train went chattering by, a whirl of movement and purpose, and Karl thought of the holiday with Michaela and James. He remembered lecturing Michaela on artificial intelligence. She had dropped her phone twice during the trip – once while running on a cobbled street in Aix-en-Provence – and the screen was cut into spiderwebs. 'One day they'll take it personally,' Karl told her, 'one day they'll be intelligent enough to design a giant phone, pick *you* up and drop you on your face on the pavement.' Michaela reached down from the bunk and started to arm-wrestle him, an arm-wrestle nobody could win. Karl had worried secretly, when James met Michaela, that he might be excluded from the relationship that emerged. But instead, they'd become a three-person gang.

Outside the train which was dragging the three friends back home, the sky had bruised to purple. Churches, little villages, supermarkets were presented briefly and then whisked away again, all of them given a momentary exoticism by the rose-tint of the dying holiday. There was wistfulness in their laughter, because none of them knew when they'd get away like this again, but the blush of the booze was still warm for all of them; the return to real life seemed far off, still, though England was only a few hours away. Anyway, real life was working out pretty well. 'Information is the money of the new century,' Karl – half-cut – had heard himself say. Michaela repeated it in a squeaky voice, deliberately foolish and much too loud: she just had no internal volume control, always spoke like someone wearing a pair of headphones. There'd been a sharp knock on the door and in came the guard, an Italian man they'd first met on the platform, with a maroon jacket and a completely bald skull which reminded James of a skeleton in a doctor's surgery.

'You make too much noise,' said the guard, 'people are sleep here, if you keep to make the noise you have to leave train.'

'We don't want any bother, mate,' Karl had said, knowing that he sounded – as usual – like a minor gangster in a Guy Ritchie film, someone owing a small sum of money to a main character.

'But it is some *botherrr*,' replied the guard, echoing and distorting the English word in a way that suggested he didn't entirely understand it, but liked the sound of it. 'It is *bother* if you wake people.'

'Why don't you have a drink with us,' Karl suggested, brandishing a can like the one James was holding now, five years on; and to Karl's own amazement the guard had taken it and drunk almost half of it. In hushed tones the three travellers paid tribute to their new friend, who ended up staying for almost half an hour. Karl called him a 'cast-iron legend'. He made unsustainable promises to invite him to the wedding James and Michaela would have one day. He thought about how lucky he was to know somebody like James. James had got him into the driving job in the first place, not to mention bailing him out financially several times in the past.

But then, he had also helped James. He'd gently nudged him on to the weight-loss course which led to him meeting Michaela. Yes, they were one of those male friendships you heard about: not spoken about much, enjoyed in a quiet sort of way, acknowledged in the occasional arch text and sneaky compliment. Eventually celebrated when James and Michaela did get married. Karl would knock the shit out of that Best Man's Speech. He sat and watched as James ran his fingers down Michaela's cheek. It was touching, how much he loved her. Karl hadn't yet met anyone he could share everything with, like that. He didn't really want to, even. He just wanted this: the warmth of connection. He shut his eyes, a broad smile on his face, and listened to the rattle of the disappearing world outside.

It wasn't so long ago. It was hardly any time ago. Five years, just over. Karl rubbed his palms together. It felt cold. He trawled his finger down the screen to bring up James; pressed the green button, heard the dead-end message again. 'Fuck my life,' he muttered, and then, 'Fuck my *actual* life,' as if that would make it more definitive. His thumb flexed fast, almost unconsciously, on the screen, tumbling through his contacts, down to the name of the other person on that train: someone he thought he had moved on from, the way you had to move on from most people, in the end.

*

The marimba ringtone seemed loud and ominous in the geometric calm of the kitchen. Phillip, in his Italian dressing gown, paused at the tap where he was pouring a glass of water and gave her another ironic look of indulgence, as if she really should be over this little drama by now. This 'little bit of unpleasantness', her *ex talking about killing himself.* The marimbas continued their siren and Michaela felt herself clench.

'Well, go to bed if you want to go to bed, Phillip.'

But Phillip, instead, went over to the recycling bin and began the long-winded process of removing the lid and then hefting it out into the corridor. As he came back into the kitchen, she could feel his eyes on her, his nostrils twitching discreetly.

'Michaela, are you with him? With James?'

Karl's voice was different, somehow, from how she remembered it. Maybe it was the fact he was the other side of the sea, and the one-second delay that caused; maybe it was just the passage of time, the fibres of a person which the years loosened and altered.

'No. I mean – of course not. Are you?'

'No, mate. Driving.'

Both of them had known it was almost impossible that the other one would say yes, bail them out of the problem in a heartbeat, but both of them had been imagining it anyway. *Yes, don't worry, I've got this. He's fine.* Now the prospect of that gift was gone, and each of them felt slightly resentful of the other for not supplying it.

'Well, do you know what he's been doing tonight?' asked Michaela, trying to screen Phillip out of her field of vision as he left the room – slowly, still with a schoolmasterly air, his body implying that he was happily above all this. But she was being unfair, reading too much in, letting panic do the talking. There was really no time to think about her boyfriend. She needed to think about her ex. 'Is he driving for you, has he been—?'

'He doesn't work for me any more,' said Karl, a little stiffly.

'What?'

'He . . . we went our separate ways.' The line came out stilted even in his own ears. Michaela heard, in it, the memory of how empty it had sounded when she'd used the same phrase, to explain to people why she'd left James.

'So you don't even know . . . I mean, where is he living? Have you checked on him?'

'How can I have checked on him, mate? I've told you, I'm trying to . . . I've had to try and get this bloke to Newcastle.' Karl took a couple more steps away from the car at the thought of his passenger, who was rustling around more than Karl would like, grappling with the seatbelt in his sleep. He hoped the guy wouldn't turn out to be one of those people who were weirdly active in their sleep and startled themselves awake. A mate of Karl's claimed to have done an entire Sudoku in his sleep, but then the same bloke also claimed never to have eaten a piece of fruit. Karl felt, in the back of his throat, the catch of remorse. All these mates who'd never really understood James, who found him a bit quiet and boring; and Karl had ended up favouring that gang over James.

'Well, but you're still his *friend*, right?' Michaela was saying, almost as if she could read his thoughts.

He felt a rising irritation at Michaela's tone, at the suggestion he heard that he was somehow more responsible for this than she was. If she thought she could do better, maybe she should try running a business basically single-handed because Hugo was off half the time getting his skin creams.

Maybe she could try not dumping James, fucking off to Germany to live with this new geezer with big old trendy glasses (Karl had idly looked her up quite recently, on Facebook). Leaving James to deal with the depression and whatnot. The combative mental tone put him back on the front foot, and for a few moments Karl could believe that this situation was entirely of Michaela's making, that his own involvement in it was negligible.

'I've been ringing him, Mich. I'm not an idiot. I've been ringing him and nothing's—'

'I know. I have, too.' What if the whole problem was just that everyone trying to call was getting in each other's way, she thought. All at once she had a brutally clear mental image of James's face – a person who could never seemingly think ill of anyone, assume anything but their goodwill – waiting by his phone. Only wanting someone to get in touch and say, It's OK, you don't need to feel like this, James. Even though she hadn't really believed that that was what was happening – that this was a 'cry for help', like you heard about – Michaela now felt that was exactly it, and that it was terrible she couldn't supply that help. She felt something soften in the wall she had put up between herself and Karl; felt herself reach for his hand across it.

'I'm just scared, Karl.'

'I know. Yeah.' He swallowed. His tone had been too harsh. He was going to say *me, too* but something stopped him. 'Look. I'm sure it's going to be . . . we can sort this. I'll keep trying him. You keep trying him. Right?'

'OK,' said Michaela, grateful for anything that sounded, however faintly, like an escape plan. There was creaking from upstairs. Phillip still wasn't asleep. He was making a point of still not being asleep. 'Stay in touch, will you?'

Stay in touch, she thought, jabbing at James's number the moment Karl's name disappeared from the screen. How many times you ended up saying that. Staying in touch was exactly what she hadn't done, though. Not with James, not with Karl; with hardly anyone from the London life. It was a healthy thing, her therapist had said. To commit to this new life. To live fully in it. Her therapist had said that all sorts of decisions made by Michaela were healthy; it was one of the reasons Michaela was happy to pay her eighty euros a week (non-refundable if cancelled). But this was what happened when you were 'out of touch'. Someone you'd travelled with, someone who'd seen you on the toilet in a reindeer onesie, who'd told you all about his abusive father, things he had never told anyone, now no more than the voice at the other end of a panicked call, a fellow eyewitness, who had gone back to being a stranger in the silence after they said goodbye.

And someone you had lived with, slept with, loved, now wanting to be dead, perhaps already having taken his own life, while you'd been out drinking with the person who replaced him.

Of course, that was a harsh way of putting it. In the long run she believed that James would find someone else – she absolutely believed that. She'd even had the odd daydream in which she and Phillip, James and this notional but absolutely more-suited-than-Michaela new partner, hung out by the canal and exchanged light chat on a subject the daydream didn't supply. It might be better to let go of thoughts like that, the therapist had said; they suggest a part of you hasn't yet left the old relationship. And Michaela *had* largely let them go, but she wasn't paying the therapist €80 a time to tell her what she was allowed to think about in the bath.

Harsh or not, she had left James, and now he was talking about leaving her, leaving everything. She tried the number once more and then, the second the recorded voice began, dropped her phone onto the worktop and rested her head in her hands.

*

Karl shivered as a heavy goods vehicle went by, European phone numbers plastered all over its long body. He clutched himself around the ribs, as if hugging someone else for warmth. He opened the door gently and slid into the driver's seat.

Please man for god's sake message me. I'm sorry about what happened. We can talk.

As soon as he'd got the phone back into its cradle, it lit to signal a notification, and Karl's whole body jerked as if electric-shocked. But it was just Cruiz, some passenger using the messaging service, something dirty sent to the lover he was on his way to meet. Karl didn't even glance at it.

He started the car up as smoothly as he could, waiting for a gap to rejoin the motorway. He still had to get this guy to Newcastle, keep him asleep, finish the job, insane as all these goals seemed now. He had to knock the job off as fast as possible, drive like Lewis fucking Hamilton, except also be ready to stop any time a message came in which might be about James. And not get done speeding, of course. Karl's hands moistened on the wheel. His stomach felt like a bag of cement. There was absolutely nothing he could do but keep driving. That was what he always told himself, when he was halfway through a job and starting to hate it. *What are you going to do, start going in reverse?* It was the way he approached all of life, you might say. You kept moving, didn't get bogged down. You kept on in a straight line.

But the passing of the motorway, at seventy miles an hour beneath him, didn't even feel like forward motion in the light of what Karl had learned. He felt, instead, stuck. Stuck in a cage he'd built for himself: in the car, driving some prick up the motorway, powerless to stop his friend from doing something that would destroy both of them.

15

Steffi didn't remind Emil of a woodland creature any more. The calculating way she was looking at the screen was more like a NASA operative, in one of those movies where everyone wore horn-rimmed spectacles and ended up hugging and whooping. He realized that he'd underestimated her. It was easy to do that when someone was a waiter, when most of your interactions were just them bringing a scrap of paper to you, so that you could perform whatever thirty-second wizardry the latest cover demanded. And wizardry it was. Emil, without wanting to be big-headed about it, was like fucking Gandalf with a skillet. He could achieve things with a courgette that were not of this world. It was only because Juno was an idiot that Emil wasn't already further up the hierarchy. And because of Emil's English, maybe. So inasmuch as he'd thought about their relative statuses at all – like when he recommended that game to Steffi – he'd assumed that she might be quite into *him*, if anything.

But now she had gone into full firefighting mode and she was the one leading the line, while Emil was making a poor job of executing her orders. He'd been told to go around the bar and try to borrow a charger, to revive Steffi's overworked phone which was dangerously close to its death throes. Once more, though, the language was a problem. A panel of seven women around a table – all wearing angel wings, all with beer steins in front of them – had been disputing his request for some time, the conversation rerouting itself unhelpfully into other phone-related business and digressions which might as well be in Swedish for all Emil could follow of them.

'What's the ones you used to get, like before iPhones . . .'

'Galaxy.'

'No, you still get Galaxy. Nokia! That's what I mean.' The speaker, with jet-black hair and as thin as a USB wire herself, jabbed a rhetorical finger at the rest of the party. 'Nokia, they were tiny, like a bar of soap . . .'

'A *bar of soap!*' said one of her friends, mockingly. 'Are you on *Coronation Street?*' Emil didn't understand this jibe, or the tune which the group now broke into – some of them miming wind or brass instruments – but he recognized the quicksand feeling of a conversation slipping away from him.

'So you do not have . . .?' he said, appealing to the one woman among them who seemed less drunk, who was playing with her phone, perhaps carving out an escape.

'I've got an Android,' she replied, apologetic at least, 'but actually my charger is like a, what's it called, like a universal one, so it works on everything . . .'

'I can borrow?' asked Emil, the odds seemingly shifting back in his favour.

'Oh, I haven't actually got it here,' his new friend clarified. 'I was just saying, that would have worked, if I did have it.' There was laughter at this, and a bout of what were probably nicknames being fired to and fro, and Emil retreated, feeling sick of this city, sick of how superior it felt to everyone who showed up at its doors. How superior it felt to him.

He made an empty-handed gesture to Steffi, but Steffi seemed untroubled by the news. She nodded calmly and motioned with her head to the bar. 'OK, so what you can do is get us more drinks.' *This is progress,* thought Emil. You didn't propose extending an already late night unless you had some sort of interest in your companion, in ultimately going home with them. She was hard to read, but surely you didn't.

'No worries,' he said, 'you want the same or—?'

'But also . . .' Steffi hadn't finished. She reached out her left hand, the black fingernail the main survivor from what had once been a colour chart. 'Can I get your phone?'

'My phone?'

'Yes. Then I can get onto my Facebook, because Facebook is chewing up the battery so fast my phone is basically a corpse now, it's on life-support, but if I log in on yours, I can start hitting up his sister and his networks and things. I can work out who might know where he is and help.'

Emil blinked. He'd taken in enough of this to understand it, and it was hard to deny the logic. All the same, the actual act of taking his own phone out and passing it to this girl – who he hardly knew – was a vulnerable one; much more vulnerable than it had felt simply to let her call someone on it. There were things there which it would be best if she didn't see. Which would not strengthen his case. Still. She wasn't going to be rooting around in there, was she? She was hell-bent on finding Mr Suicidal – sexily hell-bent on it, he had to admit, but also inconveniently so. Fine. Maybe if he went into Facebook, she wouldn't be looking around the rest of the stuff. He got his phone out of his pocket, opened the pale blue Facebook icon, signed himself out and put the phone on the table in front of her.

'Passcode is 2510,' he said, 'it's day of the Basque Country.'

'Thank you,' said Steffi, 'and yes, another beer please, and I will pay you back when this is over, when we find him.'

When this is over and *when we find him* were not quite the same two ideas, Steffi admitted to herself, feeling once more the strangeness of another person's phone. Of this object that had been, maybe, all round the world with him. It was almost as intimate as holding someone's hand. She forced her brain back on to James. It was possible this was all too late. That somebody had found him, and it was bad news. But surely, they would know. The internet would be saying *something* about it. No, this was still at stake. And it didn't matter how late it was, even though she would keep hinting at it to discourage Emil from getting ideas. The fact was, she quite obviously couldn't go to sleep while all this was going on. And that thought was cheering in its own right. *No point in going to sleep.* Insomnia couldn't touch her while she was handling this crisis. The night seemed so thick when you were trapped in it, but being up and busy reminded you of how brittle it was. Soon, there would be no night left.

She pulled herself up mentally. Come on, Stef. This is not about you. It's about James. We have to save James. Even that thought, formed in the brain, was sheepishly glamorous, though – there was no denying it. They had to save him, and nobody seemed to have made themselves captain, and so she would do it. She would be in charge.

Before she logged herself into Facebook, though, Steffi – glancing back at the bar, to check Emil was oblivious – ducked out of the icon with a little swipe of the finger and brought up his home screen. He had hesitated for long enough to make her think there might be something note-worthy on his phone, something worthwhile for a detective to pry into. Almost immediately her eyes narrowed, then widened again in interest, and she peeped back over her shoulder once more before letting her keen fingers scuttle onto the screen again.

16

They were somewhere halfway up the country, and the train had eased up for another of its little breathers, shuddering like a cow in a field as it came to rest. James took the last mouthful of the third beer, wiped his mouth, put the can back neatly with its fallen colleagues in the plastic bag. Three full ones to go, plus a pie, and about eleven biscuits. He could feel the pressure in his bladder; he'd have to go out at some point, unfortunately. More insistent than that, though, was the familiar grumble of his stomach. Not just the stomach; he felt the hunger as he always did, as if every single cell of his body was holding out a pleading hand to him: *Come on. Give us* something. That gnaw of hunger, his old enemy: it was almost right that he was meeting it one more time. Once more for old times' sake. It was a feeling that was his, that was authentic; a thing about him that nobody could quite understand. If the last few hours were going to be about memories of what he'd been – and some of that was inevitable, despite his desire not to wallow in it – then you couldn't really leave out the hunger.

The beer, the pies, the biscuits had seemed like a decent picnic, he'd thought. *A good spread*. He thought grudgingly of Sally, again. Once in a café she had shouted, 'I've got a craving for some ripe juicy plums!' so loudly that a couple nearby had asked to be moved and, when this was not possible, left the restaurant altogether. James and Sally had probably been very annoying, they later agreed, but there was a fuzzy happiness in even that admission. Annoying *together*.

Their last big, fun dinner together had been four years ago. Incredible to think it could be that long, but Sal was in Australia, of course, and then there was the falling-out, and the worry (*I don't know how to get Sal to like me again*) had calcified into a load, a burden (*I can't get her to*). In much the same way as so many other small troubles had, nourished by his silence, grown into bigger and stronger things, into the things he suddenly found he couldn't live alongside any more.

Four years. They'd been on good form that night, James and his big sister; they had had to be. The scattering of the ashes in Edinburgh had been an occasion they'd planned for a long time, and almost jauntily; there was a jauntiness, in fact, to their behaviour throughout the day. This was because of an unspoken pact to maintain each other's spirits, and to act as a joint counterweight to Mum's. Mum had been withdrawn, almost wordless, on the early morning train they caught to Edinburgh, resistant to the whole exercise – to their referring to the little box as 'Dad', speaking to it, to their texting little messages back and forth about the other passengers and sniggering. To the whole notion of scattering him, saying goodbye, in this way, although he had repeated his wish more than once after telling James. James and Sal understood it, of course – the grief, the massiveness of the blow. But the real goodbye had already happened. The funeral day had been the day for tears. We have to make it a happy day this time, Sal had said, and James, pining to see her even though it had only been a couple of months, agreed.

And so they'd made a trip of it, the same kind of trip Dad had loved, the exact sort of day he would have liked himself. By dinner, the balancing of the clashing moods had exhausted them all, and it was something of a relief when Jean left the two of them to find somewhere. She'd get something at the hotel, she said; it would be good for them to spend time together. Sal and James sat in a cheap Italian restaurant full of odd maritime artefacts: a figurehead which Sal would go on to have a nightmare about, a ship's wheel which diners kept catching their hips on as they were shown to tables. The second time this happened, both of them laughed out loud, and then their eyes met and admitted to each other that it had been a slog. That they were still bruised and incredulous he was gone; that the day's levity had been purchased at a psychic price which they would feel, like a tough exercise, for a long time to come. And that, however much he would have been delighted by the scene, it was something hard, to watch their father's remains float away over the old tenements and grubby station roof.

'We've, er . . . we've done well today, I think,' said James, and she reached out to take his damp hand on the tabletop.

'You're looking great,' she said. 'I guess the . . . the exercise programme is working. I mean. You know.'

And he did know, and it had been fine; it was inevitable that people complimented you when you were thinner and expressed concern for you (often behind your back, but sometimes even to your face) if you put weight on. Even though Sally knew this was demoralizing for him, and unhealthy, and all the rest of it, she still slipped up. But it didn't matter. It was her, so it didn't matter. The conversation moved on; in fact, moved on a long way, became the last great one they were to have, unless you counted the terrible one that burned the bridge between them.

It was that bit about weight, though, that came back to him now. James's fist tightened for a second and, in almost unconscious defiance, he brought the second pie out of its wrapper. He didn't even really want it; the first pie hadn't been particularly enjoyable, and it would be surprising if this new one outperformed it. Still. *Eff you all,* he muttered, or thought: he wasn't sure which.

People talked like it was so simple. Exercise. Cut out the snacks. People who had themselves lost weight, in particular; they were the worst for it. They acted a bit like religious converts: as if they were in possession of some insight which he could not fully understand but which he only had to accept in order to feel as good as them.

And it wasn't as if he had never made an effort. *I made so much effort,* he thought to himself, as the train rocked back into motion. *I tried so hard, did what you're meant to do.*

He meant it about weight loss, but perhaps he meant it about everything.

It had taken James a lot of nerve to go to the fitness class. He'd nearly changed his mind and gone home a couple of times. Once when the chirpy gay guy on the reception desk looked at him humorously and said, 'Here for weight loss?' And then in the changing rooms, with all the other men whose air of shame, of having turned themselves in for some deserved punishment, made him feel even worse that he himself was here. All that stopped him from turning straight around and going home was that he'd promised Karl he would give it a try. Karl had been the one who'd sent him the link. GAIN CONFIDENCE THROUGH EXERCISE, it said, with a series of images of fat and fattish people, like James, exerting themselves with what seemed like unforced glee. It was rare to see bodies like his own in promotional material. The email had taken him aback because James and Karl had never discussed James's weight before, as they had never discussed many things before – but as with many of those subjects, it didn't mean that Karl had not given them any consideration.

'I just thought you might give it a try, fam,' said Karl, 'because the thing is, as I see it, you don't like being the size you are, but you're never going to do anything about it because so many people are utter dicks about bigger guys exercising, but this is designed to get round that very problem. So in short, yeah. Also, it's only a taster course, and if you do the first one I'll take you for a curry after. Which will hopefully really piss off the guys who run the course.' James blinked. It was very difficult to argue with any of this, but as he glanced around at his fellow inmates, he wished that he had, and that he hadn't put the weight on in the first place, and that he was anywhere else: really anywhere.

The man taking the course hadn't seemed a good choice at first, either. He was lean, sporty; had various numbers tattooed on his forearms, like a prisoner. He wore a black athletic singlet that said FINISHER, and underneath gave details of some preposterous race that he'd taken part in: *12 hours, 52 miles, 2,500-m elevation*. Yet this frightening specimen turned out to be called Giles and the numbers on his arms were, it transpired, his kids' birthdays. 'By the end of these three sessions,' said Giles, 'I'll have won you over to the idea you can feel confident exercising. Or your money back.'

It was a little joke, since they hadn't paid for these introductory classes. James glanced up to see who else had laughed at it, and caught the almond eyes of Michaela on the other side of the circle. She was wearing an all-yellow outfit with sports logos on; she was solidly, meatily built, but like quite a few people there, she looked as if she'd already done slightly more exercise than James would have hoped. The glance lasted for a moment, and James looked back at the clownish size-twelve trainers he'd bought especially for this assignment.

That first session was only half an hour long. He was surprised to find that he was sorry it was over. He walked back towards the changing rooms, his new sports shoes squeaking across the polished floor. Maybe it *was* possible, after all, to get some sort of regular exercise without feeling as if he was being publicly paraded for his imperfections. Next to the men's changing room was a vending machine. Michaela was squatting, hands on hips, peering into it with exaggerated attention.

'If I got down like that, I, er, I don't think I'd ever get up again,' said James.

It was nerve-racking to make a joke, but he saw her shoulders relax and she turned – smiling, although vexed. Her skin was a little shiny and James made an effort not to think about the sweat on his own back. He'd chosen a shirt in the darkest of dark shades, on Karl's advice. 'Which one do we reckon is blackest?' asked James, laptop on the table. 'Ash, charcoal . . .?'

'Don't know if those will be dark enough, mate,' said Karl, 'not for the amount you're going to sweat at something like that. Have they got one called "the feeling you get as you close your eyes for the final time"?'

'What were you trying to get?' asked James.

'Lucozade.'

James's eyes scanned the crisps and chocolate bars arranged on the four horizontal shelves. He knew this type of vending machine, made by a company called Roofe and Bamford. They had them in various mainline stations where James often found himself doing drop-offs. With his eyes closed he could probably have recited the order of the different snacks, in the very unlikely event someone challenged him to do that. It was reassuring to find that, even here, in a gym, these larders of temptation were still to be found.

'And you put in the number, and . . .?'

'And a quid, yeah, and the Lucozade moved forward by like a quarter of an inch.' Michaela folded her arms across her round breasts in pantomime indignation. 'And now it's just stuck there.'

James had a technique for these situations; if you were travelling, hungry, as often as him, you needed a technique. He wouldn't normally do it with people around, but enough mild euphoria was still swimming around him to make this seem a special occasion. He levelled up the flabby point of his elbow with the rough area of the Lucozade bottles, and hammered it into the Plexiglas. The orange bottle toppled like a felled skittle into the gully at the bottom of the machine. Michaela clapped.

'You did that like someone who knows their way round a vending machine!' She broke off halfway through, squeezing it to her lips. 'Oh! I didn't mean, I obviously didn't mean . . .'

'No, no, it's fine,' said James, delighted. 'I . . . what can I say. I have no money, but I have a certain set of skills.'

This was an over-quoted line from a famously silly film, plus he wasn't even sure he'd got the words right. And yet she laughed a huge rude laugh and he thought about her on the way home.

The next session was only three days later: the idea was to rip off the plaster of their shyness. This time James looked for Michaela when they formed the circle. She was wearing black leggings this time, but the same canary-coloured T-shirt. The leggings hugged tight to the contours of her thighs and James began to be embarrassed by the things he was imagining when he looked at her.

They were put into pairs and asked to pass a heavy ball back and forth. James was too far away from Michaela to get into a team with her, but he was almost sure she glanced at him. He ended up with a huge Polynesian man who embraced the task with abandon, shoving the ball hard into James's waiting arms, so that James felt moved to push it back equally hard. The two of them, wordlessly, gleaming with sweat, ramped it up, and Giles made everyone stop and watch them as an example of how to 'give it some proper welly'. As he walked back to the changing rooms, James was fizzing with an unaccustomed joy. Neither of them was sure afterwards they'd definitely planned it, but he wasn't surprised to see Michaela by the vending machine.

'I was going to put my money in,' she said, with a smile of pure mischief that James already felt he knew and recognized. 'Then I thought, what if someone was passing, with certain skills . . .?'

She whooped with laughter as he elbowed a drink out of its cradle, with barely a run-up this time; even more when they realized that he'd also dislodged a packet of Skittles. Her laugh was the sort that made people tut to themselves on the train, or compose a scathing tweet at a party. It was exhilarating to be on the inside of a laugh like that.

'We should probably go,' said James, 'we're essentially stealing snacks here.'

'Yeah, I can't afford to get banged up,' said Michaela. 'I've got to shower and go meet my girlfriends.'

The way she said this, it sounded as if she was trying to draw a line under the conversation. But then, as they turned away towards their respective doors, she mentioned casually that she was thinking of organizing a little drink after the third class, and was that being a bit weird and premature because they'd all hardly met? James said no, it was a good idea, and he ended up giving her his phone number. The day after next she texted him to say she was worried people would 'judge' her for wearing yellow three times in a row, and James – after mentally redrafting the message for a whole hour, while driving – wrote back: 'Yellow suits you'.

After the final class, he was waiting for Michaela by the machine with a bottle of Lucozade he'd bought, and she asked him if he wanted to have dinner.

*

'Dinner' was a less straightforward proposition for James than it was for most people. His ideal situation would probably have been to continue dating her exclusively by the vending machine. He'd done well in a setting where the only requirements were to make very small amounts of light-hearted conversation and ram his elbow into something. A restaurant was likely to demand too much of the first and none of the other.

Karl helped him choose a dark navy shirt from Reiss ('You can't wear black to a date, you're not in the SS') and steered him away from trying to prepare conversational nuggets. 'I'm just worried she'll ask something and I'll blank,' said James. On a date last year a woman had asked James for his fantasy dinner-party line-up, and he'd panicked and chosen Stalin and Noel Edmonds.

'You don't have to worry about that, fam. It isn't an exam, you're literally just having a bit of dinner.'

James wasn't sure how sound Karl's romantic advice was likely to be, given that even in the past month he'd had a credible death threat from a spurned girlfriend, but he needn't have worried. Having dinner with Michaela turned out to be just like talking to her in the gym, except with flamenco guitar in the background.

Michaela was wearing a one-piece burgundy outfit. She was barely in her seat before she'd ordered a raft of starters, all of which their server seemed hugely impressed by: 'Beautiful, beautiful,' he said, and, 'Yeah, super good choice,' and so on. James wondered if there was anything they could order which would make the waiter say something like, 'I really wouldn't have gone for that, personally.' Michaela continued to make herself responsible for ordering throughout the evening, removing any sense James had that he was being assessed on what he was eating. She also made herself responsible for a lot of the chat. He'd met people who blathered away to fill silence, but it wasn't like that with Michaela; he'd met people whose opinions suffocated the conversation, but it wasn't like that either. She just seemed to have a sort of relish of speaking aloud, reading out bits of the menu, enjoying the sounds. 'Chorizo is honestly the tastiest word, isn't it?' 'Ooh, prawns, *gambas*. Yes please.'

James supposed it could be annoying to someone else, but it was exactly what he needed in a partner. He'd always aspired to be the sort of person with the confidence to speak without overthinking. It turned out that having a girlfriend with that quality was just as good. And she had large, beautiful eyes, which ignited in recognition of shared experience every time he said something about his life so far – even though he himself felt most of it was pretty banal. When he said, for example, that he'd been a coder – a computer programmer – but he hadn't had the heart after the company broke up, Michaela nodded in eager solidarity. 'I started out as a journalist, but everyone on my course was a psychopath; they all drank four or five Diet Cokes in the morning,' she told him, as if this was one of the known signs of the pathology. When he said that he'd been with one or two people in a short-term way, nothing serious, he again seemed to have hit the right note. 'I've only had one serious one,' said Michaela, pausing between clauses to see off a mouthful of seafood with noisy appreciation, '. . . sorry, that was yum – and I probably wasn't as serious about *him* as I should have been. But, you know. Good as a warm-up boyfriend.' James yelped a little nervous laugh at the phrase, hearing all the naughty fun it implied at some unknown party's expense, and too little of the sorry echo it might have one day.

The only question she really taxed him with was about the exercise course itself. 'What's your long game with this?'

'Sorry?'

'With the exercise thing, the whole health thing.'

'I don't think I've got a "long game",' said James, repeating the phrase in such a hesitant tone of voice that Michaela let out one of her ear-catching laughs. 'I just, my friend persuaded me to do it, I suppose. And I wanted to feel better. More confident.'

Michaela nodded. 'I want to do a 5K. I was doing the Couch to 5K thing, but the woman's voice was too annoying. *Good work! You've got this!*' Michaela speared a sautéed potato as if she were stabbing the offending voice artist. 'I thought to myself, I could run without some bint from the telly patronizing me. I googled fitness things that weren't too cringeworthy. I'm going to do this 5K in Blackheath in July. You should do it.'

'Five kilometres,' said James, 'is, what, three miles? I mean, I drive people shorter distances than that in my car.'

'You're a taxi driver?'

'Private hire. You can't just jump in. You have to book me in advance.'

'Do I, indeed.' Michaela grinned, and he had time to admire her two big front teeth, which he had noticed with every laugh he'd got out of her these past two weeks. Then her face became serious. 'You absolutely could do it. We'll do it together.' The word *together* was like a bell ringing in James's brain.

'All right,' he said, and the next day she sent him a training plan, and that was that.

★

The night before the 5K, James took off work. By exchange of texts they confirmed that they were both loading up with carbs, and would both make sure to get as much sleep as possible. James ate a lasagne for lunch, then a Sainsbury's moussaka for the evening. 'Bloody hell, dude,' said Karl, 'you're running round a park, not going to the South Pole.'

He'd sponsored James for £50, and James gave back a twenty-pound note, feeling that it was too much; but the following day he found the twenty in his shoe, and when he tried to return it again, Karl retaliated by putting it into James's sandwich. He had to cry out to stop James from eating it.

They'd arranged to meet in the 'runners' village' constructed out of little marquees near the start line, but there were far more people than he'd envisaged. James realized too late that the dropping-out of his phone signal, which he'd seen as a temporary whim of the network, might in fact last for the whole morning. He thought he saw Michaela half a dozen times, or heard her obscene laugh. It was maddening knowing that she was here some-where, but he wouldn't be able to find her. Well: she would wait for him on the finish line, James told himself.

By the final kilometre – after about forty minutes of running, by far the longest stretch he'd ever done – James was starting to doubt whether that was true. Even if Michaela was prepared to hang around, they would surely move people on once they'd finished. But in a way it was lucky, because the sight of him would be enough to kill what was between them. His chest hurt, he was panting like a dog invited to chase a ball around a field, and the sweat had glued his shirt to his back. His race number was half-off, drooping from the vest; other runners were passing him as if he wasn't moving at all. The banner for the finish line appeared in front of him at last, but then seemed to get no closer for a long time, and when the line eventually came he stumbled over it and then slumped down to his hands and knees.

It had been a terrible, painful slog to achieve a distance which many runners would do a couple of times a week. But even three months ago he wouldn't have been able to run if an axe-murderer was after him. Through the exhaustion he recognized, with a swelling of the chest, that he'd surprised and surpassed himself. Just: where was Michaela?

He had to get clear of the finish area, with its crowds of recovering runners, before his phone signal came back. There was no text from her, and he began to have misgivings. After waiting for a couple of minutes, he pressed the button to call her.

'Where are you?' She sounded groggy, confused.

'Where are *you*?'

There were the muffled noises of Michaela moving around; she put the phone down for a second, or dropped it. Then her voice was back, and loud.

'Fucking hell! I've missed it!'

Her plan to get a good night's sleep had worked; it had been much too good, and she'd slept through the race. The race *she* had dragged *him* into, and for which she had been preparing much longer than him. She made these points in the strongest possible terms, cursing herself, her phone and its manufacturers, her mother whose deep sleeping was a genetic inheritance, an owl whose hooting had woken her at 2 a.m., and all the five thousand people who *had* completed the run. James, sweaty and disarranged, listened helplessly as her roll of accusations went on – for reasons he couldn't quite follow – to the Deputy Prime Minister Nick Clegg.

'There'll always be another one,' he said, sounding to

himself like Dad, consoling the kids after an event ruined by rain. 'If we look online, there'll be—'

'OK, I know what we'll do,' said Michaela. 'Stay there. Meet me at the gates.'

By the time James had worked his way round to the start, where he had stood full of nerves just over an hour ago, Michaela was there: canary training top, race number, water bottle, trainers. 'I'm going to run it anyway,' she said.

'I mean . . .' James glanced around uneasily. Volunteers were clearing rubbish from the course, or funnelling spectators towards the cafés and the exits. 'I mean, it does seem, er, maybe a bit late, just in terms of . . . in terms of the race having finished, I guess, and . . .'

Before James could wrestle his sentence to a climax, she'd started her watch and was haring off down the course on her own. A few people called out, laughing, but nobody tried to stop her as James instinctively felt they would if he did something like this. He continued to think it might all be a joke until the yellow dot disappeared from view and he began, grinning to himself, to cut through the park to the finish. When she emerged from the trees half an hour later, a few people had got wind of the stunt. There were a dozen witnesses at what had been the finish line, including an amused official who sounded his klaxon.

'Last place!' he said. 'Congratulations!'

The other bystanders clapped and cheered, and James – feeling a warmth of pride, of ownership – let Michaela fall into his arms, giggling, her breath fast and hot and her body damp. 'Well,' she said. 'We bloody ran it.'

'We did,' James agreed. The sweat had dried on his back

by now and he felt shivery, but he put his arm around Michaela's shoulders and kissed her on the neck. 'And now we should – not to spoil the illusion of being in the Olympics, but we should probably shower.'

'Come back to mine,' said Michaela. 'My shower isn't the best, though, but . . .'

'I haven't got any clothes at yours,' said James, instantly wishing that hadn't been the first thing that came to mind – an objection, logistics. But Michaela smiled her large smile and squeezed his hand.

'I've got some of my brother's old stuff. He's got terrible taste, though.'

'That's good,' said James, 'so have I.'

He followed her down the steps to the flat, taking in the frosted glass of the door, the dark knotty floorboards. In the lounge there was a low green sofa and an M. C. Escher print, and a record player. One day – it would still have been hard for him to believe it at this point – James would live here with Michaela. And one day beyond that, he would live here without her.

She showed him where the kettle was, and what was in almost every cupboard, as if he was planning to stay a fortnight. Then she padded across the hall. Her shower went on as long as a classical concert. James looked at the calendar, on which Michaela had circled today's date numerous times and drawn two generously proportioned runners in cartoon form, arms outstretched in triumph. James felt goosebumps on the back of his neck. Without really knowing why, he flipped back through the old months, back to April. The three evenings of the course were marked out with the words GYM THING, and on the third one Michaela had scribbled, in red pen, a large number of little hearts.

The shower was still running, but he could hear Michaela's footsteps outside. He felt her in the doorway before he turned to look. She was standing naked, water streaming off her. Her wet hair clung around her face, sending rivulets down her shoulders. She shielded her unruly bush with mock bashfulness.

'Starting to wonder how long I'm going to be in the shower before you get in with me,' she said, and James, who'd never showered with a companion in his life, felt blood rushing all the way through him.

*

He swung his legs over the side of the little bed and leaned on the door handle. It felt strange to be standing up, either because of the booze or the long time lying in such a confined space. Like a sailor back on land. The corridor was narrow, the space between cabins and windows barely a space at all; again, James wondered if it was only being fat that gave him that impression. If most people even bothered commenting internally on it. He looked out of the window. The sky was mauve, the sort of darkness that looked like it would give way to grey rather than to genuine light. Through the long window, James made out a row of thin back gardens. A trampoline in one, a Wendy house in another. He thought for a second of all the people asleep in the houses, people he would not meet. Would they hear about him on the news? He wasn't sure if standard suicides got onto the news. There must be too many of them. Sixteen a day, he'd read on a Samaritans poster. There'd be nothing else *in* the paper if they were all reported. It was commonplace, which was something he had reminded himself each time his nerve threatened to waver over the past few days. It was a normal thing to do.

As he took his eyes away from the window, a strange sight drew them in. The Welsh woman, the conductor, was sitting with her back against the wall, her head drooping forward. It was hard to believe it was the same person who'd been so full of chirp as she ushered them on board. She reminded him of the man outside the Pret at King's Cross, for whom James bought a sandwich a couple of mornings a week.

He cleared his throat and stooped a little. 'Excuse me, are you all right?'

The woman looked up, startled. Her make-up looked sallow under the stark perma-lights. She got to her feet, dusting down her trousers. 'Oh! I'm sorry. I didn't think anyone was awake. No one's normally awake. The rugby boys are well gone, bless them.'

James looked closely at the conductor. There were pronounced lines under her eyes and the eyes themselves were flecked with red. In this light she looked as if she had been awake for a month. *Maybe it messes with your body,* James thought. *Your body or your brain. To be working these hours.* She must be permanently jet-lagged, if she was always on these trains. To reach a hotel bed just as it got light. Get up in the dark.

'Are you all right?' he asked again.

She smiled. 'That's sweet of you to ask.'

'Is there anything – can I do anything?'

His question had been instinctive; it took him by surprise, and her answer did, too. 'You haven't got a phone, have you? I feel stupid asking. I've left it in . . . I'm in a really stupid situation.'

The phone was still in his hand. James had begun handing it over before he realized.

'Oh, it's – you need to take it off flight mode,' he said. 'But, um.'

The unseen contents of his inbox welled up inside him and he had to stop himself from burping with a physical effort. It was still not too late to say she couldn't use the phone after all, but on what grounds? Claim there was no battery? No, it didn't feel possible. This must be a case of genuine need, or she wouldn't embarrass herself by asking a passenger. If he could help her, why wouldn't he? He didn't have to *look* at the phone. He handed it over.

'I'll just be . . .' He gestured towards the toilet.

'Promise I won't make off with it.'

'No, I didn't think . . .' said James.

She had hurried off before he realized that, of course, it had been a joke. Never mind, he thought, pushing down the silver handle to open the toilet door. He flipped the catch to lock it and stood over the low bowl.

Maybe it messes with your body, your brain, he thought again. But this was all nothing but guesswork. He knew nothing about what it was like to be a conductor on a train. For all he knew, perhaps they did sleep on the train, for a couple of hours; maybe there was a team, one person relieving another. Maybe she had a cabin. Or maybe she just walked up and down endlessly among all the sleeping strangers, like the people on those trains that used to take the plague dead out of London. She could have worked in this job for twenty years, and be sick of it; or this could be her first week and she was overwhelmed. He couldn't begin even speculatively to guess at what sort of crisis had provoked her to ask for his phone. A love problem? It was always the first guess, but she could be looking down the barrel of eviction, like Karl's mum all those times, at the mercy of her bloodthirsty landlord, before he started to earn more from the company. It could be a money thing. It could be a family problem that it had fallen on her to solve; something that was too much for a single heart. Really it could be anything, or it could be nothing. She could have an unrequited crush on someone in Mexico whom she was ringing ten times a day; or she could be trying to find an organ donor for a cousin. None of it was within his reach to know, and none of it concerned him, any more.

Oh, the old James had stuck his nose in quite a lot, yes. It was how the driving started. A rain-lashed night, on the cusp of his thirties, the torrents driving diagonally into his face as he left the third-floor flat. He'd just finished an hour-long appointment helping a 74-year-old man called Gavin use his email. It had been their fourth session. It was rewarding work and he never charged the full amount; one time he didn't even bother to take payment.

James sat there as the old man tapped out, one finger at a time, messages to his son – who was in the RAF in

Canada – and his little granddaughter who lived on a military base there. He'd showed Gavin how to attach a photo of himself for the little girl: a photo James had taken on his own phone. He reminded Gavin how to keep his inbox open in a browser window, so he'd see when a reply came in, and set up an alert that would make a noise to let him know, just in case. Gavin told him, as usual, that he feared his son had married 'a bit hastily, like', and that he 'didn't recognize the names of half the shops and restaurants round here any more'. Gavin had said these same things every time, but James didn't think there was a problem with his memory; he thought Gavin enjoyed the repetition. As he was showing himself out, down the gauntlet of stairs which felt an awfully long way for a man in his seventies to go, James wondered whether the son would get in touch, whether anyone would get in touch, until he was back there the following week.

Outside the tower block, rain in his eyes, fallen leaves being mashed to a paste in the gutter. James pulled down his hood and quickly tucked his phone into his pocket; a bit of rain could really damage them. He was on his way to the bus stop when someone, a woman, raised her voice behind him. He heard something in it, an appeal for help. He gritted his teeth against the lash of the rain and turned around. She was a tall, reedy-looking woman with a smoker's yellowed teeth, what Mum might call a 'lived-in' look; but not much older than him, he thought, although it was hard to be sure about anything in this weather, in the murk of the night. She had her hands over her stomach and he saw that she was pregnant.

'Please help me,' said the woman, 'I think I'm going to lose the baby.'

'Sorry?' asked James, feeling immediately out of his depth and looking around, through instinct, for someone who might not be. There was no one. The few passers-by, if anything, quickened their strides, looked at the pavement, sensing in this tableau something vaguely threatening, something they didn't want to be part of. They had their own problems, their own plans. The woman reached out and touched his sleeve, communicating some sort of need that James desperately hoped he could meet.

'I need to get to the hospital,' said the stranger. 'I don't know what to do. There isn't anyone to help.'

The second sentence, its plangent note, spark-plugged James's brain into life. He could do this. He could get her an ambulance. No: a taxi. There was a cab just across the road. James moved as fast as a man of his burgeoning size could at this sort of notice. The driver was making a gesture to ward him off; he wasn't even keen to wind the window down and talk to James, but James persisted, tapping on the glass.

'It's advance only,' the driver began. He sounded like he had to say this a lot in life. 'You've got to—'

'It's an emergency,' James blurted out. 'There's a woman who needs to get to the hospital, straight away.'

In the back of the car he wasn't sure what to say. The woman seemed calmer now; she took deep breaths, occasionally letting out a little stifled sob or muttering something to herself. James realized that he didn't have the slightest idea about labour, childbirth, any of it; nor did he have a clue what to say to somebody in her position. He asked if he could call anyone, or do anything else, but the woman hardly seemed to hear. The driver stepped into the silence, commenting on the whole business with a clumsy but welcome cheeriness. 'I've seen this sort of thing before and it all worked out,' he said; James wondered how he could possibly know that, but it was better not to ask. 'I've seen things you wouldn't believe. We've had all sorts. I've had people crying, people bleeding, all sorts. You'll be all right, love. I've had someone with half their leg hanging off.' This seemed to be the driver's idea of lightening the mood; he gave a brief barking laugh after it. 'You wouldn't believe the things you see, doing this. The people you meet.' On he went in this vein, jinking expertly into gaps in the traffic, almost knocking down two pedestrians like skittles in a 50/50 situation at a zebra crossing, continuing to describe the 'all sorts' he had witnessed, until James and – he hoped – the patient began to believe that this was all quite everyday and manageable after all.

James walked the woman into the glaring light of the A and E, and soon as he explained the situation to the receptionist, matters were taken out of his hands as if the whole thing had been prearranged. Two women in scrubs took the lady away, walking her slowly and with care into an anteroom. Someone else immediately headed towards the room with a clipboard and a bag of medical equipment. A trolley rumbled by with an ancient, paper-white person on it, face covered by an oxygen mask. The receptionist asked James what relation he was, and James explained he didn't even know the woman's name – why hadn't he asked her name? – and they said that it was all right, they could take care of it from here, and there was a coffee machine in the corner and he was welcome to take a seat if he wanted. But James had the sense that he was now surplus to the drama; in fact, it was almost like he'd dreamed it all, and was now waking to find he hadn't really done anything at all. He walked out of the door and back into what was now a drizzle. It was ten o'clock, and someone shouted drunkenly from the entrance of the Old Oak pub across the road. James looked around and wondered how to get home. He couldn't tell whether he had passed this strange little test, set by the universe with no warning, or failed it.

That unease had followed him around for the next week or so, especially as – of course – he never heard the end, never found out what happened to the woman. But there was something in the experience, when he reviewed it, that was useful; that was trying to teach him something. He realized that what he liked about doing the freelance computing job was helping people, contributing in some way to the giant network of humanity he'd originally tried to help build at the old start-up. The driver's confidence in taking charge, his near-relish for the task of grappling with this strange human situation, was something James didn't associate with himself. But the will was there. He'd like to be somebody who could see someone, a newcomer, approaching his car, and think: *Let's see how I can help*. He looked up the firm the next day, and he was working there by the end of the month.

★

But that was gone, he thought, as he emerged from the toilet to find the conductor waiting, phone in an outstretched hand, as if to emphasize exactly how little intention she had of running off with it. Even now, he had little curiosity about what she'd needed it for, which of the infinite possible crises he might have helped to defuse. It felt naïve, now, embarrassing, to think about how much energy he'd put into worrying about other people, all this time. 'I hope it helped,' said James, glancing down at his shoes.

'It did, and anyway, well, thanks again,' said the Welsh woman all in one tapering breath, so the last clause was almost inaudible. *Gina*, said her name-badge; he noticed it as she turned to go down the corridor. She was gone, her footsteps swallowed by the clanking of the train, and James felt all over again the meanness of this space, and turned back to the door of his cabin.

To open it, he shifted the phone from right hand to left. Its upturned face glowed at him. He had no intention of looking at it until he looked at it. It was a reflex, the way it was for anyone who had a phone. It was an involuntary motion that made him flick the screen down, down, to see what had been unleashed by the message he'd sent four hours ago. The collective bulk of the messages hit him in the guts and he shut the door behind him and sagged onto the bed, hearing the springs mutter in grievance.

'Christ almighty,' he said, loudly enough that it could have been heard outside.

He shoved the phone back into his pocket, where it should have stayed all along, and took hold of his breathing, which had gone fast and shallow. Even in this three-second glimpse, there had been the names. Karl, Michaela. Sally, even, in Australia. The people he was trying not to think about.

Eighty-two texts and fourteen missed calls. A deluge. In January he'd received just two texts in an entire week, and one of them was to offer him two-for-one pizzas if he replied with the word PEPPERONI. Eighty-two messages sent by people who had been disrupted, moved in some way, by the one he'd sent.

It was gratifying. If he let himself dwell on it. But he was not going to do that, because it was also a trap. *Where were you all when I actually needed it?* James asked the silence. And it wasn't a coincidence. They were texting now because he had forced their hand. It didn't actually mean that anyone wanted him alive, particularly; otherwise he would never have been so cut adrift from them. They just didn't want him to die in a way that would be on their collective conscience. That wasn't the same thing. Once that momentary spark of gratification had died, he felt – if anything – indignant. You didn't stop someone from killing himself by sending panicky texts when his mind was made up. It should have been their responsibility not to allow him to get anywhere near this helpless, this lonely. For the first time since he'd started to plan what he was going to do to himself, James felt a flexing of something like anger. It needn't have got to this. It never should have, in fact. He shouldn't have been left to rot like this, he shouldn't have been abandoned by all of them. By Karl, Sally, Michaela; all these people who were suddenly so keen to avert disaster so that they'd sleep easily at night. He shouldn't have been left out in the cold, exposed to everything like this, when he'd given so much protection to others. What about karma, or all those things? Not that you were meant to take those ideas literally, but you always believed there was *something*, as Mum might have said. Some safety net, some natural justice, so that you couldn't just fall through the cracks and disappear. If you were doing your best. Some invisible system that paid you back some of what you deserved.

Come on. Snap out of it. This was just feeling sorry for yourself. It was just like having a tantrum if you lost a game. He'd lost; other people had won. It meant no more than the quizzes Mum made them play with the neighbours at Christmas. Nothing had to mean anything, from now on. He was free.

Without looking at any more of the messages, without even having read more than the first few words of the top few on his list of notifications, James brought the phone back out of his pocket and scrolled onto his settings menu. His hand shook a little as he slid his thumb back over the screen and reinstated flight mode. It should have been like that all along, he told himself again.

His heart rate – after the cold-water spike of the phone screen – dropped gradually over the next minute, then the minute after that. It had been a mistake to look at it at all; it had gone against everything he told himself he'd do; but it didn't matter. He was still on track. You couldn't stop a train. It would get where it was going.

He had absolutely no responsibility to engage with any of the messages, or even engage with the idea of their existence. The flight mode was back on, the screen door was pulled back across. In fact it was more secure even than that. The phone was effectively locked in a safe. As long as he didn't weaken again, which he would not. People could send as many messages as they liked, but they would not get to talk to James. They were just talking to themselves.

At the thought that they were gone – all of them – James felt his stomach tighten, and a sort of tingling or fizzing in his limbs. It made him change his position, rolling onto his side; it was a strange feeling. But it wasn't fear, and it was shadier and tricksier than excitement. It was a chemical response, a sort of heightened aliveness, like the bristling of nerve-endings before lightning strikes.

PART THREE

THE MISSION

17

One night in the pub, Karl had remarked that – if it had come only a few years later – the internet start-up could actually have worked, could have made all of them very rich indeed instead of ending with their boss fleeing the country never to return. Could have been life-changing. If it had just happened a little later. 'I mean, yeah, trying to sell instead of give it away was a mistake,' he said. 'He didn't realize the future would be about giving stuff away and *then* selling secretly, selling information, whatever. But the actual ideas. Making a network of people, instant-messaging them. Having computers guess what you want and find it for you.' Karl swigged from his pint. His friends leaned in, nodding, humming approval. He stood, spoke, gesticulated like a textbook man-leading-pub-conversation – his listeners could have been arranged around him that way on purpose, like extras in a beer advert – and it was only James who knew that Karl was actually having a hard time. Working a series of wretched, unrewarding jobs to keep his mum afloat; forever looking over his shoulder for his father, who drifted spectrally back into the picture whenever they thought he was gone.

'It's just, phones just weren't good enough yet,' said Karl. The CD in the fake jukebox stammered over a song, the barwoman went over to thump it – like someone slapping a choking person on the back – and James thought about how some tech innovations died as fast as a mayfly and some got away with it for years and years. It was true, almost everything was luck. 'As soon as we got these it was game on.' He brandished his iPhone, the third model he'd owned in these couple of years. 'We just didn't know then, but computers and phones are the same thing. Jacob was like that guy, who was it? Geezer who nearly invented the light bulb. Thomas Edison.'

'I think Thomas Edison *did* invent it,' said James, 'at least, he got the credit for it.'

'Who am I thinking of, then.' Karl made a short, impatient gesture. 'Done the light bulb, someone else shafted him, invented all this stuff but someone else always got there first, drank himself to death like – your man, the poet – Wordsworth?'

James sighed. 'I think you maybe don't mean Wordsworth.'

They stayed up late that night, trying to follow a film which made no sense until an important revelation hit them simultaneously. 'Wait, is this entire thing happening backwards?' said James.

'Mate,' said Karl, slowly, his face clearing. 'I mean, it did seem weird the guy was suddenly a baby but we thought it was a flashback, but it was actually . . .'

'. . . it was actually a flash-forward but the action was back to front, and *that's* why . . .'

'. . . that's why he was already wet when he got in the bath! Fuck!' Karl and James cackled at the TV. 'They really need to start making films that strictly go in the right direction,' said Karl, opening another bottle, 'or we need to start watching them all from the start, I guess. Are you having another one?'

James hesitated. He'd become anxious as he entered the early thirties that booze put more weight on you than you ever thought about – weight he felt he could ill-afford to carry, as he'd been filling out alarmingly in his year as a driver – but he wasn't going to tell that to Karl, because he thought Karl was oblivious to his size worries. He used working hours as an excuse, instead. 'I'd better not, in case I get called out at nine or something.'

'Are you still liking it, the driving?' asked Karl, in a tone which contained a number of male ingredients James correctly identified: a little envy, a little regret, and a total refusal to admit either of those even to himself. Last week Karl had been giving out leaflets in a shopping centre for an energy drink which had been withdrawn from shops on the Friday, because a boy in Hull had drunk four cans and tried to attack a swan in a canal; it wasn't clear if he was even going to get paid. During the summer he'd gone to Cornwall and worked for six weeks on a whale-watching cruise, where he was forced to begin every day with the words: 'We can't actually guarantee seeing a whale, but we'll do our best, and of course if we're out of luck you can always ask for a refund!' It was meant to be a joke, but there'd been so many refund requests that, once more, he had ended up with less than half of what he was meant to get paid.

'It's great,' said James. 'You really should just get over it and sign up. You know I'd get you in.'

'Get over what, fam?'

'Whatever's stopping you doing it,' said James, in a rare spurt of alcohol boldness, 'which I assume is the fact it's my idea.' As would happen with the fitness class two years later, the conversation then flitted with a butterfly's lightness onto something else, but – again like a butterfly, in that thing about the wings that Karl could never quite remember – it had thrown things onto another course.

*

It was true that, even ten years ago, what Steffi was now trying to initiate would have been impossible: at least impossible to achieve as quickly as James needed them all to achieve it. But since Karl and James first worked in tech, things had moved on at a giddy pace; exponential, mind-bending, if you stopped to think about it, and yet – with hindsight – inevitable, as soon as machines began to talk to one another. Now, the eight billion cells of the earth's body could speak to each other as fast as thought. There were think-pieces every week about how dangerous this was, how paranoid it was making teens, how easily exploited it was to drip-feed poisonous ideas into the world's bloodstream.

And some of those were probably right, Steffi supposed; maybe the internet *was* going to drive us all over a cliff, but deep down she thought maybe humans were better than that. Could use their powers of connection to do cool things, even if they were only making up and sharing fiendishly complex sheep-pursuit tasks.

At the very least, you had to admit social media were useful for a job like the one that had landed on her tonight. She wrote, on Emil's phone, a paragraph explaining the situation. 'I'm James Chiltern's flatmate. He is in danger as some of you might know from the text. We need to get the message all over the internet because someone must have seen him, stroke, be able to help. You can message me direct and I am setting up a page to post anything that helps.' She read it back as Emil sat down next to her with the beers, touching her arm lightly to welcome himself back. She wasn't 100 per cent sure about the apostrophe in 'Chiltern's', and she wasn't sure she had used 'stroke' correctly, but those things were less pressing than whether James was still alive. As Emil watched – still at a respectful distance, but in a way she felt continually aware of – she went through James's Facebook profile one friend at a time, starting with those who seemed to be the most important (his old boss, his sister), cut-and-pasting the message to them. She began an 'event' – a weird way to describe an anti-suicide mission, like it was an anniversary party at Bella Italia, but also the quickest way. She invited them all to join it.

The pot began to bubble even before she'd finished heating it up. 'Look,' she said to Emil, who – with little to contribute except the hardware – had made his way methodically through the beer already. 'Two replies. Not useful. Just people saying how can they help. But it shows you what we can do.'

Emil nodded, a little glumly, thinking of other things they could be doing. Steffi sipped her beer and waited at her post. Above them and around them, unseen fibres thrummed; conversations began, echoed, spread, fuelling one another, the combined goodwill making an invisible shape in the air, a force. But nobody among these nocturnal correspondents had seen James, yet. Nobody knew where he was. If he was all right. If he still existed, other than as a thumbnail picture, a portly smiling man in a striped jumper, an idea of a person.

In the bar, Emil stared at the thumbnail, at this man who was commanding almost all of Steffi's attention, with something that was definitely approaching envy. And Steffi, too, looked at the photo and thought she saw more in it than the face she was used to glimpsing in the kitchen or outside the bathroom. Maybe it was the beginning of fatigue – it could jangle your emotions like coat-hangers. Once, after a double shift, she was so tired she'd cried at 'Three Times a Lady'. But it was as if the image was more real than her actual, living and breathing memories of her flatmate, and the feeling that she wanted him to come out of this alive – that was real, too.

18

MELBOURNE, 14:25

The sun was high and strident over the Botanic Gardens as Sal paced the dirt track, passed at intervals by mad hot-weather runners, dog-walkers, and sometimes the even more insane people who ran *with* dogs. Away to the left were the sports stadia, domes and polygons, looking like a series of spaceships that had landed in town. There was the familiar eucalyptus smell, the little birds that hopped onto the path: a cheeping finch, sometimes a black and white ibis, its comical long beak scanning the ground like a blind person's walking stick.

As usual, the processing space required by all these sensory pleasures took her out of her head, and so did the orderly data of her fitness watch. Two thousand three hundred steps. Heart rate slightly high, but good. One hundred and sixty-two calories. But her phone was intruding, wanting to drag her into it again; she snapped back into the now to find that she'd missed a Facebook notification and that a call was coming in right at this moment. There was no way she could *not answer* Mum, not at the best of times, let alone now: even though this was the third call in an hour. 'I mean, for the love of . . .' she said out loud, and pressed to reply.

Somehow, Mum took four rings to pick up. What the fuck else could she be doing in these circumstances but waiting for the phone? Planning a barn dance? But the words jarred, because that was something Dad used to say.

'Mum?'

Sal's heartbeat felt fast and bit scatty, like someone not very accomplished was playing the drums.

'I just – I didn't know what to do, Sally, I don't know what to do at all, so I . . . I'm just calling you again, that's all, in case . . .'

The plaintive tone, the unvarnished need for help, socked Sal in the heart with immediate remorse. She hadn't heard her mother like this since Dad died.

'All right. Mum. Listen. People are . . . all of us are trying. I've been calling James and, and tried a couple of his friends.' Sal felt like a politician trying to spin an unpopular policy change, even though it was true: she'd sent messages to Karl, to anyone else connected with James who was still on her phone. 'And I've just, literally now, just had a message come in on Facebook.'

'Facebook,' Mum repeated, doubtfully. Sal gave a deep, ten-second-long sigh, breathing out into the warmth, the stillness. She and James had spent most of an evening coaching Mum in the art of Facebook; largely James, she supposed, if she was honest. But no, it was still too much hassle, it seemed, just like it was too much hassle for Jean to even get a mobile.

'I just, I wondered if it would be a good idea to . . .' Mum took a sharp, pregnant breath, and Sal knew what was coming a second before it happened. As with Meghan, the anticipation – the unsaid, the tiptoed-around – was more infuriating almost than the actuality. Could nobody in this world, Sal asked herself, just come out and say what they were thinking? Did she have to be Derren Brown all day long? 'I just wondered whether you'd got in touch with Michaela.'

Sal held the phone away from her mouth for a few seconds, because the sigh this time would otherwise, she felt, have carried it away like a tidal wave.

'Yes. I'm still here. But no, Mum, I have not *got in touch* with her, because she is literally the number one reason why this is happening, for a start . . .'

'I know, I know you two had your . . . your feud.' (*Feud*, thought Sally despairingly; am I talking to Shakespeare here?) 'But still, she might be in touch with him, mightn't she? She might have seen—'

'She's in Germany,' said Sal, 'and if she's had the message I'm sure she'll deal with it. I don't think there's anything to be gained by me calling her. I'm going to hang up in a second and I promise you we will find him. All right?'

'Of course,' said Jean, 'of course, yes. I mean, do what-ever you think, Sally. Just please – let me know. Please keep talking to me.'

Sal felt her throat constrict as she ended the conversation. She brought up Steffi's message, read it, clicked through to the link it contained. 'Steffi.' This girl, whoever she was, James's flatmate – someone Sal had never heard of – had more chance of helping him, or thought she did, than James's own sister. Sal was indignant for a second at the presumption. How old was the girl? Barely twenty-five, to look at her. How long had she even known James? Then, as she waited at the Swan Street Bridge for the lights to change, the sun still glaring down indifferently, that indignation inverted itself, and Sal accepted she was really angry at herself, for somehow letting it get to this.

As James had done earlier, on the other side of the planet, she thought back to their dinner together in Edinburgh; that air of sentimentality and easy disclosure that came with booze, something they'd both grasped for eagerly after the repressed sorrows of the day. The wine and the head-rush and the swirling emotion had lent her a series of revelations – that *family was more important than anything*, that a brother and sister should *be able to tell each other anything* – which in her head were no less true just because she was pissed while saying them. Quite the opposite. In vino veritas. 'Which *Famous Five* book is that in?' James had asked, and she squeaked with laughter and they got a look from the buttoned-up couple two tables along, just like in old times.

When they got back to the hotel, Mum was long asleep, and Sal suggested a nightcap, a last one in the bar. She was surprised at how much of a relief it was when James agreed: she didn't want to be on her own, and that was a newish feeling. Specifically, she wanted to be with James. 'Seriously, we should be messaging every day,' she said once more, waving at James's iPhone, which was out on the table. There were often notifications, from WhatsApp or YouTube, the unending clamour of the portals Michaela used, and it was becoming part of his job now to react to those. But what he really wanted, of course, was a message from Michaela herself. That was something which, after more than a year, still made him thrum with anticipation, as if he was at school again and being smiled at by a girl in the playground. 'I mean, why not? Isn't that why we even have these things?'

'I just always worry – no, I'll get these – I always worry you're busy,' said James. 'With your twelve different jobs. Or you're asleep . . .'

'I only sleep four hours a night.'

'. . . or just that I don't have all that much that would be exciting to tell you, I suppose.'

'What? Apart from having an amazing new girlfriend? Apart from having lost all this weight and got into the running?'

'Thanks to her,' said James. Sal swallowed. She was going to have to get used to Michaela, she guessed. Dad's wake had been a terrible place to meet somebody for the first time, obviously. Michaela had just been trying over-hard, probably; surely she didn't always speak that loudly, as if into a gale-force wind, and tell anecdotes about James with such a complacent air of familiarity, as if she had known him for far longer than his own family. Yes. They'd get to know each other properly at Sal's wedding, she expected.

'I suppose,' said James, after reflection, 'I've always sort of felt that it's quite difficult to measure up to you – you've always been ahead of me. I suppose that inhibits me a bit from getting in touch.' He was surprised to hear himself say it, and she was surprised, too, and secretly pleased by her place on the family's scoreboard, in the way anyone would be. In the hotel corridor, outside her door, she embraced James for a long time, feeling the warmth, the reassuring if reduced plumpness of her little brother.

The hotel room seemed full of noises that night: the radio alarm clock ringing in each new hour with a double bleep which she couldn't work out how to turn off; church bells, from somewhere nearby, marking the same milestone two minutes later each time. The coffee machine making some sort of automated clank at occasional intervals, like an old man coughing in his sleep. Sal's body clock was out of sync; jet-lag had hit her harder on this trip than it usually did. She'd messaged Dec back home a couple of times, but he was working on a big contract and it was lunchtime in Australia, and he wouldn't really understand, anyway. She drew back the curtains and looked over the orange-blue of the sky, thinking about how it was never really dark in a city, and then she remembered it was Dad who'd told her that, told her so much else that was in her head, and she felt a cold hand on her spine and almost fell over.

She went back to the bed and sat down: they were happening again, those thoughts. She couldn't let her brain look at them directly: they would torch straight through her like the sun. Something, somebody had to distract her. She wanted to go along the hall and knock on James's door, wanted it more than anything for a moment. But no, she couldn't wake him up. She didn't want to look stupid. She sent him a text: Are you awake? Not feeling too good. With Dad and everything. The momentary deadness after the message landed, and then – she caught her breath, relieved – the moving dots as James began to type back. He was typing for a long time.

You are doing one of your speeches about business in a packed concert hall in Australia (forgive me, I don't know the names of any venues). A gunman rushes in and threatens to take the whole room hostage unless you give him a million dollars. Do you: immediately start to phone the police? Or: call his bluff and tell him to leave?

She grinned. It wasn't even a very good one; a bit laboured as a set-up. Very James. Perfect.

The small sideways shove from her brother had been all that it took for her to stumble off the frightening course, away from the bad things. Sally exhaled and lay with the phone in front of her face, tapping back a reply to James like a sixth-former flirting in her bedroom. The fear had gone, and she thought about the wedding venue – only ten miles from here – with its magnificent oak library and portraits of old men hunting; how proud she would be when everyone walked in, kissing her cheek, saying what a great day it had been. She thought about the speeches, the tribute to Dad she had already sketched out, and imagined looking at James as she said it: James sitting next to her on the top table.

★

That was not how things had been, of course. The gap between her vision of the wedding day and the reality was something she had never forgiven James for. But it was in the past, and she'd let it pollute the present. Sal looked down at the river sparkling in the sun. A horse and cart went by, tourists messing about; a grey horse and a black one, heads bowed in resignation, the driver in a red waistcoat cajoling them forwards, the passengers taking selfies in the carriage. She thought about how easily life could become nothing. You could hoist yourself up onto the handrail and fall into the water and, in moments, everything in your brain – all you'd ever struggled towards, loved, feared – would be wiped like code. Her heart tightened in her chest as she thought about James, miserable, vulnerable, about to make a mistake he could never undo. Would he think of her in the minutes beforehand? Why had she left him like this?

Come on. We're going to listen to our breathing. We're going to think of the next steps. James needed her. She had to be his protector.

She looked at the phone. The Facebook discussion was moving on. Someone was talking about Twitter. People were helping, they were engaged, even though it must be the middle of the night back home. People were sorting her brother out. Their voices were there, high notes above the aviary chatter that never ended: Dec talking about what he'd like to do to her 'sweaty bod' after the speech tonight (he was out of luck; she was 100 per cent getting in the shower for forty-five minutes), Bridget expressing her ongoing excitement about the Lorne weekend with a total of nineteen GIFs taken from the movie *Despicable Me*.

Sal would wade in. She was the cavalry; solving problems was what she did. She would get in touch with this Steffi, introduce herself. Start getting the word around.

Ways we could get help for him:

1. See list below.
2. Circulate Facebook message as far and wide as possible.
3. Get clients with celeb contacts involved, call in favours.

Sal had good networks. The thought buoyed her. This could, ultimately, be an example of how you stayed calm under pressure. A story she could learn from, others could learn from. It didn't even matter if it made her late for the rehearsal, unthinkable as that was. They could have all the time-management jokes they wanted. She didn't care if it got Meghan stressed. Meghan could suck her tits. Although thinking how well Meghan did with jokes and metaphors, maybe she wouldn't say it in those terms.

She went into her recent calls and pressed the green button. Imagine if she was the person to get through to him. If he was waiting for her, if there was something he needed to hear from her. Blood was thicker than water. No; 'the person' was not available. Never mind. Get back to the office, try again, start actioning some of these ideas. Sal was going to sort this out.

Not far beneath this capable mental voice was another, not a voice really but a noise: a series of frightening yells, like those heard from the street in a strange city. It didn't often manage to get at Sal, through all the layers of sound-proofing she'd put in the way. It was terrifying when it came onto you, as it had that night of the ashes, as it had threatened to for a second earlier today. She had become expert at shutting it out. Now it was close again; if she broke her stride for a second, she could feel the horror playing with the hairs on the back of her neck. Now it was happening, again. Now it was close.

19

'Eat some of this, love. You'll feel better.'

It wasn't that she minded Lee having woken up, being with her in this emergency: of course, he was her . . . *boyfriend*. Although that stuck in the throat when you were 68 and a widow, but 'life partner' sounded like someone who would be issued to you by the council. And when people said 'other half' she wondered: so was Alan half of me for thirty-four years, then, and have I only been half a person since then? That was why she had retrospectively settled on the word *soulmate* for Alan, which came from a Marian Keyes book they'd read in the group – although Jean would never have said it out loud.

Yes, Lee was doing his absolute best here. But in that half an hour he'd already made two attempts to solve this potentially life-altering problem with toast, and it wasn't even made right. Although he should know by now how thinly she liked the butter spread, he had – as ever –

slammed it onto the bread like someone painting a house. And his bed-hair was all spiky like a cockatoo, and he kept muttering 'oh, bollocks' as he misdialled James's fiddly number, in vain. All in all, the more he bustled about like the emergency services, the more he demonstrated that he was *in her corner*, the tighter that corner was starting to feel to Jean. As he hung up the receiver once more, Jean heard herself say something she would have thought hugely unlikely not even twelve hours ago.

'I think we should use your mobile.'

Lee scratched his head. 'It'll be the same, love, if the call isn't connecting.' His voice, roused from sleep and warming up slowly like the engine of his weary old car, was even more growly than usual, the Pennines accent even flintier. He sounded like someone reading a Ted Hughes poem on the radio. 'No matter what phone we used, if it's not connecting, you can't . . .'

'No, but we could send him a text.' Jean still wasn't quite up to using 'text' as a verb. She remembered being quietly crushed at how amused the children were when she called it 'The Facebook'. *The children.* One of the children needed her. The thought was cold on her skin, and it pushed her forward. It wasn't as if she had anything *against* mobile phones, was it? It wasn't even a 'complex' about technology, as Sal liked to insist. It was just that Jean had been left behind, and without Alan she didn't have the energy to take to new things so easily. But now, in this upturned snow-globe of a night, now that just sounded like an excuse.

'Perhaps for some reason he can only get texts. Perhaps if we text him. Where's your mobile, Lee?'

'Well.' Lee rubbed his eyes. If Jean wasn't going to eat the toast he wouldn't mind having a bit of it himself, but it didn't seem like the right thing to bring up. His hands went to his trouser pockets to check for the phone, but it wasn't there. After a few moments he accepted he wasn't wearing his trousers; he was still in his pyjamas. All this was a strange business, it really was. 'The thing is, love, I don't think I've got any credit.' There was no *don't think* about it. Lee never bought more than ten pounds of credit at a time, and the latest chunk had run out last night during the Pink Floyd documentary. He'd texted his brother about it – taking himself down to 15p – and then, when his brother asked if it was any good, Lee had maxed himself out writing: aye. Of course, if he'd known what was going to happen, he would have saved that last 15p, but anyone could be Mystic Meg after the event, couldn't they?

'How do you get more?'

'We could top up online,' said Lee, and their eyes met doubtfully. The connection was in and out, because of Jean's reluctance to ring someone up and have conversations about the router and this password and that password. On Thursday they'd tried to get the internet going, to check film times, and ended up having to call the cinema. The girl who'd answered the phone sounded amazed, even euphoric, like she hadn't had a conversation in weeks. Lee scratched his head again, and his temples, and the nape of his neck. 'Head-scratcher', applied to a problem, was not just a figure of speech to Lee; he didn't know how anyone solved anything *without* doing that. His father had scratched his own head over the closing of the coal-mines, and *his* father over his own loss of faith in God and the need to conceal it for thirty years since he was a parish priest. Sure enough, the scratch dug out a useful thought.

'Or, I tell you what. You can top up at the cash machine. By the Tesco's. I could run out, get some . . . some credit on it.'

'Are you sure?' asked Jean. 'I mean, if you *were* sure, you could – perhaps you could pick up a few things.' The Tesco had recently gone 24-hour. She started to give Lee a list of things they could do with. More milk, kitchen roll. But was he sure he would be all right? Going out there in the dark?

'Of course,' said Lee, 'don't be silly.'

It took him no longer than three minutes to get dressed. He came clattering back down the stairs with a certain assumed heroism, like the captain leading a football team out; banged the front door shut with a sense of purpose but an appropriate respect for the stained-glass panel, because Jean had told him about that before. He reappeared almost immediately to get his wallet, and made a second exit.

Jean exhaled. She'd handled that well. She preferred it like this. She needed to be on her own with her thoughts again, even though those thoughts kept circling round to the same, impossible question: why? Why was James doing this? What had brought him to this? Why did she not already know the answers?

She sat on the stairs, smoothed down her dress, looked at the phone – if only it would ring now. She would know what to do then.

I could call the police, she thought. But someone had

already done that, according to Sally; in fact, several people had done it. And the police available to Jean would only be the balding, gloomy men in the station down the road. They'd not even found the teenager who snatched Gloria's handbag from a moped, even though he was apparently covered in tattoos; they were hardly going to track down someone in London from a single text message, were they?

If he was in London. It was inexcusable that she didn't know. She felt that *even if* the phone rang, if James was there, it wouldn't be completely obvious what she was meant to say. What's the matter?, she would ask. What can I do? The question, in fact, was the same, whether she could get hold of James or not. What can I do? What should I have done already?

The walls clicked and creaked, the kitchen appliances conferred in occasional bleeps. The wind was moaning in a way which had seemed cosy to her only a few hours ago, when they went to bed, when Lee's body was warm next to hers, and there was no reason to think that anything was wrong. She tried to think what she had been doing at the very moment James sent his message. Probably she had just been drifting off to sleep. Thinking about Sally. Wondering what Sally had planned for her weekend, which was already under way. But not thinking of James, not really.

Not that she ever stopped thinking about him, let alone caring: you couldn't forget your own son any more than you could forget your right leg. And yet the leg analogy was sort of accurate. The act of parenting, as you and the children got older, was more automatic than consciously engaged in. Especially when they weren't close at hand or on the phone. And especially when the years went as fast as all her friends tediously, but accurately, kept pointing out they did. And so, when something went wrong with one of your children – out of the blue, or rather out of the purple-black of the night outside – it was no easier to anticipate than if you woke up and found one of your limbs wouldn't move any more.

Jean thought she heard something on the landing above. More sentimental friends of hers, or friends even more bereft by a loss than she was, sometimes raised the idea that the lost husband – in one case, daughter – was still 'with them' on some plane; every creak of floorboard or branch scratching a windowpane was a message of comfort. One of the book group had claimed a supernatural bond like this two months ago, when they were meeting at Jean's, and Rosamunde Pilcher hadn't got a look-in all evening, somewhat annoyingly as Jean had speed-read the final hundred pages to be ready. What was undeniable, though, was that houses never lost the imprint of the people you'd lived with there. She could never sit on the sofa without thinking she saw Alan there, snorting at the weather fore-cast. She'd never been able to move the framed print of all the cloud types that hung in the bathroom, even though she couldn't really look at it, either. She still thought, when she was alone in the house, she could hear Sally in the bedroom, practising one of her speeches ('and that's why this house should vote that the twenty-first century will belong to women'). Or James in the other bedroom, on the computer with one of his friends.

But her memories of James were grainier. When she used to knock on the bedroom door and come in with sandwiches, he and his friends would be huddled over the black keyboard of the little computer, mysterious lines of symbols on the screen. Once or twice he showed her something he'd made on there, asked her to press a button: 'A to deliberately run the other car off the road, B to try and take a different route'. She never really knew what to say to these things, beyond 'well done!' or 'this is very clever!', which always seemed to disappoint James somehow. Alan had seemed to have more of a knack for it, and as James got older – sixth form, the computing college, pottering around doing this and that – it hadn't troubled her that they seemed to share more. The trips to Edinburgh, the walks they sometimes went on. A boy needed his dad, didn't he, even when he was a man himself.

Jean made herself responsible for Sally, Alan for James. They were a team. It was all she'd wanted, for them to be a good team. And they were. They had been.

Jean looked at her watch. A quarter to four. Even *that* was probably old-fashioned, wasn't it, relying on your watch. She had a painful memory of that final trip to Edinburgh, that horrible day. Sally's phone lighting up, a smirk on her face, a glance across at James. Another phone-chirp a couple of moments later. Jean realizing: they are sending each other messages. They don't want me involved. More accurately – she couldn't be involved. Because she didn't have a phone, did she? When Sally and James had fallen out over the wedding, she had felt at a similarly helpless distance from it, and for the same reason. The argument wasn't like one in the old days, where she could step between them in the bedroom and say: all right, enough of this. It was being fought on terrain she didn't know. Life, relationships, everything moved quickly these days, and even thinking that made her a fuddy-duddy, and thinking the word *fuddy-duddy* made her even more of one, she supposed, but what were you meant to do?

She sat and waited for Lee to get back, even though she'd deliberately sent him away. She composed, in her head, the message she wanted to send her son, even though she didn't know where he was, whether it was too late, too late now to reach him when she had wasted so much time.

20

James pulled the phone out of his pocket and tossed it onto the counter, where it landed with another clatter, its screen lighting for a moment as if in reproach. He didn't want the effing thing in his pocket. If he hadn't handed it to the conductor, if he hadn't seen it. That was what had started all these futile thoughts. And now they were crawling over him like little lice under his skin. There was sweat up his back and he was too hot, even though a mean little draught kept whispering through the thin shield that separated him from the night outside.

How could a life go from that to this, he asked himself again: from the gallery of lights it had once been to this miserable little compartment, shaking and hobbling its way up the country like a sidecar on a cobbled road? How could you trace a straight line from a happy, functioning James to this finished one? Could even one domino have fallen differently and left him in that safe, perfect life he'd once

had? If Dad hadn't been diagnosed. If James hadn't promised to go and 'meet him' regularly after he passed; if
Michaela hadn't made them so late they missed the wedding
and he missed getting to the bridge; if they hadn't had that
huge row at the station. If she hadn't gone off and met
Phillip, if he hadn't had to go back to Karl for a job; if Karl
had trusted him enough not to fire him over something
that wasn't his fault.

He remembered walking through King's Cross station,
a few years ago – unaware that not so far into the future,
when he had run out of options, this would be his workplace. There was some building work going on, and a
temporary display of art had been erected to put an attractive face on the mess. One of the pieces was a huge canvas
with nothing on it except some words stencilled, black on
white, in the bottom right corner.

IF YOU DON'T LIKE YOUR LIFE
YOU CAN CHANGE IT!

The words had stuck in his head as he got into the car
that night, responding to the buzz of the radio, and started
off towards the pick-up address, Hamish Elton's address in
Primrose Hill. It was very true, James thought to himself.
He wouldn't exactly say that he hadn't 'liked' his life before
all this, but everything he had gained had been as a result
of overcoming his natural reluctance to ask – to ask other
people, and the universe in general. He'd managed to find
himself a job in which he felt valued and useful, which let
him meet people, and occasionally gave him a portal into
a world he would otherwise never have seen. Tonight, for
example, even though it was already nine o'clock, he was

driving Hamish to a party *in Manchester*. Hamish was a TV personality of some kind; according to Karl, he was 'paid to have good hair and hang around with Alexa Chung' – though James, if he was honest, also didn't know what sort of personality *she* was. It was the fifth or sixth time that James had driven him on one of these all-night escapades: Hamish seemed to work in Manchester quite a lot, but also to have the sort of job where a certain amount of party-going counted *as* work.

When they got there, James would sit in the car outside the venue, sometimes listening to classical music on the radio – he'd got quite fond of it, although he didn't know the name of anything. The swelling, mystifying melodies; the half-asleep patter of the DJs with their odd arcane knowledge ('this is a wonderful piece, really one of the best recordings of this Czech genius that we have'). Sometimes – before it all happened – he would text back and forth with Sally, asking her what the weather was like there, marvelling at the idea she was in *Australia*.

Hamish normally got back in the car about six in the morning. Sometimes he asked to be taken to another address. Once he had gone to a back alley six miles away, too narrow for James even to get the car into, and come back with a package which he asked James never to mention to anyone, and a traffic cone which James never discovered the relevance of. On the last occasion, Hamish had texted James to come in. James had picked his way, invisible, through the shouting, laughing people, the nests of beer cans and wine bottles, the glitchy music whose genre he couldn't even have named. Hamish had emerged with a girl whose name he said was Lucienne. 'Hello, Lucienne,' said James. 'Is this your man?' asked Lucienne, laughing. 'Like, your servant?'

'He *is* my man, but he's not a servant,' said Hamish, 'he's my mate.' James had felt an odd pride at the accolade. He drove Lucienne, along with Hamish, back to London, arriving at 7 a.m. The two of them were asleep in the back and James looked out of the window at the day taking shape: buses trundling out on duty, the familiar patterns of people doing what people did. He thought how much fun it was that there was this other planet he could visit – where people slept by day and drank all night – and how relieved he was, at the same time, that he didn't have to stay there, that Karl and Michaela were always back here. When he dropped off, Hamish asked him not to mention Lucienne to anyone – and, as ever, James vowed not to. It was none of his business what Hamish did, why he wanted to go anywhere, any more than it was a pilot's business to go around the plane asking people's reasons for travel. James was involved exactly as much as he wanted to be. It was this attitude of his that led Hamish, when he became suddenly much more famous, to ask if James could drive him exclusively. But it was also because they liked each other. It was a model friendship of a certain kind: they cracked jokes, exchanged notes on the radio or the weather, got where they were going, and never worried about each other when they were not in the car.

The artwork had moved by the time James took up his last job, at King's Cross; it hung in the Gents' in the Great Northern Hotel bar, adjacent to the station. James went into this bar sometimes to use the toilet during his lunch break, trying to put off going back into the building until the last second. His colleagues all seemed to have existing loyalties and friendships. There was a WhatsApp group which he couldn't join, as he'd got rid of all the apps like that; they went bowling together, that sort of thing. Waqar, his supervisor, only ever seemed to talk about two, unrelated subjects: his view that people were underestimating the importance of sex robots, and the 'chunk of change' that his flat in Watford was going to earn him. In the final few weeks, James had also started going for a drink in the bar, on his own, after his shift finished: normally a double whisky, which had a short-lived dulling effect on his brain. The winter darkness would wrap its glove around the building and James would look at the business mates in their overcoats, drinking in tight little knots; the couples going by outside, with a sense of purpose and anticipation that had left his own life. He would think about the fact that he didn't belong here in any sense, and yet was sheltering here because he didn't want to go home either, back to the dripping shower and the silence. He could feel the weight of these places pressing in on him, crushing him like an insect.

And now the YOU CAN CHANGE IT art – hanging next to one of those Andy Warhol four-way portraits – had a mocking quality. Because he *had* changed it. Found Michaela, sorted his weight out, got a job that made him feel busy and valuable. He'd prided himself, in a quiet way, on those changes, on the progress of his life towards the point where he was seemingly winning. Yet all of it had changed back, and he felt like a fool for believing in what he'd had before. None of it had been real.

When he'd phoned the Samaritans, the lady had tried to remind him that if things could change for the worse, they could also get better – as he'd seen for himself in the past. 'It doesn't have to be this way,' she had said, towards the end of the call. It was a moment in which he thought he heard her default mode – concerned, professional helpline monitor – morph into something more potent, into an appeal from one soul to another. 'You could feel better than this.' He had taken it seriously; he'd tried to hold it in his heart. Even in the past couple of months, with his general sadness so acute that it hurt physically to heave his big body out of the door – a pain he couldn't point to or even locate, a leadenness in every limb. He'd continued to *do things* as if any day might throw him a raft, might sneak a magical turnaround into the plot.

He'd kept getting up in the morning, always checking his phone when he woke up in case Karl had found new evidence and realized James was blameless; or in case Sal had been in touch with an olive branch. In case Michaela . . . in case something had happened, in the night, to turn things around. He'd kept saying hello to Steffi, when their paths crossed. Going to work, smiling at customers, asking how he could help. He'd even kept trying to find dates on the app, until the night of his humiliation.

He'd given it every chance, was the point. *I tried so hard*, he thought to himself, annoyed at the lurch into self-pity. It was stupid. The train was idling in an empty station again: a station that would come gradually to life in the morning. There were the footsteps of the conductor outside; he knew her tread by now, the flat-footed plod, that pantomime un-quiet of someone who thought they were being discreet. He wished for a second that she would knock on the door; that they could talk. Just make small talk, kill another stretch of this silence. But he'd never been much good at that; if he was, maybe he wouldn't be here. *Anyway*, James thought, *I would probably cry. If she asked me anything.* And he remembered crying on Steffi, and felt mortified all over again, and then relieved he was doing this.

He was heading to Edinburgh now, to the bridge, only because he had given the world a reasonable chance to prove that it 'didn't have to' be like this, and the fact was it *did* have to, it was going to keep being like this, and he would much, much rather not be in the game than keep on losing it over and over again.

This horrible end hadn't always been inevitable. There had been plenty of moments along the way at which anyone would have looked in at James's life from the outside and said: yes, this guy is doing well. Is set up nicely. He thought back to that first Christmas living with Michaela, the place done out in an incredible number of lights because Michaela turned out to be one of these people who treated Christmas as if it only came round once every hundred years. In fact James had made a joke to that effect, sweating through his shirt as they wrestled the Christmas tree through a hallway which was already a festive Aladdin's cave: reindeer antlers on the coat hooks, a plastic Santa hiding like a mugger behind the bathroom door. 'You do . . . er, you do realize,'

203

he panted, 'by the time we've got all this down, it will be Christmas all over again?'

'Perfect,' said Michaela, 'we'll just leave it up, then.'

James laughed out loud; he knew she was only three-quarters joking. He'd heard about people having 'infectious energy', but never lived it until now: never before felt that energy flow out of somebody into him. It was just easier to do everything when she was there. He could run further than he thought. He found he was fully awake, anticipating the day, as soon as he opened his eyes. Every appointment, every future prospect was rosier in the mind if he pictured it with Michaela there. It seemed too good to be true that she should get the same daily boost out of being with *him*. But for that longish period he'd started to believe that things could, indeed, be as good as you wanted them to be.

'We'll end up being those people who act like it's Christmas every day,' he said, kissing her on top of her head. 'We'll be on a documentary on Channel Five.'

'*Please*,' said Michaela. 'Channel Four at *least*. Ideally I'd hold out for Theroux. Here, these are going under the tree. Three for you, one – ' she tapped a little tissue-paper parcel – 'for your phone.'

'For my phone?'

'It's an umbrella. *The slightest bit of water*. I stole it from an Eighties cocktail night.'

'Don't you ever wish I was funny, like you?' asked James that evening. 'Or just – you know, just, er. Be the person at the party who is actually funny?'

'You're funny! That story you told at Karl's party . . .'

'*Would* have been great, yes, if I hadn't somehow said it

204

took place in a casino when it was really a zoo, and then spent four minutes getting to the punch line but it didn't make sense because of the, er, because there wouldn't be elephants in a casino. I mean, this is my point, really. I'm not even that good at telling the story *of* how I told a story badly.'

'Well, my love, do you know what, there are more important things than being funny,' said Michaela. It was only very occasionally she said something like 'my love', or 'darling', affection being something she preferred to show physically; because of this rarity, it always lit a little fire inside James. 'The "good sense of humour" thing is a bit of a myth. I think so, anyway. That's great on a date, someone making you laugh. But you need more. In an actual relationship.'

'Like, for example . . .?'

She squeezed his cheek. 'Are you fishing for compliments, mister?'

'I suppose that's exactly what I'm doing. Yes.'

They stood by the tree together. This was fun. James's parents hadn't really dressed their place up for Christmas these past few years, now that it was only them who lived there, although Mr Chiltern hadn't been able to see why not when Sal suggested they should at least get a poinsettia bouquet for the front door.

'Kindness is way more important,' said Michaela, 'being a good person, caring about other humans, giving a shit about the consequences of your actions. Also . . .' She fanned herself, she was glowing with sweat, almost as hot as James. 'Also, carrying Christmas trees. Those are the main human skills, and you seem to have most of them. Yep, I think you're going to be OK.'

*

The little plastic bulb above the bed gave out an off-white light, the best it could do. It wasn't a real light bulb, and this, thought James, wasn't a real place. It was an antechamber. The locations of his life were gone now, the locations and the people who'd lived there. He couldn't go back to them, any more than those kids – in the book Sal used to read him extracts from – could get back to Narnia if the wardrobe were taken away one day.

James kicked out at the counter with the heel of his shoe. It felt a stupid, feeble gesture, even though the noise was gratifyingly loud. Probably loud enough for the woman, Gina, to hear. Maybe he'd get into trouble. He imagined himself mounting a defence, borrowing argumentative abilities he'd never had, finding them now it was too late. *I paid for this ticket!* Channelling the sour passengers he himself had had to serve, at King's Cross. *I suggest you concentrate on running a service that isn't delayed every other day!* Surprising the Welsh woman with his confidence. His indignation. It was nonsense, it was feeble and petty even in his imagination.

He needed to sleep. There were only three and a bit hours left to kill, now. He attacked the lid of the fifth can, jerking it upwards with such force that it made a little scratch in his finger. *I'll just get this down me and shut my eyes.* But the sight of the phone was worse than the feeling of it in his pocket had been. It lay in its corner, daring him not to look at it, jeering that he couldn't manage it. The unread messages were like an alarm going off. He buried his head in the thin pillow. But the sound of the alarm was burrowing into his skull; he could hear it even though it wasn't there.

21

I'll keep trying to call him, wrote Steffi.

Me 2, Michaela began to type out, her finger skidding a little on the screen even though she'd kept one hand out of the bathwater specifically for typing duties. Pls stay in touch. It felt odd to be using these textual shortcuts with someone she did not know, especially as Steffi was writing everything out in full. Someone she'd never heard of an hour ago, since these days she paid no attention to who was living in the flat with James. Just to whether the rent was coming in – which it always did, because it was James.

'Steffi'. She was Dutch. She looked young and sort of keen-eyed and clever on her profile; although there weren't many photos, she wasn't much of a sharer. She reminded Michaela a bit of the twenty-something business-influencer people who occasionally came to the gallery to give them frightening presentations about things like 'click maximization'. Michaela wondered if there was anything between her and James, if maybe when all this blew over – but no. She couldn't ask for a get-out like that. The universe didn't owe it to her to find James someone new.

Michaela envied people who could nail an admin task quite as fast as this girl had set up the Facebook campaign. She'd got out of the habit of organizing things when she was with James. Nowadays she had to bluff it at the gallery when people sent Google Sheets or made her sign into Doodle or whatever the hell the new one was called, which made you remember about nine passwords just to arrange a meeting with someone who was sitting next to you. Yes, Michaela felt it really should be her who was launching this online rescue attempt. But what would Phillip have made of that? His eyebrows would have lifted clean off his face.

Even now, she didn't think he was asleep; she could picture his scornful face against the headboard, ready with some bon mot about how 5 a.m. was an unusual time for a bath. He thought baths were ridiculous at the best of times. He was a showerer. Baths made no sense, he'd said during one of their first dates, because you were just lying around in your own dirt. But what about the joy of it, she'd countered – wanting to hold her own against this man. He had already ruled that three films she quite liked were 'overrated', as well as one type of cheese and one breed of dog. And he'd managed to talk down Israel but also online liberals who were *too* pro-Palestine so she had no idea whose team she was meant to be on.

'What about the . . . just the fun of being in the bath? Or are Germans not allowed fun?'

He'd broken into his huge laugh, an even more distracting laugh than her own – a noise she loved getting out of him. Then and now. 'No, you are right. We are only allowed fun on holidays and we have to fill out forms first.'

The bath here was a beauty. The water pressure was amazing: it came out like an espresso machine, the estate agent had said – speaking in English, for her benefit. It was a weird thing to say, because nobody wanted to imagine they were bathing in coffee, but Michaela remembered it every time. The agent had gone on to show them the view the bathroom window gave of the Landwehr Canal, which was becoming very expensive to live on, so this was a bargain. Michaela wasn't really listening to that bit. She'd been enjoying the thought that she could lie here naked, looking down on people walking their dogs or jogging far below, and they would never know.

But there was no fun in that thought, now, any more than there was in the memory of her playful early argu-ments with Phillip. Nothing made sense, and Michaela didn't feel in a state of mental fitness to deal even with things that *did* make sense. Of course not. It was five in the morning. They'd been drinking. She should be asleep. She should not be trying to talk James down from this. From this mad but increasingly plausible threat. And not even talking to him, just sending messages into nothingness. She'd texted him six times, tried to call four. Each time, part of her instinct had been that he surely must answer *this* time. When they were together – and especially when they'd begun working together, too – he'd barely left it as long as the second tone if her name came up. Can I help with anything, love? Are you sure you don't want me to . . .? The almost comical devotion, which had been so lovely until it started to feel very slightly like a bind, and to which she ultimately preferred the cat-and-mouse game of Phillip's erratic phone etiquette. So she had thought.

She looked helplessly at the phone held out in front of her, and at her own knees rising from the water, reflected in the elegant silver tap. She was sitting up almost straight against the back of the bath; she might as well be in an office chair. She remembered being in the old place, in London, sitting like this – bolt upright, the water going cold – on the night she'd admitted to herself that she was going to have to leave James.

Michaela had reconstructed it meticulously with her therapist. That awful night, a night (like this one) that had seemed never-ending, preceded by bad sleeps and followed by no sleep at all. Couldn't stop crying; clown-like smudges all over her face. And James, who was the one who would have had the right to cry, James keeping it together, just asking: 'What can I do to change your mind? What can I do to be better – for the relationship to be better?' Because she hadn't told him about Phillip yet, which she later hated herself for. (Although the therapist said 'hating yourself' was unsustainable, and could we find another way of talking about it?) 'I'm so sorry, James,' she'd kept saying, aware how absolutely inadequate it was, particularly as he didn't fully realize what she was apologizing for. 'I'm so sorry, my darling.' Not just for leaving, but loving someone else, more than she loved James, even though that made her a terrible person. (The therapist had said it wasn't constructive to label herself like that, and was there a different way of talking about it?)

She'd almost wanted him to ask if there was someone new. Nearly anyone else would have done that. But James hadn't; he'd just kept talking, as if there was still something to play for, as if he could still hold onto her. Asking how he could fix it. How it could still be all right.

'I know I'm not very good at expressing things without sounding silly,' he'd said – Michaela couldn't even meet his eye; she stared at her wine-glass, which she was holding so tightly at the stem she feared it would snap. She thought of Phillip, against every good instinct in her body, thought of how soon she could see him and this would be over. 'This is going to sound silly,' James continued. 'But you're the only person I have ever loved this way. Please don't take away . . . what we have. I'm begging you not to do that. We can solve this, whatever it is.

'You can't . . . I mean. You can't, you mustn't leave me just because I shouted at you. That one time. It doesn't make sense, Michaela.'

But of course it hadn't been about the one time. It had been made of a lot of different little things, just like suddenly huge problems always were. Part of it was the way that she'd begun to feel trapped by the whole running project. If you didn't post something every twenty minutes, people started getting at you. 'I pay to subscribe to this!' If you *did* post, you got the usual internet pond life sneering at you for being fat, but if in a video she looked even slightly thinner than usual, she'd get plus-size fans making out that she was 'a bad ambassador', that she'd sold out, like all of them did when they started making money.

It wasn't even that much money. It had just felt like selling old rope, when they started. James had been able to cut back on the driving, allowing other drivers to take some of his jobs, and devote himself to building this with her. A little run, a piece to camera while she was going along, some exercise and diet tips, uploaded and tagged by James. Really no more than a couple of hours' work in research and execution, compared with a whole shift for him on the road. But it turned out that to maintain it, you had to keep ramping it up; you had to find enormous quantities of the rope. New people came along, competitors. The business had been built on nothing, so it was never far from her head that it could just return to nothing. And her friends back at the Citizens Advice would pretend to be sympathetic but they'd be full of *Schadenfreude*, like they always were when someone got out and then it blew up in her face. 'She thought she could live off that? Off doing videos about running when you're fat?' 'Not fat: plus-size.' 'Well, it sounds like it's been a big, *plus-size* failure.' Ha ha ha. People were always so fucking witty about her size when they thought they were behind her back.

Imagining the reactions to her failure – malicious, or just disappointed, as in the case of her mum – drove Michaela to work harder and harder at her brand. She posted more and more stuff, 'content' as people had started saying; she replied to every single favourable comment, every request for advice. Before she'd even put the phone on in the morning she would feel tension massing in her stomach, cramping her up: she told James it was because she couldn't handle dairy any more. He began fetching her matcha lattes the following morning, and even switched to oat milk himself, even though he eventually confessed that it was 'a bit too much on the oaty side'. Yes, she'd said, you will find that with oat products. He'd persevered with it, he'd kept on finding her dairy alternatives, googling, ordering strange-looking packets from Southeast Asia, and it became too late to tell him that dairy wasn't actually the problem at all; that he was looking at the wrong thing.

She had to keep on with the running, the diet tips, the body-positive advocacy, long after it had started to wear out her enthusiasm. James had more or less completely sacked off the driving, to be somewhere between her PA and her manager. He updated her diary with every invitation to speak, every personal appearance, trade fair, anywhere she might pick up new followers. Michaela did them all. She thought it was only for a while; that eventually she'd be so well established that she wouldn't have to work quite so much. But something like the opposite was true. Self-employment turned out to be like that fable about the ever-replenishing feast. The more work you did, the more, somehow, you had to keep doing.

The trade fair on Sal's wedding morning had been one of the biggest of the year. Michaela had a fifteen-minute slot on the main stage. It was sponsored by a running magazine whose editor wanted to feature her on the front page; he told her over the phone that 'loving your body and stuff is really in at the moment'. They'd be done by eleven; the train from Manchester to Edinburgh wasn't too bad, the wedding ceremony didn't start till two. It was tight, but it would work. You always just about got away with these things. That was probably what she would have said.

'This is what you have to do when you're on the way up,' she'd said, grabbing James's hand. 'Taking everything like this, grabbing it, even – even when there's, you know, family stuff.'

'I know, and of course I would normally . . . but this is not really "family stuff", is it? It's my sister's wedding.'

'We'll be at the station on time, we've already got the tickets. We'll be fine.'

He could, of course, have gone on his own – as the therapist remarked – but no, they did things together, they were a team. They did the morning session together. James made sure people subscribed, collected the contact details of influencers, signed them up to the socials then and there: all these tasks he'd taken to naturally, as his old computing instincts kicked back in. They were, sure enough, at Piccadilly station on time. As soon as they got into the station and she saw the crowds around the departure boards, though, Michaela felt her stomach drop into her boots.

She could see it any time she chose to torture herself: the sweat patches on James's too-light shirt, the colour draining from his face. 'Well, we're not going to make it,' he said, calmly, but with a tremor in his voice she hadn't heard before. 'We're not going to be there in time.'

'We could still make it,' she said. 'We could get a cab, we could—'

'A cab wouldn't be fast enough.' James's voice was so taut that he was almost laughing, the way people did when they were in shock. 'There's no way.'

'We could still get there for the . . . the evening bit.' She didn't know what to say. 'There's always a lot of standing around at weddings.' That wasn't going to save the situation; she wanted to take it back almost before she'd finished saying it. 'I just mean—'

'I said I'd be there at effing half past one, and I was going to go to the . . . to the bridge,' James had snapped. She couldn't help it, she giggled at him for his non-language. 'Ah, yes,' James had said. 'Well, of course it's funny if you don't like my sister in the first place.'

'You don't think I tried to like her? I was so into being liked *by* her. But right from the first time, the way she looked at me, like *who's this random brown bird that my brother's—*'

'That is absolute, that is absolutely . . .' said James, his colour up. 'She never thought anything about you. Especially – what are you saying?'

'Well, maybe it's just her way, but it always seemed like I wasn't good enough.'

'So this is your response, is it? To miss her wedding? Do you think this is going to help?'

'For fuck's sake. It's not a fucking *response*. I didn't plan for us to miss the—'

'Don't swear at me, please,' he said, sounding impossibly prim and mannered, even to himself.

'Grow up, James.'

'I don't think it's *grown up* that you swear.'

'Ah, good. All right, let's have it all out. You think I'm common because I swear, you think I'm gross because I pee with the door open, you—'

'I never said that.'

'You imply it quite strongly by shutting the door for me, mate!'

'Are we going to stand here talking about every single thing that, er, that you have been saving up to argue with me about while I thought things were going quite well, or are we—'

'You think I'm obsessed with running and keeping fit and, I don't know, I should give up building this brand that I've fucking – I'm sorry, that I've *bloody well* broken my back to get going . . .'

'Well, look at it.' James spread his arms wide. Involuntarily she scowled at the sweat patches, and he felt fat and shamed. 'Look where the running has got us.'

'What!' Michaela dumped her bag at her feet; she needed her whole body to express how wronged she felt by this conversation. 'Excuse me, what? *Where it's got us* as in, we have an exciting life, we live purely off what I put online?'

'What *I* put online for you,' James murmured, and she had walked away, open-mouthed, wanting the entire station to share in her indignation: a gesture which felt empty, because after thirty paces or so she'd had to turn around and walk back and ask James what they were going to do next.

What they did next was to wait on a crowded platform, next to a mother with two bickering children who was carrying an enormous crocodile-shaped lilo and kept visibly thinking about throwing it onto the tracks. What they did next was to stand next to the toilet, in silence, for three and a quarter hours on a delayed service that dragged them towards an appointment they were already late for, James staring out of the window with such unbroken focus that he might have been hypnotized. Michaela reflected on the fact that many of the things she'd said in the argument, many of the criticisms she'd put into James's mouth, must have been things she was thinking about herself. 'It's like I was looking for an excuse for the fight to start,' she said, much later, to the therapist. 'Which is typical me.' (I don't think it's helpful to talk in generalizations about your personality, said the therapist; I'm interested in the specifics.)

Even when they got shamefacedly to the fancy Scottish place – stone lions by the doorway, lanterns along the drive, the sort of place someone like Johnny Depp would probably get married in – Michaela had still thought this would pass, it would be OK. They'd have a couple of drinks, maybe there would be karaoke. Michaela had a 'Total Eclipse of the Heart' that could blow the birds out of the trees; a stranger had offered her a recording contract once in a Lucky Voice place in London, although it later turned out he was blind drunk and also not connected to the music industry. Surely it wouldn't have to be a big deal, because they were here *now*, weren't they? And if Michaela ever got married (which she wouldn't do in a pretentious bloody castle like this, by the way, she thought) – but if she ever married James, for example (which she realized in her guts didn't sit right as a fantasy) – well, she wouldn't spoil her own day stressing over who got there when. The whole thing was about celebration, wasn't it? As the taxi crunched over the gravel, she was almost certain their lateness would be forgotten already. But there was James's sister, in the slim-fitting, expensive-looking dress (Michaela would want something more colourful, less *wedding*). Arms folded, standing on the steps, as if she'd literally been waiting for them right here since the second they left the church.

'Right, well, thanks for making such an effort,' had been her opening words. Michaela, she admitted to the therapist later, should probably have opened with an apology, rather than trying to hug Sally and say congratulations. (Why do you think you did that? the therapist asked. Because I'm a touchy-feely person, I guess, Michaela had said, but the therapist hadn't written it down, so she felt she'd failed the question.)

'The trains . . .' James had begun.

'Yes, if only there was some way of planning around that,' Sally had snapped, like she'd had it ready for hours.

'We're not all time-management experts,' Michaela muttered – meaning it as an ice-breaker, a compliment even. But in Sally's mind it had somehow read as a sneer, and she'd turned and walked away. In James's eyes, following her, Michaela could see that in some ways he was on his sister's side. If there was a single moment, a single thought that ended it, it was that one.

★

So maybe the floor of the relationship – however solid it had seemed – was really a sheet of ice which would have cracked one day or another. And the bloody events of the next few hours and days, the ripples and aftershocks, the exchange of nasty texts between Michaela and Sal – all this was just a blowtorch. Even though, before the wedding day, she would have said that she and James were great together, were happy, that couldn't have been completely true. There must have been something missing all along.

All the same, they could have patched it up, like people did after an argument. Things were prickly, and it didn't help that James's way of addressing the charged atmosphere was to continue holding work conversations, keep bringing her the matcha latte in the morning, try to smother the memory of the falling-out with a big thick blanket of decency. But they *could* have patched it up. It was true what James had said: people didn't just tear up a four-year romance because of one wrong note, however jarring. Yet the fact was, a fortnight after the wedding disaster, Michaela had texted a friend to complain that things were still tense at home, and the friend had invited her to a boozy art event sponsored by O2, and Michaela wasn't bothered about art but did like Prosecco, and hadn't been out properly for a while because of the sodding running.

There Phillip had been, this very handsome man, with the German inflection which made him sound like a physics genius as imagined by Dan Brown. Speaking, not even in his first language, to a hundred rich tuxedos. 'At times when the world feels full of conflict, when politics lets us down, art does not become less relevant. It actually becomes *more* important'. 'Ect-ually', he pronounced it. Michaela's mate saw the way she was looking at Phillip, and smirked, and introduced them on the balcony afterwards. He said that he hoped the speech was OK, he'd been very nervous. It had made her feel powerful to tell him, this man who'd made jokes in three languages, that – yes – the speech had been OK; more than OK, fantastic. She'd noticed he was not wearing a wedding ring. She thought about how, if she'd been there beforehand, she would have made him less nervous. She'd been alarmed by the thoughts. As she took his number, she told herself she would never use it.

But that idea only lasted forty-eight hours. Then she texted him to ask when he was next in London, and it turned out the answer was that Thursday. Again, a surprise. It was a surprise for him to be asking, straight out: 'So, if you could do anything – if you could have any life right now – what would it be?' Very little teasing or small talk; none of the flirty preliminaries you might expect with a new person. The way he looked her bang in the eyes, it was as if they had already known each other for five years, as if they were the sort of friends who could pick up after a long absence. It was not just surprising, but alarming, to be thinking about him like this. It was positively alarming that two hours into their first proper drink together, which she prolonged by sending James a series of dishonest texts about 'meeting a blogger', she already couldn't imagine not knowing Phillip.

If something's not right, it's wrong, Phillip had said, with just enough forward tilt of the glasses to convey that this was a quotation (Google helped her out on the way home). He'd said it, like everything on that stolen meeting, with a show of neutrality. It was only weeks later he'd admitted: 'What I meant by that was, I want to make love to you more than anything in life.' It was even a surprise when she found an excuse to meet him in Paris; she felt as if she was merely submitting to a long-held plan as she straddled him in a toilet cubicle at the gallery where he was meant to be having meetings, because neither of them could wait till they got back to the hotel. As they walked out of the Ladies' together, an old woman with a complex assembly of necklaces gave them a strange look. 'This facility is now gender-neutral,' said Phillip, in French. 'Since when?' she asked. 'Now,' he deadpanned.

If something wasn't right, it was wrong, and something obviously *wasn't* right, or it would never have happened this way with Phillip. He was the answer to a question she hadn't been courageous enough to ask. And once that solution was in her grasp, she had to commit to it, she had to walk away from everything and begin a new life, because that was how she did things. She'd never regretted it, really. Felt guilty, yes, but not regretted it. Now, in the bath, she felt a shudder pass right through her and she reached for James's number again.

The person you are calling . . .

'Are you ever going to come to bed or do you just plan staying in the bath all night like some sort of John and Yoko thing?'

223

She let Phillip's barb die on the air. Why encourage him? Just at this moment she didn't need his sarcasm, thank you. Yes, she was sure it *was* strange to be doing this at gone five in the morning. Desperately messaging her ex's friends, contacts, anyone. But what did he care? They had nothing to get up for tomorrow. They were just going to go out and have brunch. And maybe see this Spanish movie by some female director who Phillip said would be regarded as a genius if it wasn't for what he called 'the intrinsic sexism of the arts'. (Michaela had looked up 'intrinsic' out on the fire escape.)

These plans, though, seemed as absurd to her – after what had happened – as her current texting marathon apparently did to Phillip. It flashed before her that all this happy time with Phillip, this bliss, had been an illusion, or at least had been as flimsy as the happiness she'd had back in London. Because if James had overdosed, or . . . or hanged himself, Jesus Christ (it was unspeakable even in her head), or whatever the fuck he might have done, none of it would make any sense, it would all be broken.

It was frightening to feel that about someone who was – however important in her biography, however embedded in her heart – not meant to be in her life any more. To feel that he was, after all, still part of what Michaela regarded as herself. She kicked out against the feeling, tried to push it away.

She felt so empty, like an engine trying to grind through on fumes alone. Should have eaten more, should have drunk less. Should have asked if James was all right. At least now and again. Should have seen the signs that must have been there.

And what now? What the fuck now? Michaela stared at her phone. It stared back with nothing.

22

A1(M) SEFTON PARK SERVICES, 04:34

This is not the dream, thought Karl. Gone half four in the morning, services, not even one of the better services in North Yorkshire. It had a two-burger rating for food (out of five), a two-angel rating for how happy customers felt (out of seven); its bathrooms were rated at just four smiling urinals (out of twenty). There was an amusement arcade where even the machines' jingles sounded tired, like they'd won too many times for it to be fun. There was a café called Secret Eats which, far from being secret, very publicly served lacklustre sandwiches and machine coffee. It was Karl's business to know these things; an option on the app allowed all his drivers to access it, too. This was not the dream. As he and James used to say.

It was pretty rough how his brain kept circling back to their little jokes, to the very moments you didn't want to be thinking about when you were scared for someone's safety.

There was a time he came round to see James and Michaela, a couple of months after James had moved from their shared flat to hers. It could have been awkward, the reshaped dynamic, but Karl had pulled out all the stops to ensure that didn't happen. Business was good and he had purchased, as well as a good wine, some marijuana from a contact of Hamish's. He rolled himself a bifta as thick as a Subway sandwich. Michaela was asleep and, at James's insistence, they opened the front door to let the air circulate, even though it was raining and thundery outside. James – who'd of course not touched the joint despite Karl's wheedling – was the one alert enough to see the darkish shape in the hall. It was a frog, James said in a whisper. Michaela hated frogs, they made her freak out – frogs, cotton wool, and anything to do with the circus. 'It shouldn't be in here,' said James, several times, lumbering into the hall. 'Well of course it shouldn't, pal!' Karl hooted. 'We didn't invite it round, did we!' But from the way James shushed him, from his solicitous expression, Karl realized the problem needed to be addressed. He padded into the hall. James was on his hands and knees, a waste-paper basket raised over his head, face down.

'This is *not* the dream,' Karl cackled, as the frog eluded James's crude trap with ease, hopping out of the way a good few seconds before the bin came down on top of it. 'Oh, man, this is very much not the dream.' They built, in hoarse mutters, on this idea, throwing the bin between each other, taking turns to try to pounce on the intruder with their makeshift container. 'This is, I mean, not even in the same postcode as the dream,' said James, breathing hard. 'This is – you can't even visit this, and the dream, in the same day trip,' said Karl. The joke escalated, feeding off itself, until it was harder and harder to keep the laughter down. And then, finally, when it had seemed impossible, James – with one of his slow but forceful movements – brought the basket crashing over the frog. Hurriedly they slid a thin chopping board beneath bin and floor. Karl cheered like he was watching the football. Michaela, roused, stuck her head out of the bedroom door. 'What the fuck . . .?' she asked, and in the panic of having disturbed her after all this effort, James – a bad dissembler at the best of times – shouted what would become a famous phrase between them: 'I DON'T HAVE A FROG IN HERE!'

Karl dried his hands on his trousers. He'd been doing almost a hundred. His guts were thrashing about like a tumble-dryer. There was still time. Maybe there was still time.

He pulled into a short-stay space. He swung open the door, wrenched his phone out of its cradle. It was ringing again, the third call. The DJ in the back groaned and wriggled, and Karl's muscles tensed. His back and shoulders and even knees were aching. But, as usual, the passenger seemed to resettle, his breaths settling back into that serene rhythm, his face wearing the look of someone who was not worrying about his friend, thought Karl. *He'll be dreaming about all the money he got working for an hour tonight. Or about his beautiful gaff he's probably got back in town. I bet he's got one of them bathrooms with a double sink for no reason.* He thought of Hamish Elton, the jumped-up, bigoted little piece of shit, with his penthouse which a cleaner visited more often than Elton himself did. Elton, that bleached-teeth, well-born cocksucker, who'd coked his way to a university expulsion and somehow enhanced his job prospects in the process, the way only a rich white guy could. Elton, the cause of all this trouble.

Karl went ten paces away from the car. The phone was just ringing nonstop, now; it was like a press conference with one hand going up and then another. He pressed green. It was a woman's voice.

'What's going on?' he asked. 'Have you found him, is he, what is he . . .?'

'We still have not found him,' said Steffi. 'I'm his flatmate.' Her voice was . . . Danish? Swedish? One of those countries. 'I have put a lot of messages on Facebook. You're his friend? His boss?'

'Yeah. Was. Am.' Karl wasn't sure which part of the proposition he was responding to.

'And you fired him?'

'Yeah. Look. I'm driving, I—'

'I have found out some things about it,' said the woman. 'You thought he had given newspapers a story about a guy called Hamish. But he says very much he didn't do it. He said that to me. And since he lost the job, he's been really upset.'

'*Ham*-ish.' He corrected her pronunciation; she'd said it with the first syllable 'ham' not 'hame'. What was going on here, Karl thought – his mouth forming a sort of incredulous half-smile, the way tennis players' did if they'd been wronged by the umpire so obviously that they felt sure the whole world could see it. That was sort of how he felt at the moment: like the victim of some conspiracy or trick. He half-expected one of these grinning pieces of work off ITV to jump out with a camera. Because how else could you explain the way the past five hours had gone? It was only a moment ago he'd been in the car park at Wembley. Nice and warm in the car, but not too warm for the incoming passenger. A little sign in his window with the DJ's name, can of Red Bull, phone ticking over with news of jobs coming in, already imagining the tip from this one and maybe being able to take a couple of days off in midweek, go down to the coast. And now this. It was enough to make your head spin. Not just your head; everything. He felt spaced out, like in the not-quite-on-the-planet phase between hangover and recovery.

'I mean, what are you . . .?' Karl raised his voice, then dropped it again, but it might be too late. He'd heard a noise from his parked car. The geezer was awake, this was buggered. The tip was going the way of the dodo. He wished his heart would slow, but at the same time he was dimly aware that most of its exertions were in protecting him from the truth. Most of the *cardio*, as Michelle used to say. His heart, his brain, they were all about finding paths away from what was difficult to face. That was how he'd survived the first twenty years of his life, grafted through the next fifteen. You moved on, you found another direction.

'Why are you talking like this is my fault?'

The woman on the other end let this fry in ten seconds of silence, and Karl could smell his own desperation. 'All right, so what am I meant to do exactly? I tried to call him,

I've text him, I don't know where he is any more than you do, I—'

'You need to call this man, Hame-ish.' Steffi said it with a sardonic precision, like she was indulging Karl's pronunciation, like he'd probably made it up. 'You need to say it wasn't James's fault.'

'One: it's half past four in the morning,' Karl began, but the voice was not going to let him get even to point number two.

'OK,' she said, 'so – wait till nine o'clock and maybe he's dead but it's a nicer time to do a phone call?'

'One: it's half past four in the morning so the fella will be asleep. Two: what is he going to do? He's on the telly, he's not Superman, he's not just going to fly down and grab James off a building or . . .'

Once more it was as if this woman had been given a script of his objections in advance, and worked on a set of rebuttals. 'You need to ask him to get onto Twitter and re-tweet what I have written about James, also to share it on his Facebook. He has three hundred thousand followers, many fans on Facebook also. If we can't get hold of James, we have to get more people looking. I have been in touch with all his contacts, nearly, that I know about.'

Or if not a trick, a dream – that was what this was like, thought Karl. It was very close to being nuts enough that he could believe it was a nightmare, and that he had reached that semi-aware state your dreaming self sometimes did, where even in the dream you started to call its bluff. Like that dream where he'd had a talking horse and inexplicably only sold it for £200 and was full of remorse as it got more and more famous. Yeah, he'd seen through that bollocks even as he was dreaming it. But this wasn't far off. James was saying he was going to kill himself, this woman was ringing him, talking about Hamish Elton, talking about stuff she shouldn't know about. Making demands about Twitter and God knew what else.

'Or if you give me his number,' she was saying now, unbelievably, 'I will call him, this guy.'

'I can't give you his number.' Karl felt a claw of panic stirring his stomach. He was going to have to go to the toilet here, which – if the reviews were accurate – would be even less of a barrel of laughs than taking a shit in a services normally was. But only if the guy was still asleep. And even then he'd have to be so quick or the prick would wake up and wonder why he was on his own in the car and then the tip really would be as dead as the fax machine.

'And you can't call him,' he said. 'You can't disturb him, over this.'

'So then, you need to . . .'

'Stop fucking talking about what I *need to do*,' said Karl. This woman was a psychopath, giving orders to someone she'd never met before; talking like someone had made her the Pope just because she lived with James. He blew out a hard breath, his mouth making an O. Right at this moment he would swap lives with anyone he could see. With one of the lorry drivers sleeping in their sad little encampment of vehicles in one corner of the car park. With any of the tail-lights streaking past, even with the handful of deadbeats feeding coins into the arcade machines. 'I'll do my best, all right? I'll . . . I have to get to Newcastle and then I'll get onto it. Tell me when you find him, yeah?'

'All right, Karl, mate,' he said out loud to himself – the way he'd used to sometimes, under his breath, when he was a teenager and his father was crashing around downstairs. Talking to himself had made him bolder, forced him to put on a front like you would for someone you wanted to impress. 'All right. We're going to nip in there.' The rain-hardened brick of the service station, the overfamiliar logos of the food and coffee superpowers. 'Then, we get on the road and we fucking cheese it all the way to Newcastle, we do a hundred and ten until we're on that bridge and we can hear the fucking *Likely Lads* theme tune, we—'

A car horn blasted, ripping apart the near-silence. Karl jumped, swore. It was his own car. The bloke had literally clambered over into the driver's seat and had a go on the horn. Was he off his box? You couldn't do that! You couldn't just sound the horn in a fucking car park! Karl had pretty much had enough of everyone queuing up round the block to bust his balls. And yet he couldn't get funny with the DJ either. He couldn't afford to piss *him* off, either. He needed these people, their custom. The whole great money-making edifice, painstakingly built by Karl, seemed to be swaying in front of him. He strode back to the car.

'Sorry about that,' he muttered, 'emergency.'

'*Was* it an emergency?' asked the DJ. He had undone the seatbelt, was sitting arms folded in the back seat. He was looking at Karl as if Karl had caused him some indefensible disturbance; as if Karl was a neighbour who'd been letting off fireworks in the garden. 'It looked like you were just on the phone, mate.'

'I'm sorry. There's a situation going on.'

'Right, well, the thing is, dude: if you remember, I wanted to stay asleep,' said the DJ.

'I know,' said Karl, 'but we're nearly there, it's probably about forty-five minutes—'

'But I could've been asleep for that extra time, yeah? If you hadn't stopped the car to do your phone call. The whole point was to get maximum sleep, yeah? And I would still *be* asleep if we'd not stopped.'

'I know, and I do apologize, it's just—'

'But instead, I'm in a situation where I'm sitting here awake. Which isn't being asleep.'

'Yeah. As I say, apologies.' Karl forced the words out, marvelling at this arsehole who was taking the trouble to explain what sleep was. His teeth were gritted so tight it felt like one row would take the other row out altogether, like dodgems trying to force each other off the rink. 'We'll get you there ASAP, all right. I'm just going into the services now for two minutes, and then—'

'Are you kidding me, mate?'

'Sorry?'

'I've got to get to Newcastle, pal,' said the DJ. As if there'd been any doubt about that; as if the preceding hours, the two hundred-odd miles might have just been a spin they had taken for fun. 'I want to get there and get into the hotel, be able to properly chill.'

To properly chill, thought Karl, *after all this stressful sleeping.* Jesus Christ. This geezer was too much.

'I'm just going to run in to the bathroom, all right, so . . .'

'Can you not wait?'

Karl stared at the man in the back of his car. Around six foot tall, double-breasted Paul Smith coat (about six hundred quid, Karl reckoned); ridiculous but somehow desirable baseball-cap thing he'd taken off to sleep (at least a hundred quid, probably); superior-quality bling, unshowy as this stuff went (couldn't even guess the price of that gear). This man who seemed to be under the impression that he had hired, not just the car and driver, but the use of Karl as some sort of robot servant.

But he had, in a way, thought Karl, climbing helplessly back into the driver's seat. It didn't matter how much he felt like the big guy, with Cruiz. How clever the AI he'd built, how impressive his work ethic. When confronted with an *actual* big guy – someone who could casually pay three hundred and fifty quid to be shuttled across the country like precious cargo by night; well, someone who could get his bloody handlers to pay for it, in fact – Karl was just a pair of hands on a steering wheel. He snapped the indicator on with such taut energy that he felt like the lever would come away in his hand. It flashed into his head that there was a story about a driver who'd wet himself at the wheel trying to get someone to Stansted on time. And the tip – this was the punch line, this was why it did the rounds – the tip was a fiver. Was that what Karl had become, despite everything he'd achieved, thought he'd achieved? Someone who would basically soil himself for the price of a pint, if someone more important told him to?

No. Karl squeezed the pedal down, watched the numbers climb. Enough of this. This was not the moment for introspection. It wasn't even the moment to fantasize about turning around, scooping up the guy's stupid hat and his headphones and just posting them out of the window. It was about mind over matter, now; it was about nothing but the present. If the guy was going to treat Karl like a machine, then he would be a machine, just for now. His brain could be disengaged; his cramping body could be ignored, from second to second. Karl could look after himself. He was just going to have to pray, to God or whoever else was there, that someone else was looking after James until he could take over.

★

Karl found his brain doing much what Cruiz's software was designed to do: finding optimum pathways, pairing users with desired outcomes. Karl was its user and it had identified that what he needed were memories of the many times he had been a positive force in James's life. As a result, as they whittled away the distance from here to the drop-off – Newcastle 34, Newcastle 22, said the signs – Karl's brain played on a loop the scene that did him the most credit. It had been two weeks after Michaela had moved out of the flat, seemingly gone mad in fact, disappeared to Germany, telling James she didn't want to be together any more. Not as a couple, not as business partners. Karl had been driving up and down like a blue-arsed fly for the whole period; he hadn't taken seriously the extent of the problem until James left a voicemail. He'd known without needing to listen to it that something was up, properly up.

It was obvious that James had tidied, but there was only so much of a PR job that he could do on the fact that Michaela was in the process of moving out. That her records and books were in plastic bags in the hall, that her extensive collection of sports jackets were no longer hanging on those coat hooks. There was a whole cardboard box marked CHRISTMAS, which Michaela hadn't had the heart to take with her, but which James also hadn't mustered the strength to shut back in its cupboard, so it was sitting outside the bathroom as if someone was planning to deck the place out three months early. Karl handed over a bottle of wine. 'It's not great wine, I'm afraid,' he said. 'The dude in the Turkish shop won't serve booze after ten because apparently he's invented his own version of the law, so I had to go to the . . . Christ.'

James had taken the bottle, unscrewed the top and drunk straight from it: the least James-like gesture Karl could imagine. He was almost as impressed as he was worried. He put an arm around James's shoulders. James's T-shirt was fresh on; why had he bothered to change, for Karl? Did he think after all this time Karl couldn't handle the fact he might be a bit sweaty? Or, for that matter, a bit unhappy? But it *had* been less frequent, their contact, these past couple of years. Since James had left Cruiz and moved in with Michaela. Since everything had become about Michaela. In a way, there was no denying it, this outcome – her suddenly fucking off to Germany, the absconding of his rival – was what Karl had secretly hoped for, secretly even from himself.

James read that thought, or had already had it. He smiled wryly, a brave loser's smile, as they settled on the sofa together.

'Well, I look like . . . like a proper idiot, now, don't I,' said James.

'No, you don't.' Karl felt his sense of loyalty bubble up as if someone else had attacked James. '*She* does, if anything, fam. What's she playing at, galloping off with some bloke who looks like Jürgen Klopp?'

James blinked several times, and Karl knew he had said too much.

'How do you know what – what he looks like,' James asked, 'and who is Jürgen . . .?'

There was a little silence. Karl necked half his glass. He wondered whether James had anything else in. A normal person would have *something* in the kitchen, especially a fortnight after their bird had – not that Karl wanted to labour the point – absolutely shafted him. He wondered what he would try to explain first. That Jürgen Klopp was a football manager, someone who James wouldn't have heard of; or that Michaela's new man, who bore him a passing resemblance, had already put something on Facebook about her, in German but with reasonably clear import.

'I mean,' said James – after they had sat there, Karl's arm still around him although he was getting pins and needles – for a silent five minutes. 'I mean, I pretty much gave up the driving to set up with her. Help her do what she does. So her leaving, it means I don't, I don't really have anything now. Not to be melodramatic.'

'Not to be melodramatic.' It pained Karl now to remember that detail. It was a jarring note in what was meant to be the soothing hold-music of this memory, because it reminded him once more of how colossally reluctant James would be to send a text like tonight's. How the text could only mean he really was serious. He tried to elbow that aside and go back to the comfort of the playback.

'I think you're allowed to be *melodramatic* when your woman leaves and takes her job with her, mate.' Emptying the bottle between their two glasses. 'I don't think it would be overkill if you were dangling from the rafters, mate.' Fuck, Karl had said that. But that was how you talked, wasn't it. You were allowed to make jokes. He couldn't have foreseen this, two and a half years into the future. Anyway, Karl was the hero of the story, not the villain. He really needed to concentrate on the bits where he was the hero.

In the back, the DJ seemed to have fallen asleep. Newcastle 14. All the fuss he'd made and he had been able to nod straight back off like flicking a switch. Well, the man would wake up again nice and soon. Karl couldn't wait for the moment he got shot of him in the hotel lobby. He had a good mind to turn the car radio up to 10 as soon as they pulled up outside. Or screech to a stop like in the movies. It wouldn't matter any more, if the tip didn't look like it was happening. He'd blow a fucking alpenhorn in the guy's face if he had one.

'What am I going to do for work?' James had asked, into a second bottle – awful wine, even worse than the first, because bless him, he simply couldn't tell a bottle of vinegar from something Louis XIV would have ordered. Karl felt an obvious response come into his head, so obvious that he auditioned it silently a couple of times in case the booze was putting a gloss on a load of shit. But no. It was obvious because it was right.

'Surely you get back full time with Cruiz, don't you? Just pick up the old driving again?'

James stared sadly at his glass of wine, as if the suggestion had come from there. 'Raymond's not just going to start giving me loads of hours again. I left, I'm not sure if you remember.' It was quite unusual, even this tiptoeing sarcasm, for him: Karl had a hint of the pain that was beneath everything James said. Why hadn't he encouraged James to talk more, Karl reproached himself. But now, now he could wave a magic wand and clear whatever debt he'd put himself in by getting the hump when James had gone off with Michaela. It could be like old times.

'Mate,' he said, 'I don't think you completely realize how much I'm in charge of Cruiz now. I've built them an app which—'

'I saw it. Like the Addison Lee app.'

'But *not* like that, Jamie.' Karl grabbed James's elbow. He felt the tension in every fibre of his friend's body, felt for a second how much of a physical effort it was even to walk around as James at the moment. 'Way better. It's the sort of thing we were trying to do ten years ago and now you can actually do it. Works out where customers are, works out where they want to go, pretty much before *they* do. Looks at the sort of stuff they like, suggests behaviour without them even being aware of it . . .'

'Looks at the sort of stuff they like, how?' James frowned, puzzled and intrigued. 'Going onto other platforms? Harvesting . . . how?'

'Just using algorithms, using data that they signed up to give away.' Karl's eyes were lively and James got a glimpse of his friend as he had been in the old days, computer light on his face, inside a piece of code like a surgeon inside a body, shoring it up and sending it back out healthy into the world. James remembered how Karl used to talk about information being the cash of the future, which was just as well because he and his mum had never had the cash of the present, i.e. actual cash, and one of these decades they were going to get their turn to live well.

'Is it legal?' asked James.

'It's legal *enough*.' Karl's fingers were flexing as if around an imaginary wad of banknotes. 'They don't even, I said it wrong, they don't even *sign up to give the information away*. They just don't read the terms and conditions. No one does. The first time they sign up for the app, they're trying to get a ride quickly, they're late for something, they tick whatever boxes you ask them to tick. We've all done it. The amount of forms you sign online. It could say "I understand you get to take my dog away" and you'd tick it.' He took a breath, gently topped up James's glass.

'The point is. I've got a lot of data, a lot of contacts. Come back to Cruiz: you'd basically be working for me. Raymond's heart isn't in it and Hugo can't work any more than he does because, in all fairness to the guy, he spends about seventy-five per cent of his time scratching himself. I tell you what. Hamish Elton wants an exclusive driver, like one of those VIP things where he's got you on call. Remember Hamish? You could do that and then whatever else you wanted on top.'

James was looking at his hands, the way he sometimes did when there was something he probably wouldn't be able to say. Karl put his arm around those large shoulders again, and this time he felt James's whole body go slack with relief.

★

It hadn't been quite like old times. They hadn't ended up living together again, nor had they ended up hanging out quite as reliably as they used to. Karl was dating, now, or more accurately having lively but unrepeated sex with people he met using his phone. And he was more and more consumed by the monster he'd built, the artificial intelligence that people didn't recognize as such yet because they thought it was a term from fiction. James was also busy, because Hamish Elton was the sort of person who'd order a taxi to his en suite and back if he could get one. Still, they texted when they could; they went for curries, sometimes, now that James was resigned to letting the weight pile back on. It was a real, working friendship again. Not even a year before James's text, it had seemed to be well on track.

Karl felt his insides roiling with the knowledge that the next sign wouldn't be a number at all: it would just be WELCOME TO. Desperate as he was to reach Newcastle, he was almost equally desperate not to face what was there.

The check of the phone, the probably fruitless dive in search of a miracle get-out – *he's fine, he's safe*. And then when that didn't materialize, the horrible thing he was going to have to do. The call he was going to have to make to Hamish Elton. A call which, had he made it before now, would have stopped James from doing what he – what Karl hoped to hell he hadn't already done.

Outside it was shivering weather; listless rain, just a little, over the narrowing terraces. The occasional bottom-floor glow behind blinds; a super-early riser, perhaps, or someone like him with a problem too big to go to bed with. But Karl didn't really believe that; he envied anyone who was behind any of these walls. He'd swap with them just like he would have swapped at the services. He would take on any problem that wasn't the silence of the road, the memories of James, the cold unanswerable question of where James was now.

It was a lonely feeling when life caught you out. And that was what had happened, Karl admitted to himself for the first time since he'd seen the texts. What was unfolding was just what he deserved. Because he was only a hero if you stopped the tape where he had, with James back on his feet, Karl having helped his old friend out. And that wasn't where the tape stopped. Not in real life. The tape of Karl and James stopped a few months ago, with him throwing James away.

23

LONDON–EDINBURGH TRAIN, 04:57

The country opened out when you got this far north. Dense patches of woodland, dry-stone walls, clumps of heather and gorse by the side of the track. The train, hemmed in for so long, now charged through the widened space like an animal. There was little to see outside, of course. Behind the blind there was the hint of the coming day, but that wasn't of much interest to James. Besides, he couldn't shuffle over to that end of the bed because that was where the phone was, and it was bad enough that he could see it even from here. He wished again he'd never taken it out of his pocket. Soon the battery would run down, surely. But then, the phone wasn't doing much: it was just sitting there, reminding him of all the things it would now be dangerous to look at. James had all but given up the idea he would be able to get even a few minutes' sleep, now. He lay motionless on his back, feeling the rattling of the metal body beneath him, trying to turn off the mental playback of all the things he had already, stupidly read.

Michaela. Please, James, I'm begging you. Just at least . . .

Sally. James, I'm going to keep messaging you. I . . .

Karl. Fam. I will never forgive myself. Txt me, please, cause otherwise my life . . .

Mum, from Lee's phone. My boy. I know I haven't always been . . .

There had been a grim satisfaction in knowing that he was being taken seriously, at least. For a second he'd allowed himself to dwell on the mental picture of Michaela's big, scared eyes. Of her, pacing of the floor of the . . . of her . . . but that was where the picture evaporated. Because then he had to imagine where she was living now, and who she was living with. If he thought of Sal he had to recall a time when they were a team, when she would be perched by the bed improvising him a story. If he imagined Karl he had to remember the day they met in the café and Karl kicked the support out from under him.

James had known something was wrong when he woke up. At first, confused, he thought he had been roused by a knock at the door, one of Steffi's packages. But when he stumbled to the door there was nobody there. Only then did he check his phone. Two missed calls, six texts. SIX texts. And all from Karl. Sometimes Karl did get drunk in the middle of the night and send odd things for James to laugh at: videos of sheep wandering into the sea, games he'd found online where you could calculate which *Friends* character you were (James hadn't turned out to be any of them). But he knew in his heart that the half-dozen texts weren't good news, and he was alarmed to find they were asking him to meet at a café at nine o'clock.

When James got there, Karl was toying with his phone, jiggling his legs; he wouldn't meet James's eye. A man in a cardigan, who looked like a down-on-his-luck portrait artist but turned out to be the waiter, offered James a choice of twenty-two variations on coffee. He scowled when James asked for a cup of tea and a glass of water; the water never arrived.

If Karl's body was animated, his eyes were hard and flat, like he'd been drugged; the usual mischief was gone. He didn't call James 'fam' or 'Jamie'. He didn't call him anything at all.

'So, my question is, did you know Hamish Elton has been sleeping with the woman from . . .?'

He named something James presumed was a band, but the name meant no more to him than if two words had been randomly selected from the dictionary.

'No. I don't even know what that . . .'

Karl sighed. 'All right, did you *know he was cheating on his wife?*'

James thought about it. 'I suppose there have been pick-ups which – I mean, it was odd when I had to drive him to Brighton at 4 a.m. without using major roads – but it's not my business to pry. I like Hamish. I mean, if I didn't like him, I'm not the sort of person who would ever . . .'

'Right, yeah, which is lovely,' said Karl, exhaling deeply once more, 'but at any point did anyone ask you about this stuff, and maybe you gave away slightly more than you should have?'

James was taken aback by the question.

'Of course not. Why, what's . . .?'

Karl slid his phone across the table. On the screen was the front page of a national newspaper, a headline. James winced.

'Oh dear.'

'*Oh dear* is right, mate, I think you could potentially go even further than *oh dear*, it's pretty much bordering on *what a pity*.' Once more, it was Karl's voice and style, but not his tone. He wasn't playful; he sounded bitter, exhausted. 'That's us losing a major client and I'm on my knees to his management who have maybe twenty of our other big clients, and if all of those go away, that's us absolutely on the floor, mate, because someone couldn't keep their mouth shut.'

Despite the pointedness of the final phrase, it was impossible for James to believe the direction this was heading in. 'But you don't think – you can't think it was me. I wouldn't, I would never—'

'Nobody else was driving him, though, eh?' Karl stuck out his right palm, rhetorically. 'The whole point with Elton was, you were the only one on him, so we didn't have the risk of someone dropping the ball, because I knew with him there was always the chance of something going tits-up, so I put what I thought was my best man on it . . .'

'I *am* your best man,' said James, loathing how pathetic a claim this sounded. He shifted his weight; the wooden chair felt capable of giving up and dropping him onto the floor, to mirror what was about to happen to his life. 'I would never, I swear I would never . . .'

'There's no one else,' said Karl. 'Only you ever had the

pick-up details, the destinations. They're all in the article. That's what the manager said. I had this fucking guy on the phone at half five this morning. *Nobody could have known these sort of details except the driver*, he said. And what was I meant to do?'

'Well, what – what, I mean, what *are* we going to do?' James asked. They had sorted plenty of things out before, after all. But Karl wouldn't look at him. He drank down his coffee and wiped his lips; his hand went into his pocket for a Rizla. He got to his feet and James grabbed his arm, restraining him.

'Karl. Please. I'm sure we can – we can somehow . . .'

'Somehow what? Somehow destroy every copy of the paper in existence? Plus the internet?'

'Well, then what?' James disliked the imploring lift in his voice, the creeping alarm that it reflected. But this wasn't some malevolent boss like in movies, tie askew, whisky glass in front of him, hiring and firing. This was Karl. His friend. So what was happening, what James realized was happening, could not be happening. He couldn't have guessed the details, at this point. There would have been no way for him to imagine that Karl, panicking, had offered the enraged manager the one sweetener he could think of, bought himself some time with James's head. *I'll fire the driver. Make sure he never deals with any of your clients again.* If James had been able to hear Karl say those words about him, he wouldn't have believed it.

But if the details were not in his grasp, James could at least read the general direction this was going in, and he felt sweat break out at the base of his spine.

'You can't be – you can't be saying that . . .'

'I don't have a choice, James.'

The voice had been more dulled than ever, and the use of James's actual name this time – no tint of irony, as formal as if they were meeting for the first time – was like the sound of a door closing.

*

He'd broken the back of this. There was a certain confidence in the way the train was steaming along now. James knew that the last stretch of this journey always felt downhill, like you were riding a toboggan. They couldn't be far from Carlisle. There, with a series of winching, wrestling thumps, engineers would part the two halves of the train. The sky would be streaky by that point, light leaking into it. Half of James's unwitting companions would head for Glasgow, many of them jolted from sleep for this final leg. And James's half would cruise on to Edinburgh, would glide into Waverley station where he used to walk up the steps with Dad, tasting the always colder air, relishing the sense of weight lifted, of being back among all the happy old ghosts of themselves. A feeling you could only get in a place that was like home, but not home. Today, he wasn't going to get that sensation. Today there would just be the memory of it, like a tune he couldn't quite remember any more. But it felt right to be there. It felt right to be as close to Dad as possible, for this.

It was possibly because of that old fondness for train trips that James had taken the job at the station after Karl's betrayal. He'd prepared various things to say in the inter-view about his history with trains, his enthusiasm for them, but the man across the desk – Waqar, his future supervisor – wasn't interested in that. He asked about James's 'core skills' and where he saw himself in five years. Neither of them could have imagined what the answer was: that even a year from that moment, there wouldn't be a James to talk about.

On the 'core skills' question, James did quite well. 'I get a lot of satisfaction from helping people,' he said. 'In my last few jobs I've always tried to get people out of tight spots, or . . . or give them advice, whatever I could do.' He thought briefly of the woman he'd taken to hospital and wondered what had happened to her in the end; of the people he'd neglected to charge.

'So you was a taxi driver, yeah?' said Waqar.

'Private hire. So you had to book in advance, you couldn't just—'

'And then before that you was working for – you was a software engineer, you was working as brand manager for a health and fitness company.'

The phrase sounded even sillier, in the dejected plastic and steel backdrop of the staff canteen, than it had when James had printed the CV out in his kitchen. He hadn't really expected the interview to be in the canteen. There was a man opposite who'd left half of a delicious-looking doughnut on his tray, the jam oozing from it. James's stomach kept growling, affronted.

'*Brand manager* is a bit of newspeak, really,' said James, 'but—'

'You what, sorry?'

'I mean.' It was too hot in the canteen, hot and stifling. The doughnut was almost close enough to touch. 'Well, my job was really to run the business, while my – my business partner, er, she was the face of it, my actual partner in fact, but . . .'

He swallowed. Waqar repositioned his head to suggest something approaching discretion.

'It says in your reference you're . . .' Waqar licked his lips in simulated thoughtfulness, and scanned the words Karl had fobbed James off with. 'A valued friend to a lot of people.'

'I have certain skills,' said James, but Waqar looked blankly at him and James winced, both at the present moment and at the memory it nudged in his mind.

He'd got the job. It was a relief: in the insomniac fortnight since Karl had fired him, the emptiness of days, the sense of lost purpose, had scratched at James all night, flipping him over and over, eventually out of his bed to trudge around the dark rooms in search of nothing. What he hadn't realized was that when he started work, those feelings would be even stronger.

The shifts were from nine in the morning until five, sometimes six or seven, and James's job was to sit behind a grille selling tickets, pushing them through a little hatch for hurried passengers to snatch. Cheap red blazer, white shirt that felt cold when he put it on in the morning; belt which dug into his expanding waist. The first time Steffi saw him in the uniform, he felt ashamed – like a massively overgrown schoolboy – and hurried out of the kitchen, spilling some of his coffee, which he then had to go back and mop up while she smiled sympathetically and busied herself with her phone.

There were some customers he enjoyed serving. Often they were tourists – perhaps elderly Americans, not in a rush, full of questions, and with no firm opinions on how much train tickets should cost. He enjoyed saying things like, 'York is a lovely city', or suggesting, 'You might like to wait and get a cup of tea, because the one that leaves in half an hour is direct.' But there was a heaviness in knowing that, even on those occasions he shared an enjoyable conversation with someone, he would almost certainly never see them again. You couldn't *meet* people this way, like he had on the road. Besides, most visitors to his booth were not in the mood for conversation. They were in danger of missing the train, and snapped their destinations at him. Or they wanted to change their bookings. Or they were appalled by the price that he read out from the computer, as if James was a criminal mastermind who owned all the nation's trains and had devised this grid of charges himself. Or they didn't come to him at all; they went to the machines. Every task James was doing could be done by the banks of machines: in a few years, this job would probably not exist at all.

Days went by in which he spoke to no more than ten people, for less than half a minute each, and without learning a single thing about them other than the fact they intended to go to Peterborough. His colleagues muttered 'All right?' or 'How you doing?', as if they were cordial but non-intimate neighbours, passing on the staircase: because really that was what they were. This must be how some people spent their work lives – lots of people. *This must be where you end up*, he would think to himself. *If you've got it all wrong. Done it wrong.*

At lunchtime he would eat the cheese sandwiches he'd brought, watching people swarm around the German sausage stalls and coffee huts that formed a mini-market at the front of the station. The food people took away from these stands looked and smelled tastier than what James was making for himself, but there would be the shame, there would be the calories flickering across the dial in his brain that could not be turned off, and he didn't have the energy to think about it. He always saved half a sandwich for the homeless guy, who would then ask James for £12 to get into a shelter. Sometimes he gave him the £12, not seeing why not. After work he'd go to the bar with the businessmen and the now ironic artwork. He'd walk home in the temporary consolation grip of whisky and try to watch something on TV. He would lie squirming in bed, unable to sleep, getting up to pace the kitchen floorboards and move things pointlessly between cupboards, thinking about the fact that tomorrow would be just the same.

The frosted-up pavements, mulched leaves, grey nimbostratus low over his head like a metal beam: it was the perfect stage set for this new loneliness. But James hated the word 'lonely', how juvenile it sounded in his own head. *What do you want?* he would ask himself, staring into the mirror in the morning, careful not to say anything out loud and disturb Steffi, but wanting to shout it, to wake himself up from whatever this was. *What do you expect to happen?*

A few weeks before Christmas came a Wednesday morning rush hour with an unusually high concentration of travellers. The cheap office chair clinging at him; he felt as if he'd been in it for ten hours already. A cup of tea from the machine, half-drunk. James had just directed a twenty-something couple, in striped scarves and unofficial wizard merchandise, to the spot where all the Harry Potter fans went, the magic platform. 'You get even more of these freaks at Christmas,' he overheard Waqar saying. And James thought briefly about the unwelcome prospect of Christmas: going home to spend it with Mum and Lee, the heavy jollity of adults pulling crackers. Sal was staying in Australia with Dec. James imagined the cold of the house, the dead weight of time after lunch. The questions: so, what have you been up to? The whisper of Dad in the empty seat at the table, in the Boxing Day walk they wouldn't have on the Downs, because Lee preferred them to 'go for a spin' in his rubbish, cigarettey old car. The knowledge that Dad would be disappointed in him, if he could see him. Wouldn't feel he had paid out on the promise he had made, to all those years Dad had put in.

A customer was drumming his fingers urgently on the grille. James snapped out of it. He'd only lost concentration for five or ten seconds, because he would never go longer than that, because he respected the work. Even this work.

'Single to Leeds.' Grey suit. Shirt unbuttoned at the top, a bit of chest hair peeping out. Barely half a second to comment silently on James's weight and disarrangement. *The guy had let himself go*, he might say to his gym mates later. *I don't know how people get like that.*

'Do you have any railcards, or—?'

'No, mate,' snapped the traveller, 'and I'm in a rush, so . . .'

James had told him the price, taken the card, put it into the machine, but there was a delay getting signal. The card readers did this at busy times; they got overloaded.

'Can you hurry up, please, mate,' said the businessman, or whatever he was. His fingers were drumming on the counter now. He was casting looks left and right as if to imply that other sales assistants were serving people much more quickly, whipping tickets into the air like magicians with playing cards.

'It's just a problem with the . . . I mean, unless you have cash?' asked James.

'Yeah, of course, of course I've got eighty quid just sitting in my pocket. Jesus wept,' said the man. He grabbed the green and orange tickets as soon as James dropped them into the hatch; left at trotting speed, shaking his head. Three minutes later he was back, panting, thrusting a finger at James.

'I'm making a note of your name, mate. I've missed my train.'

'I'm sorry to hear that,' said James, 'but – Leeds, wasn't it – there's another one, actually, in—'

'There's another one in *too late o'clock*,' said the man in incoherent anger, 'so I'm in all sorts of shit, mate, because you couldn't do your job properly.'

'I'm sorry about that,' said James, 'but as I said, the machines don't always – we can't always – also, I'm going to have to ask you not to use language like that.'

'You mean, your fat fucking fingers don't always press the buttons fast enough,' the guy said.

A couple of people glanced in James's direction. The blood burned in his cheeks. Surely someone had heard this. Surely the whole point of a supervisor was to protect him from things like this. There were even signs up around the station about not abusing the staff. But when he spoke to Waqar, Waqar said that there was a procedure for complaining about customers. 'You gotta download a PDF. I can give you the link. Yeah? And obviously the more info you can give them about whoever this guy was, the more chance they've got of doing something about it. Yeah?' James nodded. He didn't say anything. There were tears in his eyes, and he turned his back and began to rummage in his locker for something that wasn't there.

That night, James did look up the relevant form. File a Customer Abuse or Harassment Report, said the heading, in a cheerful font which would have been at home on the website for a boutique hotel. As soon as he started typing, a pop-up box asked whether he would be interested, after filing this report, in answering some questions about how easy it was to use; he could win a case of champagne.

As he was typing the words 'made an obscene remark about my weight', trying to pretend he was doing this on behalf of someone else, James's eye was caught by a GIF in the top right of the page. *Begin your magical journey!* it said. The Scott Monument on a rainy, glistening Princes Street, fireworks above. He thought about watching those fireworks with Dad, the night Dad had asked him to scatter the ashes. The wild spots of light across the black sky, the gunpowder smell far off. James had grinned into the dark-ness, but when he looked across, Mr Chiltern – who had always loved fireworks – was shaking a little, his hands clasped together.

He clicked on the link. He thought about what it would be like to leave his workplace, walk straight down the road to Euston, get on the train to Edinburgh and disappear there, disappear for good. It was only half an idea, for now, but it was surprising how much comfort it gave him. The next morning, as Waqar greeted him with some minor jibe, James looked straight past him at the few hundred metres of road between here and that escape. It was so close, it could be so real.

*

And now here it was; he just had to keep his nerve for what was not even two hours.

A minor jolt, a stumble of the train, was enough to make the phone's screen light up again – like someone flinching in sleep. James flinched with it. No, it couldn't be a new message or a call. Flight mode was still on. But people would still be sending messages, trying to contact him. Four hours ago, the flight mode had felt like barbed wire around the phone. Now it felt slight and porous; it felt as if all the stacked-up messages would come crashing through at any minute, like police hammering on a creaking door.

He took a gulp from the final can and slammed it down on the little ledge with an angry energy he wasn't expecting.

The can, as if surprised itself, fizzed out a little fountain of beer, which ran down the sides and pooled on the ledge.

It would almost be better to read the messages, to take the filter away. He could take it; he wasn't going to get blown off course now. *I'm in my right mind.* It was just as he'd said in the text. He knew what he was doing. He'd been thinking about it ever since that man screamed at him in the station. This wasn't a whim, and he wasn't going to back down from it. He sat up. He stood up. No, of course it wouldn't be better to read the messages. That was a mad thought.

Just need to get out of here for a bit. Get some air.

He raised his eyebrows. 'Air'. What was he going to do: float out of the window, go for a little jog? But anything would be less stifling than being in here. He'd been an idiot to think he'd be able to sleep all the way. What drowsiness the beers had initially lent him was gone now; he felt more alert than at any time on the journey, and the only water-mark of the booze was the swilling of it around his pipes, a bodily lethargy. Alert to what, though? To the creaking and clattering, the train's hard breathing up the hills, and what now seemed the achingly slow passing of the minutes.

Need to go out.

With an uncharacteristically quick motion, James bounded up from the bed, causing the mattress springs to complain once more; they didn't seem to like it when he arrived *or* when he left. Well, that was nothing new. Without looking at it, he scooped up the phone and buried it back in the trouser pocket, where it belonged. He hauled himself to the door and out into the corridor, out to the long narrow window. Outside the sky was toying with the new day's light, trying it on, unconvinced. His last day. The thought wasn't troubling at all; there was no more heft to it than any other thought. He felt better already, just being out of there. *We could go for a wander up the train*, he thought.

Past the other cabins, the little doors like hospital wards. Each one with a life behind it, of which James knew nothing. Another corner of the internet, another invisible player of the computer game. Nobody would have walked past *his* door, after all, and imagined a man about to commit suicide. Past the restaurant car, closed for the night, the bar shut up. Such an *Orient Express* idea, so romantic, the 'restaurant car'. Paper tablecloths, proper cutlery; an attempt at a little world. James felt a sort of atavistic yearning, not a feeling but the memory of a feeling, a fondness for something that had gone. Through a set of sliding doors and into the seating compartments.

This was where you slept if you couldn't afford a cabin, or hadn't booked one in time. People were crashed out across pairs of seats, like transit passengers marooned at an airport. A man with thin hair was sitting, arms folded, suit jacket with only the top button undone, as if a business lunch might break out right here in the small hours. A woman was bobbing up and down in the aisle with a restless baby girl, shushing, patting, trying to lull her as she clawed miserably at her mother's face in search of something she couldn't name yet. The woman had skin like Michaela's, large emotive eyes like hers, lips like hers. James tried to imagine how tiring it must have been: to have been here this whole length of time, but with a creature pleading for help all that time. What would make someone take the overnight train with a baby?

It occurred to James that he could offer them his cabin, just for the couple of hours that remained. He didn't really need it. It was better being out here than in there. He could happily walk up and down for the rest of it. He looked at the woman, attempting a reassuring face; it seemed to fall as flat as everything always did. She took her eyes away from him, brought the infant right up to her face and kissed her tiny nose, and the idea of initiating any sort of conversation seemed so ill-conceived that he felt ridiculous. He turned and walked back towards the corridor, noting the onrush of a new town: the train's pace easing, the closing-in of houses, hotels. He jumped; Gina was standing there, looking out of the window. Next to her was a little trolley stacked with trays. Foil-topped orange juice cartons, a silver coffee jug. She was on her phone – she must have found a way to charge it, he thought – but at James's approach she stuffed it with apparent haste into her jacket pocket.

'Not quite breakfast time yet,' she said. This might be the last time ever that someone glanced at his body and assumed he was thinking about food. 'Didn't manage to drift off?'

'Yes, um, not easy to go to sleep,' said James. Carlisle, he thought, this would be Carlisle. This was where they split the train. 'Still. Not long . . .!'

'Are you all right?' asked Gina, as he had asked her before.

He glanced sideways at her: the reddish eyes, round face. The bluntness of the question had him outflanked, for a moment.

'Yes,' he said – it was true, in a way. It would be true pretty soon. Without knowing why, he added: 'and you?'

Gina allowed the shadow of her smile across her face. 'Well. It's hard sometimes, isn't it.'

'It certainly is,' James agreed.

In the game they were playing, the game everyone on earth was playing, the character of James still had a number of options, and the correct one could change an incalculable amount. *Do you: ask the woman for more details about what has been troubling her? Or start to talk a little about your own unhappiness; about the fact you're on your way to kill yourself? Or just let the conversation fizzle out and go back to your cabin?* Press A. Press B. Press C. For a second he wanted to play the game. Push the button, see what happened.

'What . . .' He moistened his lips with his tongue. They were standing close, next to one another, like people at a bus stop, fenced in by the trolley; the rushing countryside on one side, the cabin doors the other. A narrow space for two people to share. James dropped his voice. 'What . . . are there things which are particularly difficult?'

It felt gauche, the way he'd asked, but there was something in the process of asking that he liked, in the brief reconnection with somebody he used to be.

Gina made a sort of swishing motion with her hands, as if birds or insects were flying all around her. 'I mean. Short version. A guy left me completely in the lurch, never married, he took my money, I owe money to everyone in the country . . .'

'I'll let you off mine,' James mumbled.

She smiled. 'Thank you. So, apart from you. Yeah. Live

on my own. No real – you know, hard to see how things can get better.'

'And the long version?'

'The long version's the same but with more swearing,' she said.

He laughed, perhaps a little louder than he intended. There was a creak and a mutter from behind one of the doors, and shuffling; it sounded as if someone might come out. The train, meanwhile, was gliding into the station. It felt at its smoothest, its happiest, when it was stopping somewhere. The floodlights were flickering over the track, as if they hadn't been given clear instructions on whether to keep going or not. It was that sort of time: between one thing and another. Gina slid open the glass panel at the top of the door.

'Stuffy in here,' she muttered, sounding very Welsh as she dropped the H; she said *here* like *year*. 'Too hot in year, too cold outside.'

There were technicians, in orange hi-vis jackets, waiting to perform their surgery on the train. Hot drinks in polystyrene; the trail from a cigarette. He could hear them talking in dry monosyllables. This was the end of a shift for them, or perhaps the start.

'It *is* stuffy,' James said.

'I should be . . . it's been nice talking to you, though,' said Gina. Before he could think of anything to say to that, she was gone, back into standard class, leaving the trolley parked where it was.

He stood in the gap where she had been. There was a little crunch and thud as the engineers began the brief task of unhooking one half of the train from the other. He didn't want to go back into the cabin and sit there by himself, not immediately. His hand went instinctively for his pocket to pull out the phone. The mad thought came again: *it would be better to know*. He fumbled with the settings, removed the flight mode. Adrenalin swelled violently through him. As soon as its gag was taken off, the phone began to gush with the messages it had been forced to keep from him. The screen filled with text captions, which slid down to admit more, then more, the names piggybacking one another. There were numbers his phone didn't even know. The collective effect of all the voices was like landing in cold water.

It was too much, having Karl and Michaela in his pocket. And Sal, all of them. He couldn't keep carrying them around if he was going to let go of them properly. He couldn't have them in here. He went back out into the corridor.

The train was still static. James fished the phone out, thinking once more how light it was. He extended his arm out of the gap at the top of the door. The air was cold. With a light flick of the wrist he threw the phone out onto the embankment, and they were all gone, really gone this time. It was amazing how easy it was. That was how easy the jump would be.

24

Steffi's laptop and phone sat next to each other on James's kitchen table, buzzing and bleeping like two alien creatures flirting. She rubbed her eyes. There'd been a surge of notifications. People were talking about James in all sorts of places. Lots of people. And most of this was her doing. *I'm going to try his old school friends, there's a group for us, everyone would be devastated . . .*

There were reasons for optimism: for a start, several people had pointed out that their messages were showing as 'Delivered' now, which might mean nothing, but at least indicated that the phone was switched on, wherever it was. But it was just talk. And so much talk. The conversation circled, doubled back on itself, was stalled by the arrival of newcomers, like at a party when an anecdote has to be started again and again. Steffi had been at a party back in Amsterdam where a girl spent almost the whole evening trying in vain to finish a story about meeting Michael Bublé, having to start it ten times, and she'd got so frustrated that she took a piss in a pot-plant. The host never spoke to her again. This reminded Steffi a bit of that.

Some people were so *dense*, and then some people thought they knew everything, and some were in both categories. Brightly suggesting that 'someone should check on his home', or that 'workmates might know something'. Like she wouldn't have covered these elementary steps; wasn't sitting in his home right now; hadn't been at this all night.

All night! It was light outside, at least she assumed so. Here in the kitchen of this basement flat, it could be any time. It was good to feel that the night was over. She didn't have to worry about sleep. The irony was, she *was* now starting to be weary. Her eyelids were heavy as she looked at the latest pointless comment, suggesting 'the police could get involved', as if Steffi might not have heard about that useful service. The coffee hadn't helped; almost the opposite. And Emil also hadn't helped. He was in the shower now.

Another message landing, with a little electronic plop, in the pond. Another useless one. *This is terrible, what are we gna do?* What indeed, thought Steffi wryly: thanks for your input. But there were possible breakthroughs, too. A gossip journalist had been in touch, via Michaela: she claimed to have a phone number for Hamish Elton, the client James had been fired over. Steffi and Michaela had been pinging messages back and forth. It seemed like Michaela was either somewhere where it was tricky to text, or she was just a bit incompetent spelling-wise, because some of her messages were like your grandmother might send with her Nokia. But then, Steffi couldn't imagine what this would be like if you loved James, or had loved him. If you felt responsible. Well: yes, she could. She did feel a little responsible.

She remembered him sitting there, in the chair right opposite, big shoulders hunched. It was so disorientating to see him crying. It would be strange with anyone, but he was so far from the emotional type. 'I just don't understand what I'm doing wrong,' he'd said. 'What it is about me that's wrong?' Stuff just gets like this sometimes, Steffi had said. It's how life goes, isn't it, she'd said. I'm sure you'll get a better job. I'm sure you'll meet someone. What else was she meant to say?

They hadn't been insincere words, either. With the limited data she had on James, it seemed fair to think that he was a good man, deserving of whatever sort of change of luck he needed. And Steffi imagined that, on the whole, people did get what they deserved, even if they had to wait around for it. That was what you were generally led to believe by fridge magnets and memes. They were all about keeping going in pursuit of your dreams, seeing out the bad times. None of them implied that there could be an outcome in which you just admitted the bad times had won.

It was just hard to believe that he'd been here in this very room, thinking about it. That he'd been sleeping the other side of the wall, planning it, perhaps looking up ways to . . . and she with all her amateur-sleuth pretensions had picked up on nothing, had taken none of the opportunities which must have existed to make him see sense.

Still, she was more than making up for it with this vigil, she thought, standing up and going over to pile coffee into the cafetière again. She didn't drink coffee much normally; this was James's. So was the cafetière. The amount of stuff that would need to be cleared out, or sold, or rehomed. The number of people she would need to talk to. The idea that he wouldn't be back, that key would never rattle in the lock again, she wouldn't hear him exhale and bend to pick up her coat and hang it on the hook.

She went over to the tap and splashed water on her cheeks. The water did its job and she pulled herself up sharply. The final mental image of James had jolted her. It was *someone's life*. She hadn't 'more than made up for it'. If he never came back, it was partly her fault and partly her loss. It was a loss to all of them. This had been an adventure, yes, a challenge, but there was no value in that. If James was dead, it was terrible. It would haunt her. At last Steffi understood that fully. She refreshed the page and her tired eyes narrowed in concentration.

Someone in Germany had forwarded a message from someone in Egypt whose mate in London had seen a man, perhaps matching James's description, walking into Euston station. Not King's Cross; *Euston* again. This was the second mention of Euston they'd had. She'd already called the station and got a recorded message with train information; surfed the multi-choice menus in vain to try to get through to a human. She'd sent Twitter messages to the operators of all the trains that left Euston that night. She could follow those leads up again. There would be a person out there who knew where he was. If he was anywhere.

Across from the kitchen, Emil stood under the jet of water, rehearsing the next move in this long, weird game.

I'm tired, should we lie down in the bed? No, that was going to sound creepy. *Maybe we could get dinner sometime?* No, that was too formal. It made it sound like he was about to get a suit on and open a box with a ring in it, and he didn't even know her surname yet. Anyway, 'dinner' for both of them evoked toil rather than romance. 'Dinner' was what you had to turn up at 5 p.m. for; it meant being screamed at to get a calf's liver on a plate, because people who had some sort of brain malfunction thought that would be a nice thing to eat. It was how they'd started this night, mad as that seemed. Getting in, chatting with Juno, going to the *mise en place* to ensure the fontina hadn't run out because Juno had once thrown a live lobster at someone for not checking. How could that still be this same night?

Well, it wasn't really. That had been 5 p.m. and now it was – holy shit, 6 a.m. Thirteen hours. This was basically a new day. Depending on how you looked at it. His great-grandmother, who was 102, always insisted the new day didn't begin until you'd been to sleep. She hated it when she was awake past midnight and someone said it was now the morning. 'The goddam day starts when I wake up,' she'd say. But the thing was, it looked like Emil wasn't going to bed at all, unless Steffi came with him, as he continued to hope might happen. He couldn't just leave her there. And Steffi was so caught up in this quest. Watching the screens like a cat watching a bee, mesmerized by each new whisper. Even though he still thought it was highly unlikely they could find this guy just by spreading it round the internet, it was almost as mesmerizing watching *her*. It was attractive how much she wanted to win this. How much goodness she must have in her.

This whole night was like he'd ended up in a romcom but he wasn't sure what the director wanted. And now what about this for a scene: here he was, in a stranger's shower. If Emil had been shown an image of himself here, when he showed up at La Chimère those thirteen hours ago, he would have been pretty confident there must be a sexy reason. As it was, he'd got in here just because it was the only thing that was going to keep him awake.

Could we take this further? Would that do it? Or was that more like what the cops would say if they'd pulled you over? So much of his English was from movies; it was impossible to judge tone. He couldn't tell, if this *was* a romcom, whether he was the hero – destined to end up with Steffi after exactly ninety minutes and three well-spaced mishaps – or if he was the decoy, the charmless barista she escaped from to meet the actual hero.

Well, he was going to have to make a move pretty soon, because before *very* long he would be back in work all over again; this endless day would send him back to the restaurant like someone in that board game who kept going to jail. Christ, it was going to be a tough eight hours. The brunches and then – because it was the weekend – the roasts, with those weird huge dry 'puddings' smothering the wilted spinach and greens. Having to do a separate load of vegan gravy because everyone was vegan now. But he couldn't afford a slip-up, even a small one. He wanted that *sous* position so much. He realized the truth of the thought as it formed, grasped it for the first time. *I want to be the sous. I am a great cook. I am better than Juno. I should be in that job.* He was better than all those people who never replied to his WhatsApp message. He was going to surprise them all. It would be like that film about the Romans he'd seen, where the quiet one, the outsider, let all the big names stab each other in the arse – some of them literally – until he was left as Emperor.

He found a towel in a cupboard. He hoped it wasn't one of hers; it looked like a man's, he thought. He dried himself with the dead man's towel and looked in the mirror at his wet, matted hair. It suited him, wet hair. The one time Arantxa had almost agreed to be 'more than friends' was when they'd got caught in a storm. He'd been unlucky it had stopped raining just when he was about to put his hand down her top. Emil looked at himself with approval. The shower had done its work. He would go in there and ask Steffi if he could kiss her. Just kiss her on the back of her neck while her keen beautiful eyes kept patrolling the screen. Just on the top of the head, even. They'd see where it went from there. And in four hours he would go into work and smash it. Like always. Keep narrowing the gap on people who didn't even know he was right behind them.

He stood in the doorway of the kitchen. Steffi had not moved an inch, as far as he could see. The computer's cold blue light was on her face and her spine was very straight, like in the Alexander Technique leaflet they had in the staff room at La Chimère, as if Emil had the time or money to pay someone to teach him how to sit down, for Jesus's sake. He cleared his throat. *Come on, just ask her.*

271

'Hey.'

'Hey.' Her eyes didn't leave the screen.

'I was wondering . . .' he began.

'Sorry, did you turn the shower dial right to the end?'

'Shower dial.'

'Yes, the . . .' Still without looking at him, she mimed it. 'The thing that makes the water come out. Did you turn it real tight? When you were done.'

'I think so.' Emil felt his rush of mirror-confidence ebbing already. 'Yeah, I think so.'

'It's just, it has this thing where it sputters out at weird moments,' said Steffi.

The moment was slipping away. He moved over to where she was, peered over her at the screen, a picnic of thumbs-ups, praying hands, hearts.

'Lots of people seem to love this guy that they don't want him to die,' said Emil.

Steffi nodded.

'I don't get it,' said Emil, 'why if he has all these friends, why you would, why is the reason he . . .?'

Steffi shrugged, looking cross. 'Because people – it's complicated.'

Emil was aggrieved to find he was feeling jealous, again. Of this online team with their little nocturnal project, with their sense of shared goal. The buzzing chat thread, mutual back-slaps. And . . . he couldn't really be jealous of the guy himself, could he? Just, the guy *was* occupying more of Steffi's thoughts than Emil was managing fully alive.

He slid his chair in next to her. 'You're doing such a good work,' he said. 'You're a hero.'

'Shut up,' she said, biting her lip.

'Shut up like, you are happy?' Emil persisted. 'Or like, it is really shut up and not jokes?'

'I don't know,' said Steffi, eyes not moving from the screen. The thing was, being a hero was no longer the point, had nothing to do with anything. This was not something she could walk away from with a degree of credit, if it went wrong. This had turned out to be kind of a game after all, in the most brutal sense: she was either going to win or lose. And if she lost, she'd lost a guy's life.

'I'm going to see if his sister has heard anything,' said Steffi, her fingers skipping like little fish over the keys again. Emil nodded, sighed too quietly for her to hear. He wondered whether this was going to end up being nothing more than a feature-length version of the usual story, a story which ended up with him masturbating furtively in the toilets at La Chimère, washing his hands, and then – before resuming service – posting something to all his contacts back home to let them know what a wild time he was having over here. Steffi brought up Sal's details. It was getting hard to remember a time before all this; before this was her purpose, her mission.

25

Sal stared at the message from Steffi without making any attempt to take it in. Little pockets of data kept sliding onto her phone. Mum was pleading with her to call. Meghan was sending about three texts a minute. 'Flagging up' the schedule for the event itself. Some more interview requests that had come in. A potential offer to speak at a conference in Brazil. All these things introduced as if this was a normal work day, Meghan having obviously decided to play dumb from now on about the fact that Sal's brother was unaccounted for between alive and dead.

Bridget and the girls were discussing whether to do a supermarket order online in advance of the Lorne trip, as if there was a risk the nation of Australia might run out of Pinot Grigio and toilet rolls in the next six weeks. Dec was trying to find out why his Filth Window messages hadn't been reciprocated, or even acknowledged: U off with someone else babe!? That emoji with laughter-tears leaping

275

out of a face. From the cab's radio, the incredulous shtick of the youthful DJ. 'So, can this be right, Ryan? You're telling me you've *never* used a toaster?' Almost all the world was continuing. The show of normality was almost totally convincing. But this, and death, couldn't both be true at the same time. It couldn't be that all this was happening – and the sun shining, the river shimmering – and yet Dad did not *exist any more, for ever* and now James might go the same way. The jarring of these mad ideas with the bland brightness of everything else.

Sal let out a little dry heave. She wasn't actually going to be sick; that was just what it felt like. She gripped the underside of the seat. She just had to focus on breathing and on the tasks, the five tasks, as always.

1. Make this list.
2. Breathing exercises.
3. Circulate the Facebook page as far and wide as possible, getting Meghan to post it to—

'You want radio off?' asked the driver.
'No, it's fine. Leave it. Thank you.'

1. Make this list.
2. Breathing exercises.

'We're going to listen to our breathing,' she muttered.
'Sorry, say again?' called the driver.
'Nothing. I wasn't talking to you.' He was going to lose a star from his rating if he spoke to her again. She tried to

summon the voice of Trishna, the meditation woman. *Hear the breath coming in, going out. And listen for each other's breaths. And think how we are all connected.* Trishna's husband was a slush fund adviser and they had two properties. I'd *be at one with the universe if I had an infinity pool*, Sal had thought. But she was good, no denying it. Her tricks did work, at these occasional moments, the ambush of panic. And they were occasional. The panic was a very specific problem which she was on top of, 98 per cent of the time, and she'd get back on top of it here, too, as soon as the breathing started to level out.

Hear the breaths coming in, coming out.

Listen to your own heartbeat and think about the different parts of your body and how they're—

The phone was juddering in her lap. MEGHAN. Not Steffi, not anyone useful. And yet what if there *was* news. She picked up the phone.

'Hi, just checking in. All good with the rehearsal and the—?'

I mean, for the actual love of fuck, thought Sal.

'Yes, Meghan. Everything is pretty much perfect. Couldn't be better.'

A small hesitation at the other end of the line. Once more, it was impossible to tell if even this fat dart of sarcasm had found Meghan's arse or gone sailing merrily over. 'All right. So I just needed to flag up that one of those emails I sent you is hi-pri, it's pegged as *immediate response*, so I don't know if you're able to be doing that in the car, but . . .'

'Hi-pri,' echoed Sal, feeling everything from the past five hours building in her neck, in her shoulders. So much for the breathing. 'Do you think it's more or less *"hi"* fucking *"pri"* than stopping my brother committing suicide, Meghan?' She saw the taxi driver twitch in his seat, in amused pretend-nonchalance. She didn't care any more. He'd be lucky if he got *four* stars. He was heading for three, here, which in Uber world was like spitting in someone's face. 'Would you be able to *"flag up"* whether that's important? Just my thoughts are kind of on that at the moment, rather than doing a photo op with a fucking women's association representative from Bendigo called Nancy, you know?'

There was a silence from the office, and Sal thought the call had been cut off, and then realized. 'Oh. Meghan. Don't . . . I didn't mean to make you cry. Hey.'

'I'm not crying.' The voice was fuzzy, reminding Sal of her own twelve-year-old self when she got a freak bad score in Biology, 34 per cent, read out in front of the bitchy girls. 'I'm fine.'

Sally shut her eyes. This day was too much. Everything was too much. 'Meghan. Hey. I went too – that was – I've been coping quite badly with the – James is . . .'

'The thing is, I know I fucked up by mentioning him. In the interview, when the guy was there.' Meghan was breathing hard; her voice was thick with misery, and Sal felt ashamed. 'But then also it feels like I fucked up by *not* saying anything about it from then on, so, you need to help me here. I mean – sorry. You don't *have* to help me. You're the boss. I just feel like I don't know . . . I've got a dress for the dinner, but I can just take it back?'

'What do you . . . what?' Sal felt as if she was sinking through the seat.

'I guess that you don't want me to come to the dinner, now, which is all good: I can tidy up my place, I guess.' Sal pictured Meghan, deliberating over the dress purchase, coming into work today with the outfit carefully folded and still in its shopping bag. She cringed at the image.

'This is a conversation we can . . . I'll be back soon,' said Sal. 'But of course I want you to come, love . . . Meghan.'

'Really?'

The wish for approval in her voice chimed with what Sal had heard from her own mother an hour before, and Sal was hit by a terrible sense of who she was these days, who she had become. Someone who has cut off their brother. What had she done? The conversation at the next get-together, six weeks later, after the honeymoon and before the return to Australia: Sal chock-full of self-righteousness, relishing the combat, her own eloquence in his miserable, tongue-tied face. 'It's not the *point* that you got there for the evening. It's the fact you missed a defining moment in my life because you'd rather be in a sports hall.'

'I wouldn't have *rather* . . . I would of course have rather been . . .' James had been floundering, in the doorway of the restaurant; getting in people's way. 'I mean, I wanted to get there even earlier than that – to talk to Dad . . .'

'Right, the wedding wasn't even your main plan for the day.'

'You're being – this is rather harsh, Sally,' said James, looking at his hands.

'I'd almost respect it more if you had the fucking backbone to argue properly,' she muttered, walking away.

'. . . but this is on me, not being neurotypical,' Meghan was still talking, and Sal had the unpleasant sensation of having missed an important step in the chat. Her voice was steadier, at least, Sal thought. The river ran peaceably along the right-hand window, boats like sleek fish cutting their way through the stillness, coxes yelling through little loud-hailers. Kids were kicking orange footballs back and forth. 'This is, when you're autistic,' said Meghan, 'you just literally don't know if you're being weird or normal, sometimes, and . . .'

Did Sal know about the autism? Yes, probably. At least: she'd *been told* about it. It must have been something Meghan had mentioned, and Sal had failed to really respond to. She wondered now how many things like that there were. How much she'd tended to trample over, to get to the things she needed.

'I'll see you back in the office, OK?' She tried to make it sound kindly, not chastening. *Maybe I don't* have *a kind mode*, she thought; *maybe I'm a bitch, pure and simple.*

'Just to flag up, the woman's name actually *was* Nancy,' said Meghan. Sal tried to smile. She dropped the phone back into her lap and felt her hands as cold as stone.

'Everything OK there in the back?' asked the driver. 'We'll be there ten, fifteen.' *Mind your own business*, thought Sal once more. *Three stars. On your way to two.* But even that was bitchy, wasn't it. What was wrong with her? She swatted aside, angrily, another attempted-hot text from Dec. This wasn't the time to hear what he would be thinking of doing to her while she was at the lectern. She didn't even want him to *be* watching her tonight. She didn't even want to do the speech, not at all. These thoughts landed like paint-ball bullets, one at a time, across the crowded vista of her brain.

Breathe. Come on. List.

3. Make this list.
4. Get back, talk to Meghan about . . .

No. She still had to sort out James. She still had to save James.

5. Make this . . .

The joke didn't seem funny any more. It didn't work as a joke when the stakes were this high. All the times she thought she was good at 'troubleshooting', she just didn't know what real trouble was. And all the times she'd been called a control freak, they were right, but they didn't understand why: because what she couldn't control was terrifying. Because what we couldn't control was death and that was too much for her brain, that was what sometimes made her so frightened that she could not make a mental connection with anything else, made her stop in the street and want to buckle over.

6. Stop James from dying.
7. Stop James from dying.
8. Stop everyone from dying.

'So we want to know what totally common thing *you've* never done,' the voice on the radio was saying. The voices of people in their early to mid-twenties, death as far-off an idea for them as the eventual heat death of the universe itself. A shame, in other words, but not a real issue: not as bad as locking yourself out of your apartment, say.

She herself had been younger than this drivetime DJ when the terror first hit her – hit her with a series of surprise blows. First Auntie Pam had died and Sal had writhed about from 11 p.m. till the sun came wandering up into the sky, unable to believe that a mile away Pam was spending her *last night on earth*. That this time tomorrow her bones would have turned to ash and that, every day that dawned for the rest of the world, she would not be there to know what was happening. Then a girl in sixth form had died – of leukaemia, like Pam – and the teachers had sobbed at the back of the hall in Assembly. And John Smith the Labour leader had been taken off by a heart attack, and when the news came through Dad had stopped the car and rested his head on the steering wheel for a long time, and later applauded when they did tributes to him on the news.

On these occasions everyone else had been sad, like Sal was, but only because they would miss that specific person; because it was tragic that they specifically were gone. Whereas Sal, each time, had felt her fibres fill with ice. *If that person's dead then eventually we all will be.*

The phone pulsed: 'Steffi'. Sal glanced at the message. No, it wasn't news; just more chat, more 'comparing notes'. She turned the phone face down on the seat. The traffic lumbered forward, stopped. Forward again, stopped again.

And then Dad himself had gone. The night before the

funeral was like Pam all over again. It was impossible that there would be cricket matches in the summer, and the Edinburgh festival, and those cloud-filled changeable days he loved – they would come round again and again, without him. At the moment the curtain closed around the coffin, and she knew it would slide into the furnace, she hadn't been able to look. She'd heard James muttering some sort of promise. Afterwards she regretted every day that she hadn't looked. Alone in that hotel room, the night of the ashes, it had come for her again. The impossibility of it. That he wouldn't ever be here again. She would never see him again. And one day nobody would ever see her, Sal, again. And so not one thing that was happening, actually mattered. Was actually worth doing.

But you couldn't live thinking that, could you? So you constructed this story where you were a business expert, specializing in time management. You filled every second with some sort of meaning. You used every minute, every hour well. Because that felt like winning. You concentrated on gossiping about the Chinese woman at the laundry chute, you booked the seaside weekend with Dec, you relished the thundering applause after your speech. Enjoyed your bank balance. Posted impressive summaries online. If all these things could be real, then death couldn't also be real: it was too stupid, it didn't make sense. So for almost all of every day – all those hoarded minutes, all that time you managed – everything seemed fine. Life seemed like the truth; what came next, you could forget.

The sun was still on good form, outside, drenching Exhibition Gardens with egg-yolk light; it seemed to stay high in the sky for so long, down here. And to stay so hot. They were almost back at the office.

'We're going to listen to our breathing,' she muttered.

'Sorry, ma'am, you want to listen to what?' said the ever-helpful driver. She wouldn't dock him a star. She'd give him the five. It wasn't his fault.

'So – let me get this right, Gideon,' the female presenter was saying, over her colleague's rising yelps of stage mirth, 'you've *never eaten chocolate, been on a plane, or seen a cow?*'

ı.

ı.

ı.

There was no list to make. Steffi was the one in charge. Another dispatch from her, now.

Guys. We are gaining more and more people and maybe we are close to a breakthrough. If you have ANY information about James please say it.

There were things Sal could do. She could create a job for James, bring him out here. Give him a new start. That was all he needed. She could call Mum more often, and be more attentive when she did call. She wasn't in charge, she should stop thinking she was 'in charge', but there *were* things she could do. When this was over.

She picked up the phone. Even the act of sending another text in James's direction – even if you don't want to talk to me, please please talk to someone – reminded her of what was lurking further up the chain of conversation: the five, six, seven old texts from James, every month or so, trying to rekindle things between them, expressing the hope that they could 'sort this out'. Every one of them unanswered by Sal. Not because she was deliberately being heartless, she'd thought; just, you moved on.

Her hands were still cold. She scooted down through the numbers, to 'Mum Home'. She could start by making her own mother feel better. When had she stopped doing that? Picking the phone up with the aim of actually engaging in conversation with Jean, rather than ticking it off a list. She could actually make everyone feel better, if she took the time to think. She pressed green and raised the phone to her ear.

26

But Jean was trying to call James, once again. She put the phone back into its cradle and retreated from the table back onto the second stair, where she had spent most of the last three hours. She drew her knees up in front of her. This was a fine state of affairs, wasn't it. Jean gritted her teeth to warn off the onset of self-pity. It wouldn't do any good to let herself cry. It was just all a bit much, this, wasn't it. Who was she left with, if Sally wouldn't reply, if James was wherever he was, and Alan . . .?

No. Come on. She could hear Alan's voice. *I don't see why we shouldn't get to the bottom of this.* It was no good thinking about him, and yet it was also the only thing that really worked. If only he could be alive again just for special occasions. If she could just have, say, three more chances to chat to him, even just three in the rest of her life.

'Are you sure you won't have some more toast?' asked Lee, who'd now showered and put on a creased T-shirt, and those awful chinos she still hadn't made him get rid of. He had briefly left his post, upstairs on the computer, where he was making doomed attempts to get onto the internet. This was his fourth round of toast since all the chaos began. They were going to have to get a new toaster if he kept going like this. He was trying so hard. If the loss of her son was a problem that could be solved by carbohydrates alone, as he seemed to believe it was, it would all be over by now. But this was what Lee did, she supposed. If he sensed she was a bit down, he put up a shelf. If she talked about a health complaint he immediately emptied the dishwasher.

'I'm fine, Lee.'

'Tea? Coffee? Or a bit of . . . something else for breakfast?'

'I'm all right, love.' She'd already had so much tea that she felt like one of those balloons filled with water. And what if she was on the lavatory when a call finally came. No, she'd stay within five seconds of the phone, and then perhaps it would be almost as if she did have a mobile, and was able to join in properly like all these other people; be a proper mother when James needed her. Which she'd always tried to do, even when it hadn't been easy.

It felt unjust that it should come down to not having a phone. She couldn't have imagined that staying up with the latest gadget would be part of what it meant to care for someone. Look at her, sitting helplessly with her equally helpless old machine. They were alike: analogue creatures in a digital crisis.

Lee kissed her on the top of her head. 'I'll keep fighting with her,' he said, meaning the computer. In his heart he knew it was not a winnable fight. Jean's internet connection would never be reliable until she changed provider, as he'd several times suggested she might do. This current lot were useless. He'd had more or less enough of their quirky little error messages. 'Oops! Something seems to be wrong.' Like he was a ninety-year-old being looked over by a kindly doctor. He didn't know whether he was getting crotchety or whether customer service messages were getting more juvenile. Either way: when he moved in here properly, he'd sort this out. If he moved in here. If he was able to start that conversation.

He sighed, glanced at his phone. There was nothing more from Sally. Nor from anyone. The new twenty pounds of credit had hardly been touched because, really, there were only so many people they could text. Five of the texts – dictated by Jean, tapped out by him – had gone to James, and who knew whether they had been seen, whether that 75p had just gone down a well. Of course he'd spend a lot more than that if it could somehow solve this problem. He'd do anything for Jean; he'd said as much in Zizzi only last Wednesday. It was just not at all clear what they *could* do about this.

Surely you couldn't talk someone out of doing away with themselves by sending a load of texts. Surely if he was serious, it was already too late. But Lee couldn't quite bring himself to believe it, even now. He'd only met James a few times and the bloke had seemed cheerful enough, if a bit of a mumbler. At Christmas he had been a bit quiet, perhaps, and looked too warm all the time – Jean had had the heating cranked up, in preparation, since about the first of October. And he'd sidestepped a lot of the conversation, even Lee had noticed that. But none of that was enough to make you think things were this badly awry. Of course, you couldn't tell. Lee remembered, way back, when his Geography teacher had put his head in the oven only five days after his wife won a beauty pageant in Wigan. And that was before they'd had mental health and all this business. No, you couldn't tell anything about other people. You just had to listen, he supposed. He crunched his toast and thought about going downstairs for another round.

★

Jean was looking at the wallpaper: the pattern of tiny little silver dandelions. She was so beautiful, thought Lee, levering himself – nimble, spider-like as usual – into the gap next to her on the stairs. He touched her elbow. There was a silence; or rather, there had already been a silence, but now that there were two of them it felt like a formal one.

He cleared his throat. 'No joy with the internet, I'm afraid. I do think we – you – but I mean, I'll do it – we should look into the options, because there are better ones out there. Donal pays about fifteen pounds a month and his grandkids are never off the internet watching these rappers, *and* they gave him a free voucher for a balloon ride, only they've not actually gone in a balloon because his wife gets the heebies even going out on the balcony.' It was too many words, far more than he'd intended, and anyway Jean didn't seem to be listening. She was twirling a strand of hair around her finger, concentrating intently on the sight of it.

'I think when this is all over, and James is all right,' said Jean, 'I think perhaps I might see someone.'

Lee scratched his chin. He gnawed a bit on his stubby nails. He scratched his hair, which since the shower had been sitting like soggy cereal on his head. He swallowed, and tasted the toast.

'Someone – instead of me, love?'

'What? No!' Jean almost laughed. She reached for his hand. 'I mean, someone to talk to. A . . . a professional, counsellor sort of person.' It was a stranger, bigger thing to say out loud than it had been in her head. 'You don't often get a chance to . . . think about what you're feeling. Do you. People our age.'

'Oh! Oh, I see what you mean.' Lee felt himself exhale. That certainly would have been a very harsh way for her to do it – but it had happened to him before, after all. He hadn't known Fiona was leaving him until she was next to someone else on a wedding seating plan. 'No, that sounds like a good—'

'People now do it all the time,' said Jean, trying out the idea, warming to it as it took shape. 'I think most people, if they'd had the sort of pregnancy I had – and if they'd had the sort of time I had when James was a baby. Well, for the first years, really. Now, you'd talk to someone about it. But it just wasn't really – it wasn't seen as being anything unusual.' She wasn't sure it even *had* been anything unusual. She hadn't known what was happening, at the time. Just a tunnel, a lot of mornings she couldn't get out of bed and had to ask Alan to get both kids to nursery, to school, to the Downs. Times she would put James's food in front of him and he'd throw it on the floor and she was horrified by the fury that welled up inside her. But that was what people said it was like, being a parent. It had come as a shock because it hadn't been so hard with Sally – that was the thing. Jean had secretly thought she was just better at it than the people who complained. Until she had James.

'Well, it's definitely something to look into.' This was one of Lee's favourite phrases; it could be substituted for action almost indefinitely. But Jean wasn't talking about what might be nice to look at. She blinked several times.

'Because they think, don't they, that things can have an effect for years and years. If you don't discuss them or . . . or sort them out at the time.'

There were so many problems that she hadn't even known existed, or at least had never articulated to herself, when she and Lee had gone to bed last night. As recently as that. It was startling to be learning this now – to find that in the space of a few hours, so much could become new and unfamiliar. It was striking and odd to feel that way at her age. She felt as if she'd been picked up and spun around. She could learn from everything that happened tonight; there was still time to learn.

'I think I should get a mobile phone, as well,' she said.

'We can get you one of those,' Lee said. This was more like it. Something he could advise her on, and buy from a shop. Perhaps the 'we' was being too presumptuous, but Jean didn't seem to mind. She had rested her head on his shoulder.

'It would just stop me feeling like I'm not part of things,' said Jean, though the sentence didn't sound like something she would have said twenty-four or even twelve hours ago. 'You know. It's a big world.'

Lee nodded. It *was* a big world, though he personally hadn't been further than Greece and he'd found it a bit too muggy for his liking.

'Oh,' said Jean, 'also, I think you need better trousers than those.'

They looked down together at Lee's long legs, at the brown chinos bought from House of Fraser more than ten years ago; slightly too tight now, and slightly too short from the moment he glanced in the fitting-room mirror and said, 'Yes, these are perfect.'

'So.' Lee cleared his throat again. 'So the list, just to be clear: get you a counsellor, a therapist, whatnot. Get you a phone. And get me some better slacks.'

She smiled, despite everything. Outside, there was a faint rattle of gravel and the purring of a car out of one of the neighbours' drives. It would be the Bradshaws. They were always up early and going off rambling around the Lake District, back again the Sunday night; excursions which seemed a lot of hassle to Jean. But it would be nice. To have a plan.

'It's just the helplessness,' said Jean, looking in grievance at the phone on the table, her useless ally with its big thick cord. 'It's just feeling that – I mean he could be in his flat and I wouldn't know, he could be somewhere in *Bristol* for all we know, really – who knows what he might need, if he's in such a state.' She imagined her son, trudging around the streets, perhaps injured or under the influence of some drug she didn't even know about – because that would explain all this, wouldn't it. The sort of person you might walk past on your way out of the Hippodrome, in town, and think: *How do people end up like that? He must have a mother.*

'We could go and look for him,' said Lee. 'We could go out. We could go to his flat. In London. In case he *is* there, in case . . .' He tailed off, because the prospect of what they might actually find at James's place was less attractive a thought to dwell on. But the quest itself *was* attractive. He imagined himself, a fast (but safe) driver, guiding them sure-footedly past Big Ben and, what else, London Zoo, those beefeater fellows in the hats (he was vague on the layout of the capital; it had been twenty-eight years). He could see Jean hugging James, all a bit of a misunderstanding, everything blown over now.

Jean was frowning, but she hadn't yet said the idea was stupid. 'We can't just drive to London,' she said, sounding – Lee hoped he wasn't imagining it – sounding as if she wanted to be persuaded otherwise.

'Why not? I only had the one beer last night. We'd need to put some petrol in the old tank. But . . .'

'No, I mean.' Jean's eyes had a spark in them. 'I mean – just to *go to London*? Where would we . . . I mean, I'd have to pack a bag. We'd need to get ready properly.'

'We can get ready properly.' Lee was already on his feet. 'I'll go and warm the engine up, is the only thing, because you know what she's like, the old girl, but I'm sure . . .'

'It would take . . . I'd need a bit of time to get ready,' said Jean again.

'That's all right, love.'

'But what about if he calls here, though?' Jean frowned. 'What about if, you know . . .'

'He can call my mobile. We can take the mobile. You can have it on your lap.'

'I don't know if he's got your number, Lee.'

'He has.' Lee felt himself growing into the role of a man who could lead them out of this, who had all the answers. 'He will, because all those calls and texts from us – his phone will have saved the number. He can contact us if he wants to, love.'

Lee was already opening the front door to go out to the car. His hands went to his pockets for the car keys, but these weren't the right trousers; also, he wasn't wearing his shoes. He shut the door again. Jean rose slowly, feeling her muscles unwind and her brain stirring at last.

27

Finally he was dumping the DJ at the quayside hotel, pretty much six o'clock on the money. The Millennium Bridge, coiling over the river like a live electric wire, the reflection of its blue-yellow-purple light bobbing in the water. Already, along the quay, a couple of people were on their bikes. They had had their whole night, got up, for some unfathomable reason put their Lycra on, and got out here, all in the time Karl had been living through this insane episode. Karl opened the back door, like he was in *Driving Miss Daisy* or something, helped the DJ with his bag and coat, said that he hoped the guy had got enough sleep in the end.

'I mean, not an ideal sleep, to be fair, mate,' the guy had said. *Are you trying to bust my balls even more than you already have,* Karl wondered to himself. *Are you looking to set a world record for the biggest busting of balls ever achieved? Are you after a T-shirt that says I BUST BALLS and then a web address underneath? I mean if you want a perfect night's beauty sleep, maybe consider* not *driving from Wembley most of the way to fucking Scotland.*

All this went through Karl's inner censors as he ushered the DJ to the check-in desk, remarked again that he hoped it had been a good journey, thanked him for using Cruiz, basically did everything possible to keep alive the idea of a tip from this obviously affluent and privileged man, short of screaming *Give me your money!* into his face. The closest the DJ came to acknowledging almost six hours of Karl's life was a muttered, 'Cheers, mate' as they went their separate ways. For ever, as far as Karl was concerned. He'd pass it to someone else if Cruiz ever got a booking for this lanky piece of shit again. The gentleman could shove the headphones up his rectum.

The warmth of defiance left Karl in the thirty seconds it took to cross the red and silver lobby to the toilet, with its swaggering gothic 'M' picked out in steel. Sports news was showing on the TVs which played to an empty bar: subtitles over red and blue jumpers playing rugby. *Tomorrow's match in Eddie Blair,* said the caption, and then the correction: *Tomorrow's match in Edinburgh.*

He sat on the toilet with the phone in front of him, thumb racing up and down the screen, trying to make sense of what Steffi was saying, what everyone was saying. Karl's mate in the pub had been on about how a hundred people a year got seriously ill from taking their phones to the toilet, but this was the same guy who made the claim about the Sudoku, and the more Karl thought about it, the more he was full of bullshit. For a second the thought of his stupid friend lifted a little weight from Karl, but then – it leapt out at him from the lines and boxes of text, from the weightless emojis – what was this, what did this mean? We have some thoughts that he might have been at Euston. Or might be on a train from there even.

Karl felt his knees, bared in front of him, tense and groan with post-drive ache. His knees and his back. He felt as if he could pass out here. What the fuck would James have been at Euston for? You didn't jump in front of a train *at* a station, did you. But '*on* a train'? What trains were there at midnight, except night trains? He thought about James and his dad, about Edinburgh, and his heart felt wedged in his throat as he stood up, almost dropping the phone on the floor.

He'd thought he was alone in the bathroom, but standing at one of the sinks was the DJ. He was even taller than he'd looked in the back of the car; he was like a basketball player. Karl winced at the sight of his former passenger, splashing water onto his face. Couldn't he even be rid of the guy in this shitter? Was the bloke going to show up at Karl's house back in London on Monday?

'I thought you were – I mean, should you not be sleeping? I thought you were quite into your sleep.' It didn't come out with the satirical edge Karl was used to pulling off; his voice was tuneless.

'Got another gig.' The DJ raised his eyebrows as their looks met in the expensive mirror. 'Love Soup, you heard of it?' Karl shook his head, weakly; he had no idea what the guy was talking about; he felt like he would have struggled to remember his own surname at the moment. 'Nutters, mate,' said the DJ. 'They've been going at it all night, some sugar mill place or something, and now I have to do a chillout session thing at, like, eight a.m. Getting too old for this!' His tone suggested that he was, on the contrary, dealing pretty well with the years; improving with time, if anything. He turned around and looked at Karl with sharp enquiry. His eyes seemed big and inquisitive, like a child's, under the artificial light.

'Are you all right, mate? I'm sorry if I was a bit short with you. My wife always says, *Danny, I do love you, but you're a terrible arsehole.* Says it most days.' He grinned – magnificent teeth, like a poster for whitening which would make you google it and then gawp at the price. Then his face went serious again. 'But seriously. You don't look too good. What's up?'

The kindness, the concern in his voice were almost worse than when he'd been a bastard. Or what Karl thought was a bastard. That seemed unfair, now. He was starting to wish he hadn't fantasized about maiming the guy. Karl swallowed, failing to dislodge the sorrow that was rising through him, wanting to get out. With mounting shame he saw his eyes film over with tears as he began to speak. 'My mate – my mate's missing and it's my fault.'

The DJ had his hand on Karl's arm. Karl felt hot and ashamed and he tried to prevent the tears from getting any further with a sort of choking motion which made a weird, even more embarrassing sound, like a duck. 'What's his name, mate? I'll put it out there, yeah? I got a lot of people following me, man.'

'That would be kind,' said Karl, turning his eyes away, as if there was still something of his dignity to be kept. He caught sight of his face in the next mirror along, his face tatty and blotchy, almost unfamiliar to himself. 'His name's James – James Chiltern. I'll give you a picture.'

'It's going to be all right, dude.' The stranger squeezed Karl's shoulder and Karl, used to being the more powerful person in any embrace, gasped; the guy could knock down a wall with an arm like that. 'What do you need? Like, apart from me telling people. What do you need right now?'

Karl swiped his eyes clear and filled his lungs with a shaky breath. Copying the DJ, he went to the sink, pushed the tap down and wetted his face. It felt good, the cold water, and he did it a couple more times.

'I need to make a phone call,' he said, 'and I need to drive in a way that's totally illegal, and I need to pray to God, and if you're into praying maybe you could do that, too?'

'I'm into it if you want me to be, dude.' The DJ had his phone out as Karl went towards the hand-dryer. 'Just in case God isn't there, though, maybe give me the guy's details now?'

28

LONDON–EDINBURGH TRAIN, 06:30
BERLIN, 07:30

James looked out at the thickening signs of life, the gradual build towards the city. The weekend. People would be carrying out the modest plans they'd made. Walking by the river, cycling. He saw an elderly fellow down on hands and knees in his garden. This was all going to carry on without him. Not only was he untroubled by the thought: it was pleasing. Good luck to them all. Good luck with their March 9th and all the other ones.

His brain went mischievously round from this proposition to the vision of his contacts, receiving the news. It had been harder than he'd imagined to switch off that mental pathway, in these final few hours. The phone was probably to blame. It was good he was rid of the phone.

If they do genuinely miss me, maybe they'll learn from it.

The thought took him by surprise; yet, really, it felt as if it had been there all along. And it made sense. If he *was* going to leave a lasting taste, if perhaps people really did miss him and wished they had priced him more highly – well, that would be good for them. They'd get other opportunities. They would go on to make kinder decisions, enrich the lives of others. His net impact, as a reminder to do better, as an open sore, *remember what happened with James*: it was a legacy better than anything he'd managed to build by actually being around.

I'm worth more dead than alive. It sounded ghoulish, the same way the word 'suicide' did, because it felt like something to be screamed down from a ledge at a would-be rescuer. But there was nothing dramatic about it as an idea; there was no self-pity in the way it nestled in his brain. It was a calculation, and James found it quite a cheering one. He was going to give people something they'd remember, act on. A harsh way of doing it, perhaps. But life was harsh, wasn't it? Life was harsh, that was why he was here.

He was doing people a favour. It didn't matter if they understood it straight away.

★

His last attempt at dating, on the last weekend of January, had been what had decided him. Since then, he'd just been counting down.

She was called Carly. She looked friendly in the pictures James's app had supplied. Large, like James: no threat of her taking against him on first look, at least not for that reason. Red-pink hair. A disparate range of interests (animal welfare, cinema, roller derby) which he could either hold his own with, or research. They'd exchanged messages. Carly had suggested La Chimère for dinner, and it was almost a date before he realized with horror that was where Steffi worked. He'd steered her instead towards a tapas place called Bravas, and got a 'romantic offer', using one of the apps he still had from back when he booked everything for Michaela and himself. When he clicked the 'Confirm' box, a little animated heart flew across the screen, which then filled with confetti.

James had been there fifteen minutes early, hoping to get in a reconnaissance of the menu. The window was full of red glitter and mini-Cupids dangling from invisible strings; the restaurant claimed to be '*the* Valentine Venue', ahead of every other eatery in the Western world – there was even a trademark sign next to the slogan, though James was almost certain it had just been drawn on. He went in and was shown to a table, uncomfortably close to other couples on both sides. The offer included a half-bottle of champagne, but the waiter immediately asked James if he would like a drink 'to start off with', and James – feeling a burst of nerves – asked for a whisky. He drank it and sat with the empty glass, hoping his shirt was dark enough. It had been a little lighter than it looked online, and the jeans a little tougher to get into.

After a while he worried whether perhaps Carly had missed his text; but no, no sign of her outside, either. The waiter offered him the menu to look at, but James said he'd wait, thank you. He ignored the sceptical tilt of the eyebrows. He didn't think it was right to contact Carly until she was at least twenty minutes late. Even though he always avoided being late, he didn't like to be the sort of person who hassled. Besides, you weren't meant to look too keen, were you; that was what Karl would say. Would have said. James made it to the twenty minutes. He ordered another whisky. He messaged her, finally, at thirty-five minutes. Again at forty-five. At fifty minutes he asked for the bill, saying his plans had changed. Well, it was true: they had.

He hated the effort he made to look as if he hadn't been stood up. The mock-purposeful way he carried himself towards the pub on the corner, as if he'd merely been informed of a change of venue. He hated the way his shirt was sticking and his thighs complained as they rubbed together. *Why* would *you want to go on a date with me*, he asked an invisible audience. There was a thin, petty rain which seemed in keeping with the non-event of the night, of James in general. Not a big angry storm, just this. *Just this – effing – stupid, embarrassing thing.*

In the pub he asked for another whisky – a double – and then, because he was sick of the paint-stripper taste in his throat, red wine.

'What kind, mate?' asked the woman, who was tending the bar on her own and seemed stressed out that he was asking for anything at all.

'Any kind,' he said, and she shook her head a little and gave him the house.

During his second wine he gave in to temptation and – since Carly still hadn't made contact at all – looked her up on Facebook. There were numerous references to a night away with 'the girls'. The last of them had come only an hour ago, illustrated by a GIF of a woman, in an old-fashioned bathing hat, swan-diving into what appeared to be a hot tub of champagne. He closed the window and checked the date. Was it a simple case of crossed wires? No, they'd confirmed it several times. It was incomprehensible. When he scrolled down the page a little way, he came across a photo taken the past week: Carly, the hair now more pink than red, beaming, her arm around a man who looked like an underwear model.

It was incomprehensible. The word came into James's head again on the bus home. He'd had far more to drink than he was used to, and the alcohol was like paraffin. *What the hell is the matter with me?* How could he be so out of touch with everything, with everyone, that this could happen? He trudged along the street with the station at his back, where the commuter had shouted at him. It was just one indignity after another. And there was nobody to tell him he wasn't at fault. It engulfed him completely.

I'll make you proud, Dad, he'd muttered, as the curtain was closed around his father's coffin. *I'll do something good.* And now look at him, a fat wreck, in a terrible job, just back from being dumped without even meeting the other person, stinking of booze even though he didn't really drink, no meaningful friendships remaining even though he'd never consciously done anything to end them. And Steffi was in the kitchen.

'What's wrong?' she'd asked, looking up from her phone. 'Is something wrong?'

He'd gone to the fridge and started trying to talk as he looked around for a chunk of cheese. He was embarrassed

307

even by the fridge smell which escaped. 'It's just hopeless, it's just hopeless,' he said, his voice cracking.

'What is hopeless?' asked Steffi, polite, but – it was obvious enough, he thought – hoping not to get trapped here.

'Too many things are wrong,' James just about managed to say, shielding his wet face as Steffi awkwardly reached for his shoulder. He kept talking, and she tried to say useful things, but it didn't get better as he talked; it got, if anything, worse. He thought of the Samaritan conversation a few weeks back. If he didn't do something soon, this was what he would become: a supplicant, a patient.

When he woke up, a chilly clarity settled on him, and he did do something. First, he took the day off work, not even contacting them. At first there were calls from Waqar, then a couple of texts. Then it stopped. It stopped, and nothing replaced it. Nobody pursued him. Nobody expected anything of him at all. It was as if he didn't exist.

He thought about the sleeper, Edinburgh, the half-plan he'd come up with before. About what it would be like if everything went away. It wouldn't be 'like' anything. It would just be an absence of pain. You didn't need a big grand reason to do it. You just had to have run out of ideas, as a human, and be brave enough to admit it.

He booked the sleeper that evening. Boarding just before midnight on 8 March. The date went into his mental diary. He thought about exactly how he was going to do it, and started to feel better immediately.

★

About a month after they came back from their European holiday, Karl and James had a synchronized day off. To rekindle something of the freewheeling atmosphere of the holiday, Michaela came up with an idea. 'Why don't we do the Monopoly Challenge?'

'I'm not playing Monopoly with him again.' Karl was lying on the sofa, bare feet up on the armrests. 'Have you *played* with him, man. You think he's running out of money and then it turns out he set up an ISA or something before the game even started.'

'It's not a game of actual Monopoly, it's . . . have neither of you ever done this?' Michaela shook her head, outraged. 'All right. We're doing it. You have to get round London – actual London – and visit all the places on the Monopoly board. You have to take pictures for proof, text it to the other people . . .'

'I don't even have a phone,' James began, 'I mean, not one that can . . .'

'Yes, you'll have to send them by fax.' Michaela tweaked his cheek-fat. 'All right, you and me v Karl.'

'I'll rinse you,' said Karl. 'Not being funny but I used to do courier stuff, I know all the little shortcuts. Also you two will keep stopping to have sex.' James coughed several times and Michaela stretched a muscular leg to stamp on Karl's toes. 'Ow, fuck off. Yeah, you watch. I'll have finished it before you guys have even got to the Old Kent Road or whatever.'

'You have to finish at Park Lane,' said Michaela, 'and afterwards we get drunk in the Park Lane Hilton.'

'I'll be there,' said Karl, 'I'll be there with the little dog *and* the hat and the iron, fam. I'll be round London faster than that – who was the fella, first one to circumnavigate . . . you know. Discovered America. Marco Polo? Anyway, they chopped his head off in the end. Yeah, Marco Polo.'

'Not Marco Polo,' said James, 'and I think you're talking about three separate people, actually . . .'

'Whatever, mate. Prepare for defeat.'

They picked up their cars at an agreed identical moment – 1 p.m., from two different Cruiz sites – after separate battles to persuade the shift supervisors that they weren't planning to take cash bookings on the sly. ('Why would you be driving if you weren't getting paid?' asked the man at James's depot. *Because I'm having fun*, thought James proudly.) By two, James and Michaela were twisting and stop-starting through East London, where they hoped to cross off several of the low-value properties in quick succession. Michaela had downloaded a route which some previous challenger had put online: it wasn't cheating, she said, just tactics.

'I've been thinking,' Michaela said, 'just talking of phones. You know that video I put up about running whatever size you are and blah blah? It had so many views, I mean . . . *I've had* so many people asking about nutrition and how long to work out and all of it. And people keep sharing it. I wonder if I should try and make it a thing. Do it every couple of days. Build it up.'

'That would be great,' said James at once. 'Sorry, left here, or . . .?'

'Yes.' Michaela was imagining the future, a future she couldn't see in detail but which would indeed come to pass for a while, and she was nowhere near on top of the complexities of the Old Street roundabout. 'No, wait! Shit! It was meant to be . . . sorry.'

'Not to worry,' said James. 'I think . . . er. Well, everyone is online now, obviously. People share things on those platforms so much faster than even a few years ago. And you're wonderful at it because inspiring people is – it's the sort of personality you have.'

'That's a very nice thing to say,' said Michaela, wondering if being with James was exactly what her ego had always needed and deserved, or whether in fact it was in danger of over-inflating as he fed it so reliably. It was, she decided, a nice problem to have. 'I mean, it might be worth trying as a . . . shit.'

'What? Are you all right?'

'Yes! Sorry to alarm you. Just . . .' She held the phone up in front of her face, rueful. 'Look at that bastard.'

'I can't look, because of – er – well, the rules of the road . . .'

'I don't know how driving works, do I,' said Michaela merrily.

'Well, one of the main rules is that you're meant to look at the road quite a bit.'

'He's *already* done Whitechapel and Old Kent Road and now he's somehow in the West End. He's got Leicester Square and Oxford Street. He's got about eight.'

'Well, then you were right to alarm me,' said James, amused. 'That is definitely alarming.' He put his foot down for a moment – not enough for it to be dangerous, of course, but enough for the engine to produce a gladiatorial rumble. 'Battle is joined,' James said.

Over the next two hours Karl's stream of gloating messages continued to clog Michaela's phone, each producing a wail of despair from Michaela which – for a split second each time – James kept taking as more serious alarms. There he was, thumbs up, next to a sign for Vine Street; there he was, jacket darkened by one of the rain showers James and Michaela could see out of the car window, standing outside an electricity company: not even one of the official requirements, just a cocky garland. In between the shots, a stream of teasing texts reminded them of the lead Karl was opening up, his progress towards victory. Trying to match his trash-talk, fumbling with the screen, Michaela missed several key turnings. More than once she had to drag James out of the car to collect a photo, racing him down some alley, James protesting in half-breaths. 'This isn't one . . . of our . . . exercise days,' he panted. 'It is now,' said Michaela, with the grimness of someone who cared much more about winning than she realized herself.

Karl was waiting for them at dusk, in the faux-Himalayan bar the Hilton had in their lobby. After one glance at the two of them – unkempt and ragged, sweaty, at the edge even of their near-boundless patience with one another – he broke out into a high, keening laugh. It was a laugh with an unaccustomed note of guilt in it. 'Oh, man,' he said, 'I thought you would have stopped hours ago.' James looked him up and down and understood that Karl – spotless in his jacket and T-shirt and crisp blue jeans – was very good at doctoring photos, very good at technical trickery of all kinds, had the evidence of a long drinking session around him, and hadn't been anywhere at all. He wondered if Michaela would work it out, too, because if she did not, he definitely wasn't going to tell her.

★

Michaela had stayed in the bath for almost an hour and a half in the end, close to her personal record. She'd topped the water up three times. She had thought about the Monopoly day and the unwanted matcha lattes and the warm feel of him in the bed. She had watched the feed of James news, the now almost minute-by-minute updates, the false starts and red herrings. His picture; the striped rugby jumper that Michaela herself had bought him. It looks silly, he'd objected, me in sports gear. You don't have to *play* rugby, you idiot, she'd said. Just look good in it. He did look good in it. The wide stripes, although they were meant to be unflattering, had given him an appealing teddy-bear look, and there was something much more genuinely manly about him than the people you saw shouting their mouths off in football shirts. She'd always known better than James himself where his best qualities lay.

That thought, at about the ninety-minute mark of the bath, had prompted her to try James's number again. Her texts were saying 'Delivered'; it was something to hold on to, it was better than the forbidding silence, the gloomy green boxes, of earlier. And this time something in the attempted call had been different too; something had felt different in the quality of the silence, the electronic deliberations. For ten seconds, as adrenalin coursed through her,

Michaela thought she was going to be able to talk to him – hours after that had ceased to seem a possibility. So long that she didn't have a clue what she would actually say, other than to beg him: stop this. Don't do this, darling. The skin stood up on her bare arms.

'Hello?' she said. 'James, hello?'

But no. *The person you are calling*, the non-voice had begun, and Michaela had shouted, 'Fuck *me*', and dropped the phone over the side of the bath.

'Maybe he doesn't want to talk to you?'

'Are you *actually, actually* kidding me,' said Michaela to herself.

She sprang out of the bath, displacing a surprising amount of water onto the white tiles: she might have been in there for a long time, but his voice had ruined the peace of it in an instant. She walked naked to open the door. Without his glasses Phillip continued to look younger and a little less in charge. He blinked at her. She could see him adjust his weight to mask his hardness. Unsuccessfully. She could always get him, just by standing in front of him like this.

'Did you want something, Phillip?'

'I was wondering if you are still obsessed with your ex-boyfriend's stunt or if maybe you will one day come to bed.'

It was the way he spoke, of course, there was always that satirical edge, but still: the coldness of it made her catch her breath. 'So, you want me to just go to sleep and when we wake up we'll find out if he's dead? Cool.'

'Look, he isn't going to die, he isn't going to be dead.'

Phillip was studiedly not-looking at her bare thighs, his Kryptonite. Michaela watched the water running off her legs and feet, leaving little rockpools on the floorboards where they met the bathroom tiles. Good. Bollocks to him and his 'the floor is the most precious part of a property'. 'But even – even regardless . . .'

She backed into the bathroom again, sat on the edge of the bath: feet wide, legs apart. She'd make him suffer. '*Regardless* of whether my friend is dead . . .'

'Your friend. Yes. At best, your friend. You are not even meant to be in touch with . . .'

'I'm not *in touch* with him! I've heard from him tonight because he might be about to, or has, killed himself!' She was tripping over the sentence construction and, no, sitting wasn't right. She brought herself back up to her full height, arms folded across her breasts.

'But you're not with him any more.' Phillip frowned his kingly disappointment frown. 'You are with me. It isn't your fault if he decides to do – whatever he does is not your fault.'

'It's *someone's* fault.'

'It's his. That's all.'

'It isn't that simple, Phillip.' Michaela glimpsed herself in the mirror. It was a shame she looked so good naked; he didn't really deserve this. But it wasn't like he was enjoying it. He never enjoyed a genuine challenge. 'Am I only allowed to care if certain people live or die, not others? Do I have to . . . apply for permission?'

This sort of sarcasm took her onto Phillip's territory. He leaned a flat hand against the doorframe, a male-in-charge-here pose, like a builder assessing the cost of work to be done. With demonstrative patience, with a skywards hefting of his eyebrows as if he were the most reasonable man yet born, he reset the conversation. 'All right. He is very unhappy and it's dangerous, it's an emergency, I agree. And I am sorry if it seems like I don't get it. It's just, it's basically the sun coming up, and I am in my gown, and you still aren't ready to sleep, so . . .'

Michaela sniggered; she couldn't help it. 'I am in my gown' was too much for her. But the moment triggered the memory of when she had laughed at James, that awful morning at the station. It wasn't her fault that men were so funny when they got high-and-mighty. The laugh was choked to death almost the instant it hit the air. She remembered the horrible situation she was in and the fact that Phillip seemed to look down on her for being in it.

'It's a pretty funny joke, sure, cool,' said Phillip, 'it's just—'

'Nothing about this is *funny*,' said Michaela. She reached for a towel and started to dry herself vigorously, just to be doing something physical. She wanted a run; that was what she really wanted. After all this time, a run. She couldn't believe she was thinking it. 'Everything about it is scary, and I would have hoped that you might support me, but . . .'

'Hey, of course I support you.' He extended an arm, he wanted to bring her in close; it was three steps from here to make-up sex. She sensed that narrative in the air. And unfortunately he was remarkably good at sex, just as he was remarkably good at knowing about art, at making her feel special in front of important people, choosing restaurants, being funny, and so on. With his head between her legs he could do things you wouldn't see on Pornhub. But she was angry, and frightened, and she wanted to hold onto those thoughts, stare them down. She brushed aside the proffered arm, headed for the bedroom. 'I'm going for a run,' she called over her shoulder. She squatted down, looking for the Lycra shorts. By the time she'd got them on, Phillip was in the doorway.

'That's kind of interesting,' he said, with unpleasantly measured emphasis. 'A run.'

'It's almost seven, Phillip. I know you're obsessed with this idea that we haven't been to bed and we'd better get our "eight hours" and curl up with our cocoa.' *Curl up with our cocoa*, that wasn't bad: that had come out with a satisfying bite. She was almost enjoying this, apart from how awful it was. 'But the thing is, the sun is basically up, quite a lot of people do run at this time, however stupid it might seem to you, and before you say I've been drinking all night . . .'

'It's none of that,' said Phillip, 'it's just, well. Running hasn't happened for a little while. The thing was that you hated to remember when you had to run every day, right? So in your life now you don't really run, we do other stuff . . .'

'I didn't say I was never going to run, did I, I just—'

'Yeah, but it's funny that it comes back now.' Phillip had got hold of this idea, all right: he loved an idea, a theory, she thought wearily. 'So now we have you suddenly thinking all about your ex and guess what, you are also doing what

317

you and the ex used to do. And I notice you, a few times, have posted things about plus-size running like maybe you are thinking of getting into this again. And meanwhile at the gallery you seem to be not quite so into the art like you used to . . .'

'Oh, fucking hell.' She was lacing her shoes, foot up on the bed. 'Is that because I was pissed at the launch? The artist was the other side of the room, Phillip! She would have had to have James Bond ears to hear me! And I didn't even say anything which—'

'It was obvious what you thought. You are off your tits on the Prosecco and I have an important artwork, with the artist right there . . .'

'Important artwork!' She couldn't help herself; she'd been sitting on it for so long, having to send out the invitations, pass press requests to the artist who never did any of them because she was always off in a field thinking about bees or something. 'Phil, it's a load of trousers!'

He put his hands on his hips; he was wearing his reasonable face again. 'Really? We're really going to talk about Denim World and whether it is art?'

'It's a load of jeans on plinths, Phil! Literally all the artist had to do was buy the plinths on Amazon! If I take the laundry basket into work on Monday, will someone give me an exhibition?'

He moved aside to let her out of the door, perhaps still not believing that she was going to leave, but as her hand went for the door handle he said: 'Seems like you get a new interest for a while and then you move on pretty fast, that's all, so I kind of wonder—'

'Fuck off, Phillip.'

'I kind of wonder how much longer of this before you—'

'Fuck *off* and – and keep fucking off till you've got a bit more of a heart.'

She slammed the door so hard that it jumped partway open again. She heard her trainers echo on the stairs. She looked down at her phone, the stream of notifications. It was struggling with the workload: the battery was down at 9 per cent. The screen was cluttered with messages, rolling news like a TV channel, but – like one of those channels – almost all of it was noise, repetition. It took ten seconds' scroll to determine that the networked cells were still all fizzing off one another, coordinated by Steffi. But another thirty seconds and 1 per cent of the iPhone's energy confirmed that things had not really progressed, there was still no sighting of James, there was still just this international spider-graph of chatter.

Down the staircase through the neck of their building; out onto the street. Michaela slammed the outer door. She was breathing fast. Her limbs, caught by surprise, had begun spreading the rumour of the planned run: there were twinges of displeasure in her calves. But the breathing wasn't about that. It was about the argument and the lava of feeling it had unleashed into her. The brief stimulation, the kick of the conflict, had faded. It felt like the dried sweat after exercise, cold and sad, and the morning sky – concrete-coloured, low – was not going to bail her out.

She thought briefly of Steffi, a stranger, sitting at Michaela's own kitchen table, perhaps boiling what used to be Michaela's kettle, labouring patiently to untangle a mess Michaela had helped to create. It was the right thing to do, quite obviously. It was the selfless thing to do and it was only necessary because people like Michaela had been selfish. She ground her teeth. She sparked her muscles into the first running steps, despite the opposition from the pit of her stomach, which had had no fuel but empty calories, booze, for almost eleven hours. Down the steps that brought you out on the Landwehr; nettles poking through a wire fence, discarded empty bottles, then the reward of the water. Fuck Phillip. Really, fuck him.

She hated it all, and this was an attempt to run away, but it wasn't going to work – she knew that already. Running away was what had brought her here, and look where that had left James. Look where it had left *her*: helpless, lost, plodding along by a canal at seven in the fucking morning, somewhere in Berlin, far from anyone who loved her except one person who, seemingly, didn't actually love her much at all. She hated what he'd said, the implication that she was some sort of chancer – someone who drifted from one life to the next, heedless of the fall-out for everyone else. She hated the part of her that believed he was right.

No, it was no good thinking like this. The body wouldn't run if the brain was holding it back. She remembered saying that into the phone, James holding it out in front of him, gasping as he trotted along backwards to film her. 'More of running is in the mind than you think.' *Quite a lot of it is also in the legs, I can assure you*, James would remark later, de-sweating his shirt like a dishcloth before putting it in the wash.

It had been months, though. She'd been doing Pilates

instead. She'd done a couple of spin classes recently but stopped twenty minutes in because she felt like she was dying. She'd done some swimming. The whole point was that running wasn't her prison any more. And now that she was trying to break back into that prison, her body understandably didn't want to know. Her once-concrete calves felt flabby and lethargic; her stomach was – she didn't feel right at all. She managed to jog-run fifteen minutes. The voices of birds broke the silence; the water was very still. She checked her phone. She didn't feel right.

She was doubled over on the path. It had come on so quickly. She felt the rising of the gorge, the resistance of every muscle. She felt that she could see her own face, sickly yellow. She retched; nothing. It had been years since this. The horrible minutes of trying to let go. Her palms felt like wet sponges. Spots of greenish light played across her field of vision. The actual moment, it was true, you didn't know much about. Her body went limp and she vomited onto the footpath, just missing her trainers.

'Jesus,' she said.

The third time wasn't as bad, already. After that she knew it was over. She felt like things might be all right if she stayed right here for the rest of time. Her joints moaned like old furniture. A sharp-edged pebble was nibbling at her kneecap but it felt like too much even to shift the two inches it would take. It had been stupid to run with booze inside her. It had been a stupid, stupid night.

There were footsteps on the path.

Phillip was wearing one of her old hoodies and a beaten-up pair of trainers she'd never seen before. No glasses.

A pair of khaki shorts she'd also never seen before. She looked at him and laughed, without being able to help herself. The taste of sick was in the back of her mouth.

'How did you find me?'

'How do you think I found you?' Phillip was guiding her up, slowly, and she felt herself leaning into him. Her head felt too light. She was tired.

'You followed me?'

'Yes, but it was not fun. As you know, I'm not good at running. And I'm not good at it, especially, at seven thirty in the morning. It's lucky you kept stopping.'

Michaela laughed out loud this time. The thought of him tailing her doggedly, stopping each time *she* stopped to check her phone, like the Pink Panther or something.

'You were right to go. I was being absolutely a penis. I'm sorry.'

'I was being an *absolute* penis,' Michaela said.

'What?'

'It sounds better like that,' she said. 'It's weird if you say "absolutely" in the middle of the . . . anyway.'

'I was being an absolute penis,' Phillip said, thoughtfully, auditioning it. 'OK. Why don't you ever correct me?'

'I don't know. Because I feel like you know everything.'

'I don't know anything,' said Phillip, 'I just talk like I know.'

She felt his hands on her clammy back, through the sweaty T-shirt.

'I'm all shitty,' she said. 'I've been sick.'

'Yeah.' Phillip's arm was around her waist. He slipped the hoodie off his arm and wrapped it around her shoulders.

'We need to get you some water and also you need to keep warm.'

'Don't *you* want to wear it?'

'*Scheiß drauf,*' muttered Phillip as his glasses fell out of the pocket, onto the path. The two of them looked down at the glasses lying there.

'I would get those,' she said, 'but I-I still sort of feel . . .'

'Yes, it should be me who picks the glasses up,' Phillip agreed, 'but the only problem with this is, I also cannot be bothered to do it.'

They laughed, the two of them together, and she touched his cheek, and for a moment none of the past eight hours needed to have happened.

'My God,' she said. 'I can't believe we – we haven't been to bed.'

'As soon as you left the flat I stopped being an idiot and have gone onto Facebook and tried to help. I've got five people to do the re-tweets already, like big people, big names, and here's the serious news: you know Ai Weiwei? The artist. At Christmas you laughed because someone sent round the picture of . . .'

'Ai Weiwei in a Manger.' She smiled, smelling Phillip's aftershave on the hoodie she was now wearing. A morning breeze skipped lazily off the canal and sniffed around the backs of their necks, like a dog half-interested. She let herself breathe in and out. 'You said it was puerile because he is . . .' She summoned enough energy to do a pompous-Phillip voice. '*One of the most important artists.*'

'Yes, so, again, absolutely – an absolute penis.' Phillip took her arm. 'Well, his manager is going to tweet on his behalf and some other guys are going to spread that, too, and we will find James. James will be OK.' It was the first time Phillip had ever used his name, that she could remember.

'Thank you,' she said.

'I love you,' said Phillip. He coughed. 'I was thinking, a crazy thought really, but just if something happened to you, while you were out, drunk a little bit still maybe, and you fall in or something, and I would never forgive myself.' He dusted down his tone, re-found a little of the tease. 'But in the end nothing like that has happened, you were just sick because even *you* cannot run after all those beers. So maybe we should go home now?' Another cough; she couldn't tell if he was catching something, being outside around dawn for what was probably the first time in his life, or if the unfamiliar action of backtracking was sticking in his throat. 'I mean, go home but keep working on James. Keep trying to be in contact.'

Michaela stayed where she was, half folded up by his handsome frame, and although she was listening, and still thinking of James, there was something else, too. She was thinking about how late her period was this month, and how drinking had never ever made her sick before. The gentle pace of the run had been nowhere near enough to upset her internally and it was hours since the last beer. No, something else was going on here. They said you could tell, when it happened. On futuremums.com. They said some part of you just knew right from the first moment.

And if this was the moment, if 'it' *had* happened, then what? Then everything that had happened with Phillip tonight would have to be forgotten, because this was a line. No more flitting in and out of things. Real life would begin.

Or: she was trapped. Real life would smother her. She would, for the first time, be bound by the decisions she had made, unable to flip the page and start with another fresh one. This could be the best or worst thing ever to happen to her. And yet if something had happened to James, she wouldn't even be able to think about it, let alone tell Phillip. No, she wasn't going to tell Phillip for a little while.

Phillip was holding her hand, and he didn't know what Michaela was thinking. The birds were singing in that impassive way they had; the day was much the same as any other one, to them. Phillip was bobbing her hand gently back and forth, holding it firmly in his, thinking (Michaela assumed) that he had done well to regain control of this situation. And he had, she supposed, but she had a secret *so* secret that even she wasn't sure it was real yet, and she wasn't going to tell him. The lesson of tonight was surely to communicate better, and that was all well and good, but she wasn't going to tell him. This was hers, for now.

29

Meghan was sitting at the desk, computer in front of her, as if no time had passed. 'Hey,' she said.

'Hey.'

Sal sat down, at right-angles to Meghan. Meghan's tongue came out, tracing the lips.

'Are you all right?' asked Meghan. 'What are you going to do – what are *we* going to do? About James?'

It was odd hearing her say the name. Everything was odd. The swivel chair creaked underneath her as she scuttled it, gently, closer to the table, to Meghan's outstretched foot.

'I don't know,' said Sal, and saying it was in some ways a relief. 'I don't really know, Meghan.' She moistened her lips. It would be good to have a drink of water. She wasn't going to ask Meghan for that, though; Meghan did enough. 'I had kind of a panic attack at the rehearsal.'

'That sucks.'

'Yeah. I can't handle the whole . . . anything to do with death, all of it. I'm terrified I can't get to him. I don't know what to do, Meghan.' For a moment it felt like a crazy move to be talking, like this, to her assistant. Meghan had removed her glasses and was looking straight into her eyes; there was a keenness to her stare, and Sal dried her hands in her lap.

'What do you want to do?' asked Meghan.

'What do you mean?'

'If you could do anything right now, in this second, what would you do?' Meghan held her gaze; kept holding it. 'I have to do therapy because I once smacked someone at a barbecue? Like fully smacked her in the mouth with a chop? And that's what the therapist tells me to say to myself. Every day. What would you do, if it could be anything? If money was no object and if there were no reasons, like, practically, to not do it? Because then you start to work out how, actually, the things stopping you from achieving those desires – how you can get around them.'

The phone buzzed on the desk. Both of them glanced down at it, and their faces were very close together for a moment. When Meghan spoke again, Sal could smell her breath, which was agreeably tangy, like sour sweets.

'So . . .?'

'Well, if I could do *anything* I'd – I wouldn't go to this dinner. I wouldn't do the speech. I'd just sack it off. I wouldn't even tell Dec. I don't want to be answerable to anyone.'

'And what would you do instead?' asked Meghan, in a reasonable, throwaway voice that wasn't quite hers.

'I don't know. You tell me!' Sal heard the heaviness of her own attempt at levity. Her voice sounded loud and affected, like a supply teacher's, like a recording of herself that was embarrassing to watch back.

'Well, you *could* do anything – anything's possible?' Meghan gestured out of the window, intentionally or other-wise enlisting the whole of Melbourne in her escape plan. 'You could tell Dec you have to deal with this, he's not going to hear from you for a while? You could tell them, it's a family emergency – which it is – and, tough, they'll have to have their event without you. It happens.' Meghan shrugged. She looked a little surprised by her own speech, as if she had part-convinced herself.

'And then what?' Sal asked. She imagined Dec on the phone, angry. The event organizer, her management. Putting them all on mute. Calling Mum, getting through to James somehow. 'We just run off to the country for the night? We go off grid?'

'I mean, yeah – I don't know,' said Meghan. 'I'm just trying to help you to – I'm just wanting to explore the options with you. And tell you . . . it's not on you. It doesn't all have to be about you.'

There was a silence. Untouched on the table, the phone performed a little thrashing dance of irritation. It was another missed call.

'I mean, they're – like, this is no offence, but they're either going to find your brother, find James, or they're not,' said Meghan. 'You're a long way away from it, here.'

Sal imagined the reprieve it would be, to run away from this for an hour; to receive a message saying someone had found him, he was all right. It felt unbelievably close, this other world in which she decided not to be in charge. The phone buzzed again: it was begging her. She picked it up. A missed call from Mum. The three letters dug their fingers into her heart again. She scrolled down through the notifications, eighteen in all. A computer programmer – someone with a tick after his name, someone important – was saying that he remembered James from a company years ago. Would love to reconnect, to talk about a job. Sal felt her breath catch behind her ribs. She looked out of the window. Among the chrome towers, the tip of the Skydeck was like a gold-painted fingernail. Every one of those towers was a cell of information, of intelligence. A nest of brains. She thought about Trishna, the meditation lady, talking about how they were all connected. It was true, Sal thought. People were trying to help. They were trying to help her brother.

'So the car's booked for half an hour from now?' she asked.

Meghan blinked. Her tongue flickered across her lips for a minute. 'It is. Yeah. We've – I've left quite a bit of time.'

'Do you want to change here, or when we . . .?'

'I can change here,' said Meghan. 'But also, to flag up, there is a room for you to use when you get there.'

'All right,' said Sal. She picked up the phone. 'I'm going to get changed there, then. I'll – until the car comes, I'll just keep on with trying to see if there's any news.'

'Of course,' said Meghan. She got up and went quietly towards the door. Sal watched her go. The shambling way she held herself; the heavy, deliberate steps. Meghan glanced back once, meeting Sal's eyes with an accusation Sal couldn't quite read.

1: Make this list, thought Sal, feeling that strange pocket of other-life close up again, as if a zip had been pulled up. James might not be found yet but normality had settled again, smothering her, reassuring, always better than the glimpses of beyond. In the end, you could always stay in control. The moments in between were the illusion. This was real.

30

'That's right,' Steffi confirmed for the third time. 'He does live here, but no, he definitely isn't here now.' Talking to old people – anyone over roughly thirty-five – was so tiring. They returned to the same questions again and again. Still, to be fair to the woman, she *was* James's mother. If Steffi had a child, and if the kid's life was in danger, she supposed she'd be pretty frantic. Although frantic wasn't really the word for how Jean was talking: it was more a sort of controlled panic. There was a terrible plea in her voice for someone to take her in hand and tell her that this would be sorted out, it would all go away; and at the same time, so British, there was a sort of muttering apology at the very idea that she needed this, had to ask it of people she didn't know.

'So no, I don't think – I don't think it is worth for you to come here,' Steffi said. 'I think just stay by the phone and we will . . . yes, of course we will. As soon as . . . yes.

Of course, Jean. We have a lot of people looking, now – a lot.'

Emil squeezed Steffi's shoulder as she put the phone down on the table and made her now mechanical check of the screen. It was so bony and tense. Emil's fingers made a few circuits of the ball of her shoulder, crept across her clavicle. Steffi sighed under her breath, but it wasn't obvious whether it was in appreciation or impatience. Emil had a mate in Bilbao who was an apprentice masseur and once a client had sighed non-stop for the hour in what seemed like beatific release, but it turned out she was angry about the music he'd put on, and she asked for a refund and he was sacked.

'This is nice?' he said at last, and the way it came out, it sounded as if he was trying to reassure himself as much as ask her opinion.

'Sure, yes, it's nice. Thank you.' She said it with warmth, but not with total conviction; it was almost as if she was humouring him. Emil wished he knew anything about massage. He'd had the option of a summer course once, but he went for circus skills instead. What a shit call that had been. How many girls were you going to get into bed by juggling?

Emil rubbed his eyes. It looked pretty unlikely now that anything sexy was going to happen. He was meant to be back at work in three hours. Not that something couldn't happen faster than that. But Steffi literally hadn't moved since they got back here. She hadn't even been to pee. She was like a robot, except one with emotions – a super-evolved AI of some kind. She had taken it so much to heart, this whole mission. Emil wanted the guy to be saved now, for the pleasure it would give her, and because surely after all this opera (as his grandmother would say), the guy must be worth it, must be worth *something*.

She was looking at the screen; it was now difficult for him to picture her face without the slight ghost-tan it gave her. 'I mean, this person is obviously some genius,' she said, jabbing her finger at the name: Exploits. *'Any news?* he asks. That's literally the whole message, "any news". Like, yes sorry mate, we found James two hours ago and now just have our fingers in our arses!' Emil laughed, thinking that was the right response, but it came out sounding too loud – inappropriate, in this setting – and he felt as if he'd somehow trivialized what she was saying.

'You have done amazing,' said Emil.

'It doesn't feel too amazing.' Steffi's voice was a croak, even though she'd barely said anything for the two hours before the phone call. 'Like, talking to his mom. I just wanted so much to be able to say, it's cool, we've got him here.' She was dehydrated, probably, she thought. It would be really good if Emil asked if she needed anything to drink, instead of pawing her shoulder. Still, she supposed it was good not to be alone. Seven hours of this alone would have been enough to send someone mad. But on the other hand, if she'd had a better teammate than Emil – a partner in the investigation. Yes, this could have been . . . not fun, it was too serious, but – well – a *kind* of fun. A satisfying way to pass the time; something she could care about.

'But like you say, so many people are trying with it

now.' Emil sipped the coffee. No, he'd left it too long: it was such a depressing mouthful it felt like it was leaching caffeine out of him instead of giving him a final kick. 'This guy, the artist on Twitter who did the retweet. Also, Mr Legs.'

'Who?'

'The DJ: Mr Legs. This guy who came up just then. Huge DJ. I mean, that's like . . .' He searched for the right word. 'That is so many people listen to that guy. I went to see him at Primavera, and one of my friends, Gustavo, great guy but mad, he thinks because of the weed he is a pig, actually like believes to be a real pig, and . . .' The story wasn't going to cut it, he realized; Steffi's body had gone stiff again, her hands were on the keyboard. 'Like, all I mean, you are doing so great. Like a million people are talking about this guy now.'

'I don't know if it's worth it,' said Steffi, looking dejected all of a sudden. He wanted to take her arm, but overruled himself.

'Or look at this guy,' said Emil, 'he says, he wants to give a job to James, when he come back.'

This seemed to snare her. 'Where?'

He leaned across her, scrolled up so that the message was in the middle of the screen. 'I'd love to reconnect, I'd love to talk.' Her eyebrows went up in reluctant acceptance.

'That's cool. That's – look at the bio, the guy, one of the guys anyway, who do Sheep Wars. It doesn't help James but maybe he can tell me how to get further in it. That would be something.'

'*I* can do that, if it's what you need. Remember?'

'I forgot.' Steffi was almost smiling. 'I forgot you were – an expert at Sheep Wars. It seems like a long time.'

'Not even expert. Whatever is after expert.'

'Superhero?'

Emil felt his moment come, just when it had appeared too late. 'Superhero, yeah, President of the World. Give me the phone, yeah? Just for . . . you need a break. Just, I can help you, show you it.'

Steffi blinked, rubbed her eyes, half-grinned. Emil slid his chair closer to her and waited as she opened the game, the wolf in shades coming to life. She moved the phone to landscape and selected her game, saved as she was on the way up out of King's Cross underground, when life had been simpler. Emil had already got his hands on the phone and dragged it towards him: he narrowed his eyes solemnly like a doctor inspecting a patient.

'OK, yeah, easy. Just have to find the weapon.'

Steffi watched as his fingers skipped across the screen. She could hardly follow what he was doing, but it was working. The sheep watched in dismay as Emil's wolf slashed open their tyres and the chassis of their car sank comically like a ship. The wolf put on a napkin and was getting out a knife and fork as Emil laid the phone down in front of him like an engineer done with a minor task, barely seeming to register the success.

'See, easy,' he said. 'The car shit is no problem. There's one level, it's real tough, real hard. The sheep, they get . . . I don't know how to say.'

Steffi felt a flicker of annoyance, that this guy who couldn't even learn English was so much more advanced at this game than she was. 'Like, a . . . tank? Army vehi-cles?'

'No, er.' Emil swished at the air, grasping for the phrase, which he knew was within reach because he'd discussed it on the fan groups. '*Diplomatic immunity.*' With his free hand he continued to skim over the screen, dispatching the wolf on another murderous foray. 'They go to the cops and give you a piece of paper says you aren't allowed to eat them, you have to get lawyer. I didn't finish that level for like a week. That was when I stopped.'

'You stopped? You got bored?'

He laughed again, briefly. 'Not bored. Too much I liked it. So, in the breaks I always played. And then one day, I'm watching one of the guys, my flat, the – what do you call it . . .'

He mimed the swing, pointing at the ceiling.

'Hammock.'

'Yeah, this guy trying to get out of hammock, cannot because too stoned, whole place smells weed and kebab, and I say – do I want to be here? No, I want to be *sous*, and after that the name.'

'The name?' Steffi repeated.

'Name chef, like, you know, Marco Pierre, Tom Kerridge, whoever. You have ten restaurants, you have – a style of food, a way.'

Steffi glanced across at him. His eyes seemed to have got darker since she last looked properly at them. 'I am better than Juno. I could totally be *sous*.' She realized that watching him play the game reminded her of watching him in the kitchen: prepping a mountain of herbs with back-and-forth swishes of his tiny knife, like an orchestra conductor viewed on fast-forward. Planting them to obscure the overdone edge of a pork chop. He was like a different person when he was doing manual tasks. He was so fast, so focused.

'So, yeah, I stop playing the game. In the break, or on bus, I listen podcasts. Podcasts podcasts podcasts. About food. Ideas of food, cooking. From the guys who do what I want to do.'

Steffi nodded. She watched him push the phone gently away. 'That's great. You should keep doing it.'

'It's the English.' Emil's brows knotted darkly. 'Too much, I can't learn. So, never get the big job, or I go back to San Sebastián, but there it's like same four chefs since fucking Franco.'

'Franco is a chef?'

'What? No.' Emil frowned. 'Like, leader – dictator. Killed many.'

She looked aghast at herself for a second, and he burst into laughter. They shared the laugh, a tired, teetering laugh; almost warmer for the fact neither of them had the energy to finish it. Steffi touched his elbow and Emil couldn't tell whether it was deliberate.

'It isn't so hard, learning English. You get an app. Phones, apps can do anything.'

'I have the language app but it keeps making you say, like, *he drinks milk, she drinks milk, my cat drink milk.*'

'My cat *drinks* milk,' said Steffi, before she could help herself. Emil laughed sadly and rested his head in his hands.

'Why does any of them drink milk, who is drinking milk, the freaks.'

Steffi smiled. Something popped up on the computer. 'I'm just saying, you are smart, if you need to get better English, you can – I mean, I . . .'

He thought she was going to say *I'll teach you*. But she was pointing to the screen and her bottom lip had dropped a little way. 'Hey. Wait.'

Emil felt the beam of her attention flicker away; he had lost the moment. He tried to concentrate on the screen, at what was exercising Steffi, but she was already typing a reply.

'I'd kind of like to do this again, do it more,' she said. 'I know that's a weird thing to say.'

Emil gulped. He scanned his sparse larder for the right phrase. 'It's nice if we see – if we come for dinner, or to catch a movie.'

Steffi hesitated, embarrassed. 'I mean – more of *this* thing. Of helping people, finding them. Like, I'm not so good at actually talking to people, meeting them, but this, I'm good at this. I'm good at helping get this shit done.'

Emil felt the breath going in and out of him. He could still turn this into a win; he could still make the tide go the way he'd thought it was going, with a bit of courage. Come on. He thought of his great-grandmother, all the rings and bangles on her thin wrist shaking like wind chimes as she pointed her finger at him. *You are a good boy but you're lazy, you expect things to come to you.*

'That's cool,' he said, 'but also, can I kiss you?'

It was a long twenty seconds. Emil felt himself hurtle face down, from breath-held anticipation, to the fear that she hadn't even heard him, to the sudden and complete knowledge that his gambit had failed. He wasn't surfing a tide after all; he was trying to open a parachute, watching the ground rushing up.

'I don't think it's a good idea,' said Steffi, gently.

'You don't?'

'Yeah, well, I like you,' said Steffi, 'but first of all, why are there seventy-two pictures of your dick in a folder? I know I shouldn't have looked in your phone, by the way, but also, see, that makes me think you and me wouldn't be that much of a special thing.'

Emil tried to muster indignation at the intrusion, at the sheer rudeness of it, but he could only feel shame. In the blood-rush to his cheeks, he found himself wanting to rip off his clothes, but no longer in a sexy way; he wanted to rip off his whole skin.

'I chatted with a guy and things went good, and—'

'A guy?'

'Yeah. They're his – it's his dick, not me,' said Emil, scraping back in his chair and moving away from the table. 'Anyways, please – do you want another coffee, or should I go, or . . .'

'So you're bi?'

'I'm, I don't know what.' He stopped. She was motioning him back to the table. 'I was lonely, it's lonely here, so I try to find people.'

She took his hand. He stood by the table. She glanced at the screen, and then back to him.

'I guess the thing is,' said Steffi, 'kissing because it's been a long, crazy night, that's not how to stop being lonely. Being friends, that's how to do it.'

Emil nodded slowly. Steffi wasn't sure whether he had understood, and if so whether she had hurt him. But it was true. And she knew how he felt, because she had felt it, too, these past couple of years as a meaningless cog in a city of distant, automated machineries. She hadn't felt it the way James obviously had. She hadn't been 'lonely' in an active way. She would never have described herself that way. She wouldn't have described herself as anything, exactly. She'd just been living, getting up each day, assuming at some point a signpost would point her towards something of substance. And all this time, there were people out there who desperately needed the help of someone like her. You defined yourself by participating in other people's lives.

All these things, half-formed, were building in her brain, and she looked sadly and sympathetically at Emil, who (she now realized) hadn't wanted much more out of this past eight hours than one thing. But one thing she wasn't going to give him. She wouldn't be able to say any of this to him in English. Maybe one day he'd feel it for himself.

Very likely this, this little adventure, was as close as the two of them would ever be in their lives. Maybe in five years he would be working back in wherever it was, the Basque area, as a head chef in some seafood place. And she would be a project manager for an NGO that tracked down political exiles or something. They would still be contacts on each other's phones, still like each other's posts. They would think from time to time about this night, and about how their continued existences helped in some stealthy and intangible way to make each other the people they now were.

She wouldn't be able to get *that* across to him, either: not in English or in any other language.

It was a future you could imagine. 'Being friends, that's how to do it.' It was a revelation of some kind. It was a good future to imagine; better than anything she'd consciously pictured before. She looked at the screen and she wondered if James would be in her future, in anyone's.

31

Karl had known that he had to make the call before he even left the precinct of the hotel: because it would be dangerous using the hands-free while driving at the nine hundred miles an hour he was planning to, but also because if he put it off, he wouldn't do it. Christ knew he was obviously enough of a coward that he'd let it get to this stage. That he'd thrown his friend under the bus to keep himself from going under it.

No, this wasn't helping. 'All right, come on Karl, come on mate.' He tried, once more, to talk to himself the way he used to imagine his dad would talk to him, when he came back for good, when things were better. 'We're going to call Elton. Call him right now. Tell him what happened. Get him to help.'

It was the only card Karl had left, and it wasn't much of a card, and he might be throwing it onto the table after everyone else had left the game. 'No. Come on. He's still out there. He could be on that train. Come on, mate.'

It took three attempts, even with Hamish Elton's name in front of him on the screen, to press the button and launch the call. He wound down the window; cool air crept around the back of his neck. He stared at Elton's name. Every minute he sat here and didn't do anything was a minute he wasn't driving to Edinburgh.

He pressed the button. Elton wouldn't be up yet, there was little chance of that, the bastard worked about eight minutes a week; but on the other hand, he might not even have gone to bed yet. He pressed red to stop the call. The pistons of his heart were pumping like he'd done fifty bench presses, except nobody was ever allowed to know he did that. God, so many lies, so many cover-ups. Again, he thought: it caught up with you in the end. If you dodged and shape-shifted for long enough. And yes, he'd had excuses, he had to protect Mum, he had to protect himself. But excuses didn't mean anything in the end. What *actually happened* in the end what was mattered. If James was dead, it wasn't going to matter if he could go to a fucking psychotherapist and express in interpretative dance why he'd betrayed him, was it?

He pressed the button again. This time it began to ring. Karl felt his stalled breath collecting in his throat. Even if it was answered, how was he meant to start? Hi there, Hamish. Karl, here: I run the firm that drives you. That's how you think of me, if you think of me at all. A pair of eyes somewhere on the other end of an app, entirely remote from everything. But what if I told you, Hamish, that those eyes had seen more information through that app than you could ever imagine. That the fella whose name you barely even bother to remember – Carl? Chris? – actually spent years coding, and has built an AI so advanced that it knows pretty much everything about pretty much everyone who uses the app. Like you. Your movements, including the ones you shouldn't be making. The racist jokes you are OK making because it's 'between friends', because it's all 'irony'. And among those 'friends', the ones you really shouldn't be messaging, Hamish, because they're someone else's girlfriend, or wife. Imagine if someone knew every single thing about you, Hamish Elton. And the driving service that man now ran, lucrative as it was starting to be, was really just the skin of a delicious peach, one he would sell in the not too distant future.

It rang to voicemail. *The person you are calling.* Karl had had enough of that voice and phrase tonight. There was a momentary relief that the arsehole wasn't answering, but it was no relief at all, really. Karl was still going to have to do this. He'd ring once more. Then he would leave a message, the message that put things right, ruined Karl himself, and probably in vain.

. . . So what if this man, Karl, sitting on all this informa-tion, gets drunk at a dinner party where people are talking about Hamish Elton and what a great guy he is. And Karl mouths off about him because he knows Elton is a cheating, bigoted piece of shit. And then it comes out in the papers because someone told someone else. And to save his own skin, to avoid being disgraced, losing everything he's built up, Karl stitches up his friend – we'll call the friend James. Not realizing that friend is, himself, close to some sort of precipice.

The voicemail again. Karl took a wobbly breath.

'Hello, you don't know me, but a few months ago . . .' He swallowed, tasting bile. 'Well, I'm the boss of the guy who – went to the papers – told them about, you know. Anyway, I just wanted to let you know it wasn't him. It was me. He lost his job for no reason. It was me, it was my fault. And I'm going to give you all my details and you can do what you want to me. Or I can go public and say I made it up. Or whatever you want. But the guy is in trouble. James. The driver is in big trouble, in danger, so please call me back. And you can call me as much of a cunt as you want. Just please, please call me back. Please call me back.'

It was done. He felt no clearance of the load around his neck, dragging him down in the driving seat. The seatbelt was cutting into him. He hadn't eaten in hours, since well before leaving London; he felt so hungry he could walk into a field and eat a cow straight off the grass. He swung the car up the ramp, onto the empty road.

He didn't know when overnight trains got into Edinburgh, if that was what James was doing. He didn't know whether it was even possible to get there from Newcastle in whatever time was left.

*

One hundred and ten miles an hour; that's what he had been averaging for the hour and a bit since then. Your stopping distance at this speed, Karl thought was about a quarter of a fucking mile. But not many people were on the road. The scenery out of both windows was top-drawer, he'd have to admit; the coastline breaking suddenly into cold grey-blue water; trees rising from strange outcrops, the landscape wild and witchy-looking. He'd never been up this way. not this far. James was always talking about it but it was a thing with his dad, really. Shame that the first time Karl saw this countryside, he was seeing it flash past so fast he might as well be teleporting through it. Shame that the first time Karl was joining James north of the border, Karl didn't know if James was still alive. Shame his hands were so sweaty he had to clamp them to the wheel – he'd almost lost his grip once already – and that he was so hungry he reckoned he might faint. Karl's lips pursed into what was almost, almost, the grimmest of smiles. This was the polar opposite of the dream. The smile unravelled again.

He'd stopped glancing at the phone more than a couple of times a minute, partly because he was doing close to the speed of a space shuttle, but largely because instinct told him now that he'd know if there was a miracle. It wouldn't be a text, it wouldn't be chatter on Facebook. It would ring. The phone would actually ring, and it hadn't.

And he had no business asking for a miracle. This wasn't that black-and-white movie James and Michaela made him watch one Christmas, where they all prayed for the fella and an angel appeared and showed him how much he was worth. That was what all the people online were doing, he supposed; this was the modern equivalent. But who was listening? It was all very well Karl talking to the DJ about praying. There was nobody out there as far as he knew.

Yet he couldn't stop saying it, under his breath, or out loud: it didn't matter, on the road, in the silence. *Just let me have this. Please. I'll be better.* Just like he'd always said to his dad. Getting out of bed early with an alarm, flaying his brains to get his maths score up, shaking as he handed over the school report. *I'll do better. If you come back and live with us. If it's my fault, I'll do better.* Now, just like then, Karl was holding out these promises to nobody, an empty space. But there was nothing else left for him to offer.

32

Along the invisible train tracks in the sky raced the fragments of appeal sent up endlessly by James's would-be
rescuers. *Please help if you. Any information is. There must be
someone who knows.* The messages were full of emotion,
full of love, some of it panicky and hyperbolic, some of it
surprising even to the people who expressed it. A very small
measure of it, at any time over the past couple of years,
and perhaps the object would not be walking to the edge
now. But nobody could have known that until it came to
this point; that was what they would tell themselves.

Their virtual conversation buzzed in the air like helicop-
ters and, far below, the train pulled into Waverley station.

33

'Soon be arriving, sir!' 'Breakfast here! Coffee, bacon roll, orange juice!' He'd heard Gina's voice, strident and brassy again, all the way up the corridor as she knocked on the doors with the plastic trays. He'd heard the train waking up; the rugby fans had stirred into raucous voice. They banged on each other's doors like schoolboys away from home for the first time. 'I hardly got my eyes shut before she was saying get up!' he heard a man yell, so close to his door that he might be shouting it right into James's face. Not getting the response he wanted, the guy gave the remark a second airing. 'Eh – Rhys. I said: hardly got my eyes shut . . .' James listened to their heavy footsteps going up and down outside. It was hard to believe all these people had been on the train all along, even though he'd seen them board. Apart from Gina, it had been as if he was completely alone.

And even those little meetings with her felt as if they couldn't have happened, now. The brief, thin train-night had been whipped away like a cloth. He straightened up the puny bedsheet and tied up the plastic bag, which he could dispose of in the station. No mess. No work for whoever came in. He hoped it didn't smell of sweat in here. He'd done his best. It would be so good to get away from all the smells and noises and the other unfortunate things a body did. There was the knock at the door; his was the last cabin she came to. They were only a few minutes outside the station: without even opening the blind he could feel the tightening of the city around the train, the rows of houses pressing in. He opened the door. Gina was holding out the tray.

'Coffee, bacon roll, orange juice,' she said, and James thought – yes, he *had* ordered those items when boarding last night, to seem normal, and he had better take them and at least pretend he wanted them. His stomach growled appreciatively. On some level he did still want them. The mind and body kept going right up to the wire, until you stopped them, until you escaped.

'Thank you,' he said.

Gina gave him a sort of guarded, wise smile, a morning-after smile. 'Sorry about all that.'

'About?'

'All the drama.'

It was hardly drama, was it, he thought. If she had any idea what he was about to do! But then, 'drama' was a strange way to describe that, too. It was a strange way to describe any sort of actions, emotions, really: what else were people meant to do, what else did they have?

'It was . . . you don't need to apologize,' he muttered. He tugged at the tiny silver-foil tag to open the carton of orange juice; the carton spat a bit of juice onto James's jumper, and the two of them glanced at it for a second and almost laughed.

'I'll get you a cloth?' she said.

'No, no, it's nothing,' said James. Their eyes met again. He had the thought, which he could not afford to entertain at all, that they might have got on well if they'd met in other circumstances. If they'd met in life. He cleared his throat. 'I hope things pick up for you.'

'You take care of yourself,' she said, stepping a little further into his cabin as a man in an overcoat tried to pass her in the corridor. 'You take care of yourself for me.'

James nodded, without saying anything, and Gina nodded too, as if they were agreeing on something that was difficult to express. She shut his door with a delicacy that surprised him, as if – after all this time – she were trying not to disturb him.

*

Blue-grey had crept in under the blind. James pulled it up tentatively; the stone arches of the station were outside, a seagull hopping about on the platform. Recorded announcements, the words indistinct. Above them was the theatre he knew, could conjure with his eyes shut. Princes

Street, the new Ferris Wheel which Dad had never seen; the Scott Monument, where they stood to watch the fireworks. The tower like a grizzled old policeman on permanent watch. And above all *that*: the bridge. It was time. He picked up his plastic bag. It was best to get on with this quickly.

He felt light-headed and foggy in the way he normally did after a whole night awake. That was fine. They were the right mental conditions to be in.

On the platform he looked briefly for Gina – it felt sort of appropriate to say goodbye, but maybe they had already done that. A lot of things could be a goodbye, he thought. A parting with no ceremony at all, a handshake. The most banal of contacts could turn out to be a farewell. A text, in this case: 158 texts.

He thought with a flutter of misgiving of all the responses. Those he'd seen; those that would still be arriving on the dead phone as it lay on the track, a hundred miles behind him. No. This was no time for anything like that. *We knew it was going to be tricky, this bit*, he told himself, hurrying through the familiar station. Familiar, although changed; there were building works, they'd moved an escalator. The toilets were free to use now. He relieved himself for what would be the final time and looked in the mirror. This was it. He felt the jangling of anticipation in every limb. That was normal. A sticker for the Samaritans was clinging to the sink – THERE IS ALWAYS SOMEONE TO TALK TO – and he thought about the woman he'd once called, and wondered what she might be doing now. Perhaps she was just coming off another shift, or getting ready for one. Perhaps she was, like anyone else, comfortably asleep, ready to rise to a weekend, with whatever cautious promise, whatever challenges, excitements, worries that might hold for her. Again he felt a sort of detached pleasure in others, in the idea of all the little lives. The station would change again, in a few years; so many people would come and go. It was a relaxing thought.

The cold air hit him at the top of the steps. There were a couple of taxis waiting at the rank, but he was only going around the corner. The Fruitmarket was advertising an exhibition of Cuban artists: there was a pastel drawing of someone playing a saxophone. The light was grey, neutral; the city didn't mind what he did. No bagpipes till later in the day, he supposed. He and Sally had liked to make jokes about the drone of the bagpipes, which Dad had always insisted he enjoyed. *What a beastly noise*, he could hear her saying, in *Famous Five* character. A bus rumbled down the road. The castle was up there where it should be, the craggy surrounds of the city hemming it in.

He walked along by the Booking Office pub. Quarter to eight by the big clock at the top of the Balmoral. But it was three minutes fast. It always was. Dad had told him that. They set it like that on purpose to make people hurry for the trains. They'd done it in Victorian times. He remembered that Dad was waiting for him, and quickened his step. Princes Street was already quite busy with weekend visitors. A tram purred along beside him. James had told Dad about the trams on one of his trips to the bridge. *It's gone a long way over budget*, he'd said. *But you would have liked it. You do like it.*

His stomach swirled with qualms as he passed the clock and the Scotsman building came into view. *We expected this, this was going to be tricky*, he said to himself again. His heart was frisking about; there was that prickling and fizzing again in his arms and legs.

James rested his hands, wide apart, on the pale blue paintwork. All that separated him from the fall was the ledge, just wide enough to stand on, and not high at all. He could easily get up onto it with ten seconds' effort. With the traffic going by, and the Saturday bustle of pedestrians, it didn't feel like a bridge at all; it was easy to forget how high you were, how close you were to falling through the air, if that was what you chose. Everything was as James had seen it, so many times. The tall, stern tenements. The castle looking down. It was a beautiful view and so sad somehow, even if you were in a good mood. He thought again about the way the city was clenched in history's hand, all the lives knotted together and then left to drift away. There was a little gang of people in his peripheral vision, but it wouldn't matter what they did.

*

Below, the warren-like streets, the grey buildings. James gulped. It would be over in sixty seconds. Less than that. He looked at the soft light on the letters of the Scotsman building. M-A-N. Dad was waiting. He had the feeling that there was no difference between past and present. He and Dad had always been standing there, and now they would stand together again.

'Oi!' said someone, 'what are you doing? James! What are you doing?'

He thought perhaps he was already over the side, was out of his body and remembering or imagining things. He turned around a little at a time. Gina was standing there with her hands outstretched indignantly, like he'd failed to keep some appointment they had. The uniform looked odd on her, away from its context; like she was in fancy dress. Her eyes were red and pained and he was almost afraid of her, of the physical heft of her, her energy: she looked as if she could tear him apart.

'What the hell are you doing?'

'I'm just . . .' James began.

'Come here!' she said. 'Come here and talk to me!' He thought for a second she was going to physically apprehend him, and he almost believed he wanted . . . no. There was a life in which this was the start of something else, but that wasn't the right one. He folded his arms. This was one thing people couldn't take away from him. This was his decision to make, even if so many other things hadn't been.

'What are you talking about?' he said.

'Come here and stop being an idiot,' said Gina, her songful voice picking out every word in the thinnish air. To anyone else it would still look like a minor disagreement between friends, partners. The handful of passers-by glanced across and went on, some quickening their step, an instinctive distrust of whatever this was. James felt strange chemicals working in channels through him. Whatever was left of him, there was enough to fight this.

'Why exactly are you calling me an idiot?'

She took a step towards him, her eyes large and almost wild, a sudden gust of wind bothering her hair. She was stocky and solid and he could feel the internal heat of her, he could feel her as a body and a brain.

Gina fished for something in the pocket of her jacket; a small shiny thing. It was her phone. She tossed it down in front of him, almost seeming to enjoy the moment. It landed with a clatter on the stone below him. No: it was *his* phone. She had picked it up. Someone had picked it up and given it to her. While the train was still in the station. He couldn't be sure how. James could hear his own breath accelerate.

'Why . . .?'

'You should look at that.' Gina's voice contained a sort of flat amusement, like the weary acceptance of a punch line, like someone accepting a defeat that was long in the making. 'You take one look at that and all the people that are on it.'

'Leave me alone.'

'You don't want me to leave you alone, you don't want to be left alone.' She thrust a finger out at him. She was perfectly still and calm, like a statue, like a menhir. James felt himself trembling. He was freezing. He felt as if he had known her a long time. 'You need help, and you can get help. You can get help.'

'You don't know anything about me,' he said.

'You got your mother on here, begging you,' said Gina, flinging her arms in the direction of the phone, which even now had started to break-dance on the pavement. A couple of people *were* starting to look. A Japanese couple, binoculars around their necks like old-world adventurers; the mother gently redirected their young son as he stopped and pointed. 'You got your friends, you got people you don't even know about. Offering you a job and whatnot. Wanting you to come home. Wanting to help you. You don't know you're fucking born. We don't all have that help. You can start again. We can't all do that.'

'I can't *start again*,' said James. She was ten paces away. He disliked her tone, the attack, it was baffling to be spoken to like this. He could feel her muscles clenching and flexing; he could hear her synapses chattering as she tried to haul him back, and he felt that he knew something about being a human, but this was all a trick; it was what they did to you if you were weak. It was a last attempt to break him down. 'It'll all still be the same,' he said. 'They can say these things now because they're panicking. But they wouldn't – I wouldn't be any more important. When it all settled down. I'd have the same problems.'

'How do you know? How can you ever know that?' Gina was almost shouting at him. 'Pick up the phone. Pick up the phone and look at it.'

The big hands of the clock: eight, just after eight. James felt dizzy. The phone was skipping about on the pavement like a creature trapped in a jar. James looked down at it, wanting to pick it up and throw it away all over again, for good this time, over the side of the bridge. He was weakening.

He could feel in his bones the weight of the night, the time spent awake, and all these nights spent awake since things broke down. He wanted to be gathered up into silence. He didn't want to be saved.

'You should see it all on the internet.' She flung her hands up again, gesturing at all the unknown group activity above them, at all the other players.

He thought about all the paths that must have been drawn between strangers. He felt he could see Dad looking across from the other side of the bridge, and he resented that he'd been made to have this thought. He shut his eyes. When he opened them, Gina was hauling herself onto the edge, and James's knees felt old and weak. He tried to tell her to stop, to get back down, but no words came out. A crowd was building. Gina was looking down on him. Away on each side, the hills were a face, its mouth open, ready to consume anyone. Gina was standing above him now. She reached down and brushed her arm against his.

'It's not right for you to do this,' she said – gentle now, reasonable. He had the thought that there was no difference between being him and being her; being one person and another. Perhaps the thought made no sense, but it was easier on the mind than all the thoughts of the night, and the other nights. He could smell Gina's body and he could sense her heartbeat; he could almost hear the breath going in and out of her. 'It would be right for me to do it. It's my time; it isn't yours.'

'What do you mean?' James said. 'What do you mean, your time?' It wasn't how it worked, he wanted to say. If it wasn't right for him to jump, he wanted to say, then it wasn't right for her, either.

The city watched the two of them, Gina up on the edge of the bridge, James bewildered on the pavement, as they looked one another fully in the face.

34

EDINBURGH, 08:01

When the body fell, the person inside it remained a person for the few seconds it took to hit Market Street below. In that time, everything in the brain screamed that it was a mistake, that any form of life to come would be better than to turn the lights out for ever. At least, that was what survivors of suicide attempts very often reported feeling. That, and a gratitude for what might be ahead. But nobody could actually know what was in the falling person's head. That was their final privacy.

Plenty of passers-by gave thought to it, of course; to what it might be like to be that person. *I can't imagine doing that*, they said, scandalized and horrified and a little excited, clustered in their little knots on the bridge looking down, or appearing in fire escapes and side-streets to watch the emergency services arrive. Almost all of them had a momentary, guilty relief that it hadn't been someone they loved; that the wheel hadn't stopped on them, this time.

Most of them made some sort of vow, conscious or otherwise, to send a message to someone important; to make contact with someone, capture for a second what was between them, and freeze it in time, mark it. *I've not heard from him in ages*, they might think, or: *I've been meaning to say hello and I didn't get round to it*, or – if their emotions were more energetically stirred by the moment – *I should tell her I love her*. And a few of them would act on that impulse, but only if they did it straight away. If they put it off, the noise of life would distract them with someone else, and the thought would pass. And the intended recipient, the loved person, would go on down the path of their day without knowing they had been thought of.

EPILOGUE

EDINBURGH, 20:45

The police tape had been removed from the end of the bridge now; the Saturday night traffic was running normally across it, four cabs queuing nose-to-tail in a black wall, buses grumbling, the air cool and thin. They walked together, arm in arm. Just over twelve hours had gone by, and neither of them had had a night's sleep before that, either. To both of them the world had a grainy quality, dipping from high to low definition and back, voices seeming too loud; small but sudden noises, a backfiring engine, a far-off firework, had made both of them jump as they left. As they came up towards the Scotsman building, Karl – with a certain reluctance – let go of James's shoulder.

'All right, Jamie. You go and do your thing. But I warn you, if you jump off *now* I'll be pretty pissed off.'

James half-smiled. 'I promise.'

It was only a promise for this moment, and both of them knew it; at least, James hoped that Karl knew it. He went and rested his hands on the ledge where he had seen Gina fall and he thought about how he had seen his father, mentally, fall here too.

'Dad,' James began, stealing a glance over his shoulder, self-conscious about Karl. But Karl was dutifully toying with his phone; he needed to check with Hugo, he'd said. The poor bugger had been holding the fort all day and would have scratched right through to the bones by now. Karl glanced up and winked at James, maintaining a respectful distance.

'I suppose I've spoken to everyone except you, by now.' James looked down at the pavement below. A small area was still fenced off with tape, where he had stood with the policewoman and said: No, I didn't know her, I'd only met her on the train. And what were you doing on the edge of the bridge with her, the policewoman had asked. Would it be all right if I sat down, James had asked, could I maybe have a cup of tea, I'm not feeling too well. Slightly to his surprise they'd taken him to a café; she ordered him tea, and a glass of water, and found him a charger for his phone. Even as it recovered battery life, a number he recognized was pulsing on the screen: a landline. 0117.

'Mum was the first person I spoke to,' James continued. It felt a little odder than usual, addressing his father in their meeting spot like this. But everything felt odder than usual. He hadn't slept, he supposed, for thirty-six hours. He had never intended to be standing here. This was an afterlife, of sorts. Whether that was a good thing, he couldn't be sure yet. 'She was very happy. Relieved, I suppose I mean. I didn't quite realize how emotional she would be.' Nor had he been prepared for the way Karl dissolved when he walked into the café, manhandling James so hard that James almost fell off his chair and the policewoman asked, 'You definitely know this man, right?' Or the way that Sally had answered his call on stage, in Australia, and not only started to cry but – apparently – turned it into some sort of parable even during the speech, and ended up with a standing ovation (she'd sent him a video, which had 'gone viral', though she was careful to add 'that's not what this is about'). He hadn't been prepared to hear Michaela's new boyfriend shouting, 'Oh thank God, thank God' in the background. He'd been taken by surprise – surprise and embarrassment – by the amount of work Steffi had put in, by the sheer size of the collective effort she had helped to trigger. When the embarrassment faded, he ought to be grateful for all this; it ought to disprove what he had thought about himself. Maybe that would come later.

'Anyway, I've had a hard time recently, and I sort of decided enough was enough, and that we'd be together again, if you see what I mean. But, well.' But what, he wondered. It wasn't as if he'd been talked out of it. Events had just stopped him. The universe, if you believed in phrases like this, had had other plans. Somebody else had died, though; that was all he could really think about. She had been lost by other humans; they had reclaimed him, for some reason. 'But: it didn't work that way. And I just wanted to say that I'll try to take advantage of that, and – not to worry about me.' He cleared his throat. 'And I'll – I'll see you soon. Of course.'

'All done, fam?' said Karl, linking his arm into James's as

they walked back towards the hotel. It was the same one they'd stayed in on the day the ashes were scattered: James didn't know if that was a coincidence or not. There were a lot of things he didn't understand, for the time being. There was time ahead, he supposed, for clearer thinking.

'If you need anything,' said Karl, in the hall outside their two rooms. 'I'm only next door, all right.' Karl's eyelids were sagging; he looked as if he'd barely make it the distance from here to the bed.

'I know,' said James, and in the middle of the closing embrace – which mirrored the one he and Sally had once had, in this building – they stepped out of the way to let someone past, a man in a rugby jersey who eyed them with fleeting curiosty. James pressed the card against the sensor to open the door. It was more than a full day since he'd left his house. He drew the curtains across and looked out at the city, lit up for the evening, defying the gloom.

People will expect this to be a new start, he said to himself. *Or something like that.* They would talk about him 'surviving'. They'd express the hope that he was feeling better, and had moved on from the drama of today. And perhaps he would be; perhaps he would have. But a lot of it would depend on them, because, when it came to it, everybody depended on everybody else. It wasn't as if he could send a text like that ever again. Next time it would be for real; or there wouldn't be a 'next time'. Those were the choices.

For now, he was alive, and in the morning he would start to think about what that meant.

AUTHOR NOTE

We often hear that technology is fragmenting the world, reducing our relationships to screen exchanges rather than the real stuff, and so on, as if machines – rather than humans – were responsible for maintaining our mental health. I wanted to write something which explored the opposite possibility: that phones give us a power to affect and improve each other's lives that we have never had in history before. *Contacts* was of course written before the bewildering events of 2020, but the lockdown has reminded a lot of us how dependent we all are upon the core relationships in life, on our networks, and perhaps how much we've taken some of those relationships for granted. *Contacts* is about the fact that, for all its dangers, the age of instant communication gives us what is basically a superpower . . . If we only choose to use it.